The
ENCANTO'S
DAUGHTER

ALSO BY MELISSA DE LA CRUZ

Cinder & Glass

Snow & Poison

THE QUEEN'S ASSASSIN DUOLOGY

Book One: The Queen's Assassin

Book Two: The Queen's Secret

THE ALEX & ELIZA TRILOGY

Book One: Alex & Eliza

Book Two: Love & War

Book Three: All for One

HEART OF DREAD SERIES (with Michael Johnston)

Book One: Frozen

Book Two: Stolen

Book Three: Golden

WITCHES OF EAST END SERIES

BLUE BLOODS SERIES

BEACH LANE SERIES

THE ASHLEY PROJECT SERIES

DISNEY DESCENDANTS SERIES

The ENCANTO'S DAUGHTER

Melissa de la Cruz

putnam

G. P. PUTNAM'S SONS

G. P. PUTNAM'S SONS

An imprint of Penguin Random House LLC, New York

First published in the United States of America by G. P. Putnam's Sons,
an imprint of Penguin Random House LLC, 2024
Copyright © 2024 by Melissa de la Cruz
Map illustration copyright © 2024 by K. M. Alexander

G. P. Putnam's Sons is a registered trademark of Penguin Random House LLC.
The Penguin colophon is a registered trademark of Penguin Books Limited.

Visit us online at PenguinRandomHouse.com.

Library of Congress Cataloging-in-Publication Data is available.

ISBN 9780593533086 (hardcover)

ISBN 9780593700426 (international edition)

1st Printing

Printed in the United States of America

LSCC

Design by Suki Boynton
Text set in Adobe Caslon Pro

*For my husband, Mike, and for our daughter, Mattea, named after my
Filipino-Spanish great-grandmother*

*For my Chinese-Spanish-Filipino family
and everyone in our households, especially the ones who
told us kids all the scary stories about mambabarangs*

For Grandpa and his anting-anting

*For Ellen Goldsmith-Vein
for being my Hollywood mama*

Every jungle has a snake.
—FILIPINO PROVERB

1

THEY CAME FOR me without warning.

It was just another first day at a new school, which happens a lot when you and your mom are on the run. I couldn't keep track of how many first days I'd had, although the year I went to ten different schools was the worst one. That morning I was supposed to be taking notes about supply and demand economics, but instead I was doomscrolling under the desk.

Experts say the next recession will start earlier than expected. The nation's business economists predict that due to rising interest rates . . .

Strange winter weather in the Southwest United States goes beyond climate change. These "freakish" weather patterns are not attributable to . . .

Police are asking the public for help once more in the case of a missing teenage girl from Santa Ana. Phoenix Xing was last seen leaving school a year ago today . . .

Another scandal for reality TV star accused of cheating on his long-term girlfriend . . .

A shiny black beetle scurried across the floor, pincers waving. *What are you doing here, buddy?* It paused, almost like it noticed I was watching, before finally disappearing beneath the wall. I wished I could do the same. I was desperate to get out of there. High school sucks, no matter if you've been in the same town since birth or if you've just arrived like we did. I wanted *out*.

Be careful what you wish for, as my mother would say.

A crackling voice interrupted over the PA: "Can we have Maria Josephina Robertson-Rodriguez to the office, please?"

I dropped my pencil and sat up straight. That could only mean my mother was picking me up early. Already? Why? Was it happening again?

The teacher—whose name I hadn't even learned yet—nodded at me. Every head turned in my direction. *There goes the new girl,* they were probably thinking. I ignored them, trying to appear nonchalant, and stuck my phone in my pocket, grabbed my worn backpack, and stood to walk out. Behind me, the teacher picked up where he'd left off. *If supply decreases, then . . .*

The door clicked shut. I started down the long, empty hallway toward the main office. I heard the shriek of a chair scraping against linoleum and muted chatter drifting out from one of the classrooms.

I was going the right way, I was positive, because I'd come in that direction from the office only a couple hours earlier. But somehow the hall seemed to go on and on. Endless. Hmmm.

Above me, a fluorescent light flickered, making a snapping noise.

Then everything went silent. No more screeching chairs or

hushed voices. All the classrooms around me were dark and empty. *Probably no classes this period*, I told myself. *Or maybe they're meeting in the media center. Nothing creepy about it. Right?*

Even my footsteps seemed louder. Each step pounded in my ears. I felt weirdly, impossibly, completely alone.

No—it was just that I was in an unfamiliar place, making me feel unsettled. That was normal. Everything was normal. And I was on my way out, anyway. In a few minutes, I'd be home.

A door slammed behind me. I turned to look, but no one was there. My heart sped up.

When I looked forward again, the hallway stretched on as far as it had when I first left class. *What the . . .*

There were popping sounds, like balloons bursting. I spun around again, stomach in my throat. The lights at the end of the hall were all out. It was pitch-black where my classroom was. In a flash, like dominoes falling, the darkness rushed toward me. The popping sounds grew louder and sharper. Light bulbs were bursting, glass shattering onto the floor.

I bolted for the office.

It's happening.

What my mother warned me about for years.

Here.

Now.

I ran so fast I couldn't even feel my body anymore. I had only one thought: *Get out!*

Then everything went black. My eyes didn't have time to adjust, so I had no idea what was in front of me, but still I kept running. Any second, I'd reach the end of the hall. I'd be near the office, near an exit. It was right around the corner. Where was everybody? We were covered in shadows, yet there was no sound. No teachers ordering their classes to quiet down. No announcement. No alarm. Nothing.

There was only me, running, in the darkness.

Up ahead, I saw movement. Figures like shadows. Half a dozen or more. Illuminated, just barely, by the dim light coming in through the exterior doors to their left. Sharp relief filled me: I wasn't alone after all. Of course not. Why did I panic? Just a blackout. Staff was out checking on everyone. I slowed to a walk, winded, a cramp in my side.

The figures stopped moving—they seemed to be waiting for me at the end of the hall.

"What happened?" I called, out of breath.

They didn't respond.

"Um, I was called to the office?" As I approached, their bodies and faces took shape.

Oh. They didn't work at the school. Not teachers. Not administrators. And they weren't students either.

Narrow faces with flawless skin and sharp features. Slight frames with long limbs, covered in nondescript black cloaks.

I knew who they were immediately. More importantly, I knew *what* they were. Encantos. Also called fairies, but in my father's language: *encantos* or *engkantos*. Magical creatures hidden from the human realm. There were many types—diwatas were female forest and mountain spirits and human in appearance; dwendes were akin to dwarves. These were mostly munduntugs—hunters.

One of them stepped forward. Dark hair curled underneath his pointy ears. "We have very little time to waste," he said, his voice a melodious whisper. "Your father, the king, is dead. You're in grave danger. We can protect you, but you must come with us."

"Right now?" was all I managed to say. My mind was spinning. *My father is dead, I'm in danger, I have to go with them.* No, I needed to talk to my mother first. This was why we had been running all my life. To keep me safe from my father's world. And now his world had come out of the darkness and found me.

"There's no time," insisted another. Two of them stepped toward me.

The first repeated himself. "Come with us. Now."

"But my mother . . ." I began. I couldn't go without her. She needed to know where I was, what had happened.

One of them took my arm. "You must," the creature declared. "The others will be here soon." The cloak moved aside when she reached out to me, revealing an iridescent wing folded at her back. She was from the flying battalion, then. They had sent the best hunters to fetch me.

"All right," I said slowly. "But what about . . ."

"Your mother will be informed." She looked anxiously at the others.

The one who seemed to be in charge spoke again. "Of course. Now follow—"

Before he could finish, a giant gust of air blew in, like a storm coming right through the building. We all shielded our eyes but were otherwise frozen in place, stunned by the swirling wind.

The female hunter yanked on my arm and began pulling me away. She shouted to the others: "Run!"

Just as we began to move, I felt her lurch away from me suddenly, and she was gone.

The air settled, revealing another group of fairies—a group of patianaks, with sharp teeth, shimmery skin, and wings as black and glossy as a raven's. They were the fiercest and most unforgiving of the encanto warriors. I shuddered.

The hunter who'd been holding me was on the floor. One of the patianaks stood over her, his sword driven right through her torso.

Horrified, I stumbled backward, frantically trying to figure out which direction to run in. But everywhere I looked, there were more of the enemy.

The patianaks slaughtered the winged munduntug battalion with ruthless efficiency.

Back down the dark hall was better than whatever was going on here.

I turned to run, but as I did, strong arms wrapped around me.

2

DOORS OPENED. COLD air hit me. I was thrown over a shoulder and carried outside. The sky, which had been blue and sunny when I walked in that morning, had gone dark gray, menacing, with storm clouds swirling like dozens of tornadoes about to form. I was too terrified to even scream. I felt like I was outside of my body, watching it all happen.

My captors shoved me into the back seat of a black car. Two patianaks got in, one on either side of me and another in the front passenger seat. The driver was already there, waiting with the engine running.

"Where are you taking me?" I demanded as we sped away from the school. There were blinding flashes of lightning directly overhead, followed by earsplitting claps of thunder.

I lunged over to open the car door and jump out, but the patianak on my right wrapped his hand around my wrist before I could.

I tried to yank my arm away from him while struggling to get at the door with the other, but then he gripped both my wrists, and he was far stronger than I was.

I sank into the seat as if I'd given up trying to escape. When he let go of me, I leapt for the door again, but it was no use; he effortlessly blocked me. The car jerked to the right, knocking me sideways, then back to the left, so that I tumbled the other way.

"Seat belt," he hissed.

I held on to the headrests in front of me and yelled, "What are you doing?!" I looked up—we were speeding toward a red light. "Stop!" I screamed. "Stop!"

The car flew straight through the intersection, dodging other cars, which spun around behind us, blaring their horns.

The speedometer crept up, up, up, past eighty-five, then one hundred miles per hour. No way could I jump out now. This ride was going to end in a fiery crash.

We weaved around traffic. Narrowly dodged a slow-moving minivan. Cars drove off the side of the road to avoid us. I clutched on for dear life and closed my eyes, bracing for impact. We went faster and faster. Like we were flying. And maybe we *were* flying. I was afraid to look.

How were they so calm? Once it felt like we were at least traveling in a straight line, I peeked out of one eye. We were careening right into the back of a huge tractor trailer. I opened my mouth to scream right as we rammed into it—except, we didn't.

Somehow we swerved and dodged it.

I whipped around to see the truck still in one piece. When I faced forward again, we were speeding directly for a bunch of preschoolers. They were toddling across the street with their teachers, who couldn't see us behind the huge umbrellas they were holding over the children's heads. This time, I did scream.

Right before we collided, the front of the car pulled up and flew right over their umbrellas.

We were flying. Literally flying into the thunderous sky. The driver spun the wheel all the way to the right, narrowly avoiding a bright white flash of light.

And then, all at once, we were nose-diving.

I shut my eyes tight again as my stomach heaved. *This is it. It's over.*

The car hurtled toward the ground below. I bent forward instinctively and covered my head with my arms, even though that probably wouldn't do any good. The seconds felt like minutes, each one drawing out the inevitable.

But then the car yanked upward again, straightening out and slowing down. Once it was clear we were back to a stable position, I sat up cautiously and opened my eyes. We were over a huge empty lot, coming in for a landing.

Eventually the car came to a smooth stop in the dirt. At first, I was relieved to be on solid ground again, but then I had to figure out how to escape.

"Is Don Elias ready for us?" the patianak to my left asked one of the others.

Elias—I knew that name. I had vague memories of meeting him as a child; my mother talked about him. He worked for the crown, hence the title Don, which marked him as one of the lords of the court. Now, apparently, he was a traitor. Had the king's daughter kidnapped. He probably wanted the throne for himself, then. That's what this was.

My three captors stepped out of the car, one of them offering his hand to me. "Oh, now you have manners?" I didn't take it. "No, thanks. I've got it." I scooched over and got out. I was a bit wobbly on my feet after all the death-defying aerial stunts. "Where are we?" I demanded, but none of them answered me.

My heart was throbbing painfully.

They'd already killed the soldiers sent to fetch me. Would they also kill me? The hunters sent to protect me had come too late.

They gathered around me in a circle so that I couldn't flee, and herded me across the lot. I could drop to the ground, maybe. Knock their legs out from under them and make a run for it. There was no way I should let them walk me into a field. I needed the perfect moment, something to distract them, and then I could . . .

Before I finished the thought, the air in front of me changed, and for a moment everything was pixelated. Great, now I was hallucinating from the anxiety. I hoped I wasn't about to faint, because that would really screw up my escape.

But the image got clearer—it wasn't a hallucination. It was a door. An actual door. Made of dark wood, with a curved top and a gold handle. Out in a field.

Overhead, the storm clouds gathered again, as if they'd followed us there. A sudden boom of thunder, coupled with a bolt of lightning that hit the ground mere feet away, made me drop to the ground.

"Hurry!" someone said, taking my arm and getting me back up.

They began running, pulling me along, until we got to the door. One of them threw it open and pushed me through it.

All at once, the storm was gone. The field was gone. The door slammed shut, and I jumped at the sound.

We were in some kind of round room. I got the feeling we were underground, even though we hadn't gone down stairs or anything. There were no windows and no other exits. And it was oddly cozy for a kidnapper's lair. I looked around at the walls, made from the same polished mahogany as the door. There was a gray stone fireplace and an antique-looking table and chairs. Then I saw him.

"Don Elias," one of the patianaks greeted him. He was seated in a high-backed chair. A throne. So he'd already made himself king, after all. I felt a sharp stab of betrayal as I remembered exactly who he was. Elias was my father's most trusted adviser. Head councilor to the king. My godfather.

And now he meant to get rid of me, the inconvenient heir. I'd watched enough prestige medieval fantasy television shows to know how these things worked.

He sat there, large hairy hands gripping the armrests, regarding me with something like smug curiosity. The way he'd scrutinize an insect before smashing his foot down on it. I stared right back at him. I was sure he was going to kill me, but that didn't mean I had to make it easy for him.

3

I RAISED MY chin defiantly. If Elias expected me to cower and cry after that little stunt, he was in for a surprise. The corner of his mouth curled into a smile. Now he was mocking me?

"It's been a while," he said. His voice was deep. "Nice to see you again, MJ."

"Only my friends can call me that." I practically spit at him when I said it. Even though I had no friends. It was hard to make friends when you were always running away without leaving an address. I wasn't allowed social media either. Mom had made that clear. You couldn't find us online—you weren't supposed to find us anywhere.

He laughed. "You *are* your father's daughter." He pushed himself up from the chair and came toward me. I gritted my teeth and braced for a fight. It wouldn't be a long fight—he not only towered over me but was solid and muscular, too. Still, I'd inflict as much pain as I possibly could.

Then his arms opened wide. "I know you haven't seen me in too long a time." He studied me and nodded, satisfied. "You have your mother's eyes. The rest is all your father."

My mother had told me I took after my dad—that I had his same dark hair, olive complexion, proud nose, and sharp chin. But

I had my mother's eyes, as blue as the cornflowers that grew wild in her hometown.

The old man moved closer. "Is it still okay if I hug the princess?"

My eyebrows scrunched together. "Excuse me?"

He was smiling now. "It was touch and go there for a minute. We were afraid we'd lost you to the insurgent faction."

Insurgents?

The munduntug hunters were insurgents? I thought they'd come to protect me.

My shoulders relaxed, even as my mind was swirling. "So you're not . . . Hang on, didn't you stage a coup?" I motioned to the huge throne he'd been sitting in.

Elias looked at the throne, then back at me, horrified. "Of course not! Oh my, is that what you thought? That's just my comfy spot in the safe house." He reached out and gave me a bear squeeze, like a grandpa would. "You can't imagine how relieved I am that you're here with us, anak," he said, calling me *child* as he stepped back. "I made a vow to protect you, and if I'd failed, well . . ." He shook his head. "No matter. You're here in one piece."

"I thought I was being kidnapped," I said. With the immediate threat gone, I was starting to shake from the adrenaline aftershocks.

Elias narrowed his eyes at the others. "None of you explained what was happening?"

"There was no time," one of the patianaks answered, her voice raspy like the whisper of the wind. The rest nodded.

Someone else confirmed: "None at all, Elias. It was dire."

"It's true," I jumped in. "I was about to leave with the others first, and then they showed up—"

"So the insurgents did get to you?" He looked angry.

Before I could answer, another patianak stepped forward. "We thought we'd eliminated all of them. However, it looks like a few managed to breach the protective barrier before we arrived. They must have been alerted to our presence in the human realm as soon as we had crossed."

"We got lucky, then," Elias said. "Was a mambabarang among them?"

The warrior fairies all looked at one another, and then back to Elias. They shook their heads. "No witch," one of them said.

Elias sighed. "I suppose I'm not surprised. It would be too reckless. But we can discuss this later. There's no time. We must get her to Biringan."

"Wait." I held up my hand. "No one's even told me what's going on. So it's true, then, that my father is dead? They weren't just saying that so I'd go with them?" I was a toddler when my mother moved us to the human realm, so I hardly knew my father, but I felt a sharp pain in my heart, nonetheless. The pain of not knowing and then never truly knowing him.

"Afraid so, Princess," Elias said, his voice catching. It was clear Elias loved my father dearly.

My eyes watered. My father was dead. "What happened? How did he die?"

Elias didn't answer me right away, and when he did, he didn't look me in the eye. "It was . . . basically it was a natural death." He shifted his feet.

It's not like my father was old. He was an encanto; he could have lived a thousand more years. "How is that possible? Did he fall ill?" Encantos were long-lived, but I supposed they were not immortal.

"As I said, Princess, we can talk more later. The insurgents can't be far behind. I'm certain they've discovered what's happened already."

"Well, can you tell me who they are and why they're after me?"

"With the death of your father, some in our world think the throne is up for grabs. And how better to stake a claim than to first assassinate the king's heir? I have my thoughts on who might be behind it but can't share until I have more proof. It's not just you at risk either—our entire world is in danger. Without the rightful encanto on the throne, the forces of nature and magic are out of balance."

I nodded. "The weird storms."

"Correct. And every moment you're not in Biringan, it gets worse. In both worlds. Already the magic is flickering. Nothing is working as it once did."

"But why would they want that?"

"Simple. Because in the chaos, they can reign." He clapped his hands together, and the fairies rushed into action, readying their weapons and preparing to flee again. "But once you take the throne and satisfy the treaty, balance will return."

"What treaty?"

"The ancient encanto kings signed an agreement to keep the forces of magic in balance. You'll learn more when we get there." He held his arm out, motioning me toward the door once more.

I swallowed, trying to push down my anxiety. "We're going there . . . right now?"

"Yes. Well, no. First we have to get your mother."

That was the best thing I'd heard in hours. I suddenly felt lighter.

As we walked to the door, he added, "You need the amulet. The sign of your birthright."

The confusion must've showed on my face, because he said, "You don't know about the amulet?"

I shook my head.

He looked more worried now. "Let's hope it's not lost, then. And that we get there before the insurgents. If we don't, your mother will be dead."

4

"MJ!"

My mom ran for me before I even got out of the car. She was waiting anxiously at the door with two suitcases, already packed, and a belt bag over her chest. Her hair, tinged with gray at the roots, was a mess, haphazardly pulled into a bun, pieces falling out. She looked tired. More exhausted than I'd ever seen her.

"I was afraid of this," she said as she hugged me. She leaned back and took my face in her hands. "But I never guessed it would go so bad so fast."

We both looked up at the menacing sky. It was still swirling with clouds, and they were getting darker by the minute. As before, the storm seemed to be trailing us.

She started looking me over. "Are you okay?"

I nodded. "I'm fine."

"Michelle!" Elias hugged my mom. His two companions nodded to her.

"Is it true, then? Jun is dead?" she asked, her voice quavering. My father's name was Vivencio, but my mother called him by his nickname, the one used by his intimates.

"I'm so sorry," Elias told her. He cleared his throat. "You have the amulet?"

She said that she did, so he loaded the suitcases in the trunk and slammed it shut. "Let's go."

Mom and I crammed into the back seat. Elias got in the driver's seat, and then we were off again.

Looking into my eyes, Mom pulled something out of her pocket. A rough, pale crystal attached to a thick silver chain. "This is your father's amulet, an anting-anting. It's made of a very rare salt mined beneath the Paulanan Mountains of Biringan." She placed it in my hand. "Your dad gave it to me, to hold until you were ready." She got quiet, like she was remembering something, and then shook her head. "Anyway, it's yours now."

I rubbed my thumb against the grainy exterior. It was rough, yet it twinkled like a gem and seemed to glow from within.

"Here," she said, taking the amulet from me and slipping it over my head. "Keep it with you. Protect it at all costs. Because it will protect you."

"How?" It was pretty and everything, but I didn't see what protection it offered.

"If used correctly, it repels evil." She reached for my hand, and when I looked up, I saw that her cheeks were wet with tears. With a start, I realized that she still loved my father deeply and had sacrificed being with him to hide me from his enemies.

It was so dark now that we needed headlights to see in front of us, despite it still being early afternoon. I could also tell it was getting harder to control the car, with gusting winds pushing it onto the shoulder. I looked out the window, but there wasn't much to see. All the streetlights had blown out. There were no other cars on the road either.

More thunder rumbled, and it seemed to stretch on and on,

forever. Lightning bolts flashed all around us. Elias's jaw was clenched tight; his hands gripped the steering wheel so hard his knuckles were white.

More lightning again—red this time—like veins full of blood against black clouds. It made everything around us look like it was on fire. I held on to my mom's hand as the car picked up speed. We flew down the highway, passing signs so fast I couldn't even read them.

Bright flashes of yellow and red and even green and blue. Then something smacked against the windshield. I screamed. "What is that?" Whatever it was kept coming—*smack, smack, smack*. Like globs of mud hurled at the car.

No one answered me. Then I spotted what it was: frogs.

It was raining frogs.

"Am I seeing what I think I'm seeing?" I shouted.

"It's the insurgents. They want us to give up," Elias yelled back. "They think we'll be cowed by their show of strength."

Their show of *frogs*, more like. Although, to be honest, it *was* sort of gross. When the frogs hit the windshield, they splattered their amphibian guts all over the place. Eeks. Point to the insurgents.

The car veered suddenly, yanking us to the right.

We were headed straight into the mountains.

Lightning flashed. I spotted something in the rearview mirror. Another car. Without headlights.

"Someone's following us," I announced.

Elias nodded. "I know."

I started to turn and look, but he blurted out, "No, Princess!"

I sank down in the seat so my head was below the window.

Along with the car, the storm clouds trailed behind us. "How do we lose them?"

"We get to Biringan," my mother said through gritted teeth.

"What happens if we don't?" I asked.

"Everything you're seeing now and worse. Tornadoes, hurricanes, earthquakes, volcanoes erupting. You name it. Everywhere in the entire world," Elias replied. "Except none of us will actually be around to see it."

He hit the gas. I looked at the speedometer. Well over one hundred miles per hour again. And still the car behind us seemed to be gaining ground.

Elias glanced at the side mirror. "Come on," he muttered.

Just then, there was a terrible crashing sound, metal crunching. I heard it before I felt it, and noticed everyone else in the car being whipped around before my brain registered that it was happening to me, too. I felt my mom's arms reach out to protect me as the car rolled, then finally came to a stop.

I tasted blood in my mouth.

There was a second of silence.

Elias turned around. "Out!"

I broke from my mom's embrace as all the doors opened and everyone jumped out. I slipped in the mud, and pain traveled down my entire leg. My mother yanked me up with one arm. We followed Elias and the others through the woods. Branches scratched my face and snagged at my clothes, but I barely noticed. My only thought was getting away from the insurgents.

Lightning. I saw eyes in the dark. Woodland animals, peering out at us from behind the brush, as if they were spying on us.

"Nearly there," Elias called out.

The rain turned icy then, whipping against my face and burning my cheeks. We pushed on, stomping over sticks and leaves and mud, even as the droplets became chunks of hail. Elias yelled, "Watch out!" as a huge frozen ball the size of an orange hit the ground near us.

We put our hands over our heads and pressed forward. I wasn't sure how much more I could take. Hail bounced off the ground. A piece hit my mom, and she cried out. But we couldn't even stop to make sure she was all right.

Amid the chaos, the hail became snow, then a blizzard. All I could see in front of me was white. I tried to focus on Elias's dark clothing, but then I lost sight of that, too. If I hadn't felt my mom holding on to me, I wouldn't even have known she was there.

This is how it ends, I thought. *The bad guys win.*

Both my legs ached now, and I was freezing. I had the urge to lie down in the snow and go to sleep. I slowed. My mom pulled. "No," she shouted in my ear. "We have to keep going."

"I don't want to," I said, though she couldn't hear me. I could barely force myself to take another step.

My mother yelled for Elias.

Then, out of nowhere, I saw light.

First it was dim, but it got brighter and brighter, and then the snowfall thinned, until it was merely drifting down, and I saw where the light was coming from.

A huge, glowing outline of a door in front of the massive stone face of the mountain.

"There it is, MJ. The portal to Biringan." My mom encouraged me. "You're almost there. Keep going."

Elias pushed, but the door wouldn't open.

Behind us, I heard a commotion. Stomping through the woods. Flittering. Like the sound of butterfly wings fluttering together. Sounds that no human could hear, but Elias and I could. We who were from the other place. More winged battalions. More mun-duntug hunters. The insurgents were right behind us. *Hurry, hurry, hurry.*

But the door wouldn't open.

They were getting closer.

"What's happening?" my mother asked Elias. "Why won't it open?"

"They've enchanted it against us," another patianak told her.

Elias looked at me. "Princess!" He waved me over frantically.

I limped up to the door, and he pointed to my necklace. "Hold it against it!" he shouted.

I touched the anting-anting to the door handle.

At that, there was a loud click, and the door began to open.

The stomping was right behind us. The door was opening too slowly, partially enchanted by whatever dark spell our enemies had cast on it. *Come on, come on, come on.*

"Get in," Elias called out. "Squeeze if you have to!"

But it was too late. They were on us now. So many of them, even more than had come for me at school. Some were on foot and others were flying down from overhead. One of them landed between my mom and the door, blocking her. We were surrounded. And they were armed.

They charged, swords raised, and our patianaks charged back, metal clanging.

My mom ducked around the insurgents and ran for the door, bodies falling around her.

"Go!" Elias screamed at me.

I had one foot in the door. I just needed my mom. *Come on. Come on.*

Another insurgent swooped down at me, blade ready. I jumped back from the portal.

One of our warriors appeared and knocked him away from me. They rolled on the ground together, struggling. I watched as the insurgent plunged his sword into the warrior.

Elias appeared next to me, breathing heavily, with green blood all over his armor. He held out his hand. I looked around—we were the only ones left. All our allies were dead.

I was just steps from crossing into Biringan.

"MJ! Go!" my mother yelled, even as the remaining insurgents closed in.

No! I wouldn't leave her.

Then Mom reached into the bag strapped across her chest. When she pulled her hand back out, she was holding a sword.

I stared at her in awe.

She smiled. "Another gift from your father." Then she raised it up over her head, and it burst into flames. "I've got this," she shouted at me. "Go with Elias!" I could see the sky over us again, dark and swirling, pulsing with electricity.

"What about you?" I couldn't just leave her behind. She couldn't take them all on her own.

"I said go!" She turned away from me and charged for the insurgents.

This time, when Elias offered his hand I took it, and we ran for the portal. As we passed through, I looked behind me and saw my mother beyond the closing door, wielding a blade of fire that prevented the hunters from getting to me.

My mother, a warrior and a queen.

5

"BRACE YOURSELF," Elias warned me as I stepped through the doorway. Everything turned pitch-black, and then, immediately, blindingly white. I closed my eyes and held on to him, a little disoriented. I felt a lurch deep inside my stomach, like I was going to throw up.

There was some kind of turbulence, like an earthquake, and then, from beneath my eyelids, I could tell the light had dimmed. Squinting, I started to take note of our surroundings; we were inside some kind of cave. Crystal stalactites jutted down overhead, twinkling. I heard running water somewhere. A river or stream, splashing against rock. Up ahead of us, I saw an opening. On the other side there was sunshine and lots of green.

A minute later we emerged onto sandy shores softly lapped by a shimmering blue sea that matched the bright sky above. I blinked to let my eyes adjust. On the left there was a lush, dense jungle; to the right, a settlement of bahay kubos. I looked over the quaint wooden houses to see a huge structure—a castle, maybe, from what I could make out so far away—looming above the rooftops. It was searingly hot, and the air was thick, but it wasn't unpleasant. I knew Biringan was the hidden fairy realm of the Philippine

Islands and so shared its climate. And because I was of its blood, I could enter its domain from anywhere in the human world, even from Southern California, where we had just left.

At the beach in front of us, mobs of people gathered—not human people, but my father's kind, encantos. Elias gestured to them. "They're here to see you. No doubt they've heard about what happened in the human realm."

"Great," I said sarcastically. Just what I needed on the worst day of my life. An audience. They stared at me, and some of them were smiling. "Welcome back, Princess," I heard a few of them say.

Elias pointed to the placid blue sky. "We're safe here. The insurgents and their storms have been held back, for now. They won't dare attack you here, under Biringan's protection."

Mom had done it. Did she defeat them?

Was she alive?

She had to be. She *had* to be alive. *I would know if she was dead,* I told myself. I would feel it. She had to have survived.

There was a small wooden boat docked at the pier. We stepped in, and then Elias began rowing across the lake to another dock on the other side. All around us, I could see fish darting through the water around the boat, some staying alongside it and some swimming ahead.

A huge tail splashed at the surface, and then an entire body popped up out of the water. It took me a few seconds to process what I was seeing. The fish had a human upper body and nearly human face, except for the bluish-gray skin and the gills on their neck.

"Mermaids," I murmured, stunned.

"No, iha, sirenas," Elias said. Then he whispered, "Much more deadly than mere mermaids."

The sirena disappeared beneath the water.

I couldn't let the surroundings distract me from the immediate issue. "Do you think my mom is okay?"

"Your mother had the Sword of Kabunian. The Hand of God. It will have kept her safe," he said firmly.

"You'll go back, though? And make sure?"

Elias didn't answer me. He looked off into the distance. At last, he said, "If that is your wish, Princess. But first we must secure your ascension. That is why she did what she did."

I nodded as I gripped the amulet, trying to anchor myself to something. I felt disoriented, a little dizzy. And suddenly, acutely alone.

I couldn't think, couldn't process what was happening. My father was dead, and my mother . . . she had to be alive. Elias would find her and bring her back. I had to believe I would see her again.

But there was no more time to think about any of it. The boat drifted to a stop again in front of a wooden pier.

A small army was there to greet me. Guards lined the short walkway from the cavern to the road in strict formation and fanned out into the field beyond. All dressed in white formal uniforms, with long swords at their sides, they reminded me of nutcracker figurines.

A wooden calesa waited in the road beyond them. The two-wheeled carriage was painted white, with gold-spoked wheels, and the whole thing was teeming with massive, faux-floral garlands—at least, I thought they were fake. No flower could actually look like that. It seemed like the carriage itself was blooming, all the huge, vivid flowers and vines growing right out of it. Four white horses whose manes caught shades of blue and purple in the light stood at the front, unharnessed.

A guard stepped up to the boat and held his hand out to assist me. I stepped out and onto the dock, knees shaking and ankle still throbbing.

Nothing was familiar at all, even though I had spent my earliest years here. Not the vivid colors of the foliage and sky, not the hilly, lush landscape, not the undulating mountains in the distance or the river that wound through the dense forest jungle.

My mother had tried to prepare me for my role; she had taught me about the different types of encantos, and over the years my father had written me long letters about life at court. While I knew what to expect, I was still in awe of the sights in front of me.

I felt uncomfortable all of a sudden. My faded jeans looked ridiculous and out of place. I tugged my shirt down self-consciously.

Elias escorted me toward the carriage. None of the guards looked directly at me; they kept their eyes forward and their expressions glum beneath their comically large hats. When we got near, one of them opened the carriage door. I reached out to touch one of the flowers. Surprisingly not fake.

I climbed up some little steps on the side of the carriage.

Inside, the seats were wide and plush, upholstered in silk, soft and buttery, and the canopy was decorated with intricate embroidered floral patterns, edged with gold thread. I wanted to reach out and run my finger across the texture, but I was afraid to make it dirty. It was like sitting inside a museum piece.

Elias sat across from me. The door shut.

We set off down a rustic dirt road that was lined with flowers, inky blues and intense pinks, bright yellow and white and every shade of green imaginable. Onlookers stood at the edge, vying for a chance to see the princess inside the carriage. They looked like any group of regular people, until I noticed the small differences that gave them away as encanto—their elfin ears; the impossible perfection of their thick, glossy, waist-length black hair; their long, delicate fingers and spiry necks.

"Remember, Princess. Enemies are everywhere. Since your father died, we've been investigating, but until we know who the insurgents are and which court they're working for, trust no one."

My mother had schooled me in the history of Biringan and how the four courts representing the four kingdoms had been unified long ago. In his many letters, my father explained it was an uneasy alliance, and while Sirena, our court and kingdom, was the most powerful and thus the overall ruler, there were those who chafed under our reign. As the princess of the Sirena Court, diwata of Paulanan, I embodied the power and spirit of the mountains and the seas. The Court of Sigbin harnessed the power of thunder and lightning and was full of encantos who practiced chaos magic. The equinox courts were the kingdoms at the outer edges of the realm—the Court of Tikbalang was rooted in the power of the forest and known for its affinity for animals, while the Court of Lambana commanded the air and the wind and counted mischief among its talents.

The road split, veering off toward the mountains in the distance, disappearing into towering trees to the left; we took the right turn, through still more trees, where the crowd could no longer gather. As we traveled farther and farther from the world I knew, I marveled at how the landscape could be so familiar, yet not; the earth was somehow darker and richer; the blue sky and puffy clouds looked like a watercolor or a filtered photo. The birds seemed to come straight from a fairy tale. They were plumper and less skittish, and it almost seemed as if every one of their feathers was perfectly hand-painted. I didn't know much about birds, but I was pretty sure those patterns and colors didn't exist in the regular world. I was tempted to hold my hand out the window and see if one would land on my finger.

Still, I was well aware that, just like in a fairy tale, evil was lurking somewhere nearby. Waiting for the right moment.

Elias sensed my apprehension. "The sooner you are crowned queen and solidify your power, the sooner you—and all of us—will be safe."

As we rounded one of the turns, some sort of huge stone or hill appeared in front of us. It rose up into the clouds, so high that I couldn't tell where it ended. Like everything else, it was almost too perfect to be real.

"Almost there," Elias told me. "The palace is just ahead of us now."

I leaned close to the window and searched around in every direction. "Where is it?" I asked him.

He pointed at the enormous rock. "Right in front of us, Princess."

This time when I looked back, I saw immediately what I'd missed before. There, at the base, partially obscured by a cinematic fog, a glittering palace materialized from within, like it was carved directly out of the stone around it.

As my eyes focused, I studied all the detail. The surface of the palace kind of reminded me of a geode I bought at a museum gift shop when I was little—a dazzling gemstone inside an unassuming gray rock. The entire surface looked like that. Tiny multifaceted gems jutted out as if the stone had been split wide open long, long ago, revealing the jeweled interior. There were many windows, too many to count, set deep into the structure, and at least four rounded, pearlescent towers.

When we got closer, I saw a steep path set with large stones, like marble, winding up to a huge, domed doorway, which seemed to be made of glass or some type of crystal. Smaller—though still larger than any human would ever require—double doors were cut out of the glass. I watched as they opened to let in two guards marching in line. Two more stood on either side of the doors, and still others were visible within.

We parked in front of the path. A guard stepped up and opened the door. Elias exited first, then helped me out.

I stood outside the carriage and took in the castle I would now call home. I had been there before, but I was too young to remember. My mother had made sure I grew up knowing who my father was, what my birthright entailed, but this was so far from our reality of cramped one-bedroom apartments and hand-me-down furniture that I found it hard to believe I was truly from here.

And as I looked at the serious faces of the rows of armed guards surrounding me, I reminded myself that while it appeared to be a dream on the surface, it concealed a nightmare underneath. A throne without a ruler and a plot to kill the heir.

6

WE STEPPED INSIDE the palace. The round entrance hall had a sky-high ceiling that came to a steep point. A diamond chandelier hung overhead, suspended from a long gold chain. All the walls and the floor were made of quartz, vaguely translucent and almost glittery, but there were also blooming vines that seemed to grow straight out of where the floor and walls met. White sampaguita flowers climbed the walls on all sides. Then I noticed an interior doorway—at least two stories tall, arched, with double doors and huge curvy handles, like twisted branches. The handles had perfect sticklike trunks, with puffy round green tops and tiny white and pale-pink flowers.

"Welcome to the Palace of the Sirena Court, Your Highness." A butler in a barong Tagalog—a sheer formal shirt made from the linen of pineapple husks—appeared by my side. He barely came up to my elbow. "My name is Ayo." He was one of the dwendes, mischievous sprites. He held his hand out to show me the way.

I looked to Elias, unsure whether I should trust this stranger. He nodded his approval.

Still unable to find words, I followed Ayo through the big doors. They opened like magic in front of us, revealing another foyer with a wide curving staircase. It went straight, then split to the right and left. We headed up. Elias and some guards marched dutifully behind us, along with a few maids in matching gray uniforms. Like the door handles, the banister was made from varnished tree branches. It seemed to be one continuous piece of wood.

We went to the right. At the top of the stairs there was a gorgeous landing, the same quartz floor. "Your rooms are this way," Ayo told me.

We went through another amazing door, and another, until we reached a deeper interior of the palace. A sitting room with large chairs made of woven rattan, with high, curved backs, preceded yet another room, this one with a large desk and a gold chair with a white seat.

"This is your office, where you will receive your correspondences, conduct official business—that sort of thing," Ayo told me.

My heart skipped a beat. I had no idea how to do any of that. I hardly knew how to manage myself. Mere hours ago, I couldn't even pay attention to an economics lesson. Let alone manage a kingdom. I felt like an impostor.

I wished my mother was here with me and that I had been able to see my father before his death. But I pushed down my fear and sadness. No matter how intimidated I was, I had to honor both my parents by taking the throne and living up to the position. And to my ancestors. All the encantos in my family tree. The last diwata of the Paulanan Mountains had been my great-great-great-grandmother. There had not been a female heir, a mountain spirit, in the family until my birth. I had to take up the mantle of my legacy. Later there would be time to grieve my father and the separation from my mother.

"On to your private chambers," Ayo said as he kept on walking, past some more sitting spaces set up around the area and tall bay windows with seats built in, and through yet another door. That one led to another high-ceilinged chamber that not only accommodated a massive canopy bed but also multiple wardrobes, a dressing table, and a walk-in closet that could easily have been another bedroom—in fact, it was bigger than mine at home. There was a gleaming, airy bathroom attached, with another separate space just for the ornate marble claw-foot tub, as well as a private lanai with tall French doors opening onto a golden-railed balcony. It was larger than our entire apartment back home.

Even better, it was all in my favorite color: shades of purple, from lilac to deep, rich plums, coupled with lots of white—the floors, a crescent sofa, the furniture—and gold accents. Handles, doorknobs, a huge gold-and-crystal chandelier.

After a brief walk-through of the rooms, we returned to the bedchamber. A timid young girl who looked not much older than me stood near the door to the walk-in closet. Her hands were clasped in front of her white-and-silver gown. She looked down at the ground.

"This is Jinky, your lady-in-waiting," Ayo told me. "Her family has worked in the Sirena Palace for centuries."

Jinky curtsied. She was pretty, with long black hair and a gentle smile. Her skin was a pale moss green, which marked her as a mountain spirit. She seemed nice, so that was a relief, at least. "Hi," I said to her. "My name's MJ."

That caused a flurry of uncomfortable throat-clearing around the room. Jinky looked up, as if she was alarmed, and Ayo rushed forward and started making excuses for my apparent gaffe. "Ahem.

Yes." He cleared his throat again. "May I present Her Highness, princess of the Court of Sirena, diwata of Paulanan, one true heir to King Vivencio of Biringan," he announced.

After that everyone seemed more at ease. I guess I'd been too casual with Jinky. Not sure how I was going to keep up with all this protocol.

"It is good to see you returned to us," he said. "We were worried the insurgents . . ."

"They came close," I said. Just thinking about it brought back the fear, as if a winged enemy would appear from the shadows.

"You have no fear of that here, Princess," Ayo assured me. "They cannot breach the magic that protects you in this palace." To Jinky, he said, "Our soon-to-be queen is as yet unfamiliar with court etiquette." Then he turned to me. "However, all will be remedied. You have been apprised of your start date with the Biringan Academy of Noble Arts?"

Even as the one true heir, I couldn't escape school, it seemed. "Afraid not," I said.

He took out a tiny leather pocket book and flipped a couple pages. "Ah, then allow me to deliver the wonderful news!" he said, as if I'd won the lottery or something. "Your coronation training will commence immediately. You are set to begin bright and early tomorrow morning."

Tomorrow morning? "But I just got here. I don't get to, like, settle in first?" I had just escaped from an insurgent faction of winged assassins, lost all contact with my mother, and said goodbye to the only world I had lived in for almost all of my life.

"Afraid not, Your Highness. We want our leaders to be wise, learned people. And if I may be quite honest, you are a few years behind in your formal training. There's no time to spare. The coronation is scheduled for your eighteenth birthday."

I balked. "That's in a month."

"Technically speaking, less than a month," he said. "Therefore, as I said, no time to lose."

"I can't be ready in a month," I insisted. Panic rose in my throat.

Elias stepped up. "If I may, Princess, the reality is, you must. Biringan's magic will only continue to fade until then. The disorder we just endured is nothing compared to what will happen should we lose control entirely."

Ayo agreed. "Thank you, Don Elias, for underlining the gravity of the situation." He turned to me. "If you'll excuse me, there is much to be done. I'll return later this evening." At that he nodded curtly, bowed, then turned abruptly and left the room. The other maids and guards followed him.

Once they were gone, Elias asked me, "Before I go, since we have a moment of privacy, is there anything I should tell the academy about your talent?"

I had no idea how to answer that. "Like, can I sing?"

"No, Princess." He looked perturbed. "What I mean is, what is your ability? Your magic?"

"Oh! Um . . ." I tried to think. Did I have one? At any time in my life, had anything magical ever happened to me? As the mightiest warrior in Sirena, my father could command the oceans to do his bidding, and it was said he possessed many magical gifts, so great was his power. But I couldn't even make a ripple. In his letters, he had told me my talent would manifest when it was time. So far, it had not been time.

Encanto magic was rooted in the earth and in the elements, the ability to command water and fire, to communicate with animals and plant life, or to transform into different creatures. But so far, I was as ordinary as any other mortal.

"Think, Princess," Elias said. "Surely it's revealed itself by now. Perhaps you simply didn't recognize it. Think of a time you were under duress. Did anything strange happen? Something otherwise unexplainable?"

I racked my brain, trying to think of something, anything, I'd ever done that could be interpreted as magic. Nothing came to mind. Not a single thing. And the most stress I'd ever been under had just happened to me. Still, nada.

"Hmmm," Elias said, tapping his chin. "In order to be crowned queen, you must display your powers as part of the coronation. While I understand you did not grow up here, we were led to believe that your father guided you from afar. You were supposed to be taught about these things, so you'd—"

"Well, actually, yes. I have magic," I said quickly. I wasn't going to let him think my mother somehow failed. In fact, it made me mad. For good measure, I added, "I do remember something. My mother always told me to keep it a secret. I'm not super comfortable talking about it right now." I attempted an air of confidence. In my father's letters, he assured me that I would eventually discover my talent, that it would manifest at the right time. Since it had yet to reveal itself, though, I couldn't help but begin to panic. But I couldn't show Elias that.

The old man was visibly relieved, his tone brightening. "Of course. I understand. Rest assured, the staff here at the palace has been thoroughly vetted, by me, personally. We're all invested in your ascendancy. You should feel safe to share your talent when you're ready."

"Right. Good to know. So, how, exactly, do I display it? At the coronation." I needed to figure out how I was going to make this work.

"After a display of their powers, the one true heir must remove the royal scepter from a solid wooden chest. Only the rightful ruler can do so; all others will fail. Pass this test, and you are crowned."

I swallowed. "Sure. No problem." Also a lie.

It was a huge problem.

7

ONLY FOUR WEEKS until the coronation.

Four weeks to figure out how to unlock my magic or else forfeit the throne and lose everything my parents worked for. Four weeks of looking over my shoulder, worrying about more assassins, even though supposedly I was safe here. The next morning, Elias assured me all the insurgents had been routed out of Biringan, and he had sent more patianaks to hunt the rest, who were hiding in the human realm. But since he still wasn't completely sure who had sent them, I still felt uneasy. The one good piece of news was that he had also sent encantos to find out what had happened to my mother and to bring her back here safely as soon as they could.

Today was another first day of school, too.

The royal entourage, with me once more in the white-and-gold calesa blooming with flowers, surrounded by soldiers on horseback, approached the building from the main road that connected each of the courts to the middle of the island. I stared up at the towering structure. It was even bigger than the Sirena Palace, though it wasn't exactly a castle—more like a series of spirals reaching up into the clouds, camouflaged among all the mountain peaks surrounding them. I couldn't tell what they were made of.

They almost looked metallic or, as I got closer, like the surface of glossy, wet pebbles or a sleek, smooth worry stone. There were no seams or cracks, as if the entire structure was made of one humongous piece of rock carved from the mountain. The school's name was spelled out in huge, swirling letters over the wide entrance: BIRINGAN ACADEMY OF NOBLE ARTS.

I felt a little sick. Nerves. I clutched the amulet beneath my new uniform and took a deep breath. It felt like my mother was with me. If I closed my eyes, I could imagine her sitting right next to me, holding my hand. That helped.

One thing at a time. I took out the rolled-up parchment that had been delivered to my room that morning.

FIRST HOUR: *Introduction to History of Biringan, Room 421*
SECOND HOUR: *Pagkahari at Paggalang, Room 1123*
THIRD HOUR: *Astronomiya, Room 716*
FOURTH HOUR: *Biringan Hayop at Halaman, Room 622*
FIFTH HOUR: *Tanghalian, BANA Dining Hall*

Maybe some of these classes would include the key to finding my magical power. If I had any. But I was happy to note that tanghalian—lunch—was on the schedule.

We pulled up to the circular drive. Others were being dropped off by calesas, too, which made for a very strange sight for a girl from California, but even in this surreal fantasy, my ride stood out. The other carriages were smaller and less ostentatious and weren't accompanied by armed soldiers. There was definitely no chance of my showing up unnoticed.

My new classmates were whispering and craning their necks to get a look at the new princess. I'd never felt so exposed. It was like the bad dream where I showed up at school naked.

After exiting the carriage and making sure my encanto's robe was settled around me properly—over my tunic and pants and not gathered into my waistband or something—I started for the doors, conscious of everyone's eyes on me. Some took care to give me a wide berth and scurry by as fast as they could, but others were perfectly comfortable with openly staring.

While I was walking, another calesa pulled in. This one was more like mine, except decorated with palm leaves and braided with ylang-ylang and white hooded orchids. It was also flanked on the sides and back by guards, though fewer than mine had been.

I was curious but not enough to gape. The doors of the academy opened in front of me, and I walked inside. As in the palace, there was intricate woodwork everywhere, and remarkably high ceilings, but somehow, the space still had the familiar aura of school. Maybe it was the steady hum of voices in the background from students and staff talking and making their way from room to room, combined with the faint smell of books and paper—leather and ink and dust—because there were no lockers or worn-out linoleum floors. If anything, it was what I imagined the ancient Library of Alexandria had looked like, except even more beautiful. None of my old high schools had floral displays or hand-carved stair banisters or— I stopped in my tracks. A group of butterflies was flitting around one of the flowerpots. I'd never seen butterflies indoors, but I chalked that up to just one more example of what a different place I was in now. I got closer for a better look. Their wings were enormous and almost glittery. I stepped forward and leaned down.

One of the wings smacked my cheek. I flinched and heard a tiny voice scold, "Do you mind?"

"I'm . . . sorry?" I stepped back. Sprites. Or more accurately, lambanas. My mother had told me about them, but I'd never quite believed they were real.

"So rude," I heard one of their tiny voices exclaim.

I backed away, a bit stunned by what had just happened, and tried to look for my first class instead. Lots of students paraded past, colorful robes swishing around their feet. Mine was purple and yellow, the official colors of the Court of Sirena. Those wearing blue and white, I knew, were residents of the Court of Sigbin, and Elias had told me green and pink were for the Lambana Court, and maroon and black for the Court of Tikbalang. I didn't see many wearing the Sirena colors, which was fine by me, because then I'd feel obligated to introduce myself, and for now I was only interested in getting my bearings. Surprisingly, they weren't paying much attention to me anymore. I guess away from the royal calesa and with nothing to identify me as the crown princess, I was just another anonymous newbie in the hall. That, at least, I was used to.

While I was looking for room numbers, I heard a tinkling sound, like small bells or a wind chime. A few students started walking faster down one of the hallways. *That must be the bell system,* I thought. I saw a stairwell and decided to go up and hopefully find the fourth floor, the logical place for room 421.

The stairs only went up one flight, though. Hmm. I regretted not getting a map of the building, but I was so used to being able to access things like that on my phone that I hadn't even thought of it. First day and already falling behind.

"Are you lost?"

It was a student who was obviously from the Sigbin Court standing there in her blue robes. Elias had warned me that the Sigbin kingdom was the most resentful of having to bow to the Sirena Court, and that he suspected the insurgents were from that kingdom, but without concrete evidence, he couldn't make a formal accusation. Regardless, I was immediately on the defensive. First thing I noticed was the moon-shaped silver tiara perched on top of her jet-black hair streaked with midnight-blue highlights, which was pulled up into one of those complicated updos I admired but was never able to master. My ponytail felt really childish all of a sudden. I regretted turning down Jinky's offer to do my hair and to wear the golden circlet traditionally worn by diwatas on their brow. "Uh . . ." I said, unsure if I wanted this person's help.

"What room are you looking for?" She walked over to me and snatched the schedule out of my hands to study it. "Oh, wow, you have to take Hayop at Halaman? That's a remediary fauna-and-flora class for first-years."

"You mean 'remedial'?" I corrected her. Normally I wouldn't, but who comments on someone being behind in school to begin with?

She screwed up her face with distaste. "What? No. It's definitely 'remediary.'" She shook her head and pushed the paper back at me. "You'll have to go upstairs for Intro to History."

"Yeah, I figured. Thanks." I began to walk away from her. She clearly didn't know who I was, and that was fine. Hopefully our paths wouldn't cross again.

"Don't you want to know where it is?" she called, as if she was the one who was insulted by this whole interaction.

I turned around, just to avoid any more bad blood, and forced a smile. "Sure."

"Left at the next hall, all the way down, then left again," she said sweetly. "There's a door that leads to the fourth-floor stairs."

"Thanks," I said, and walked away again.

"No problem," she crooned.

I rolled my eyes as soon as she couldn't see me.

At the next hall, I went left, and then left again, as she'd said. There were no other students around, so I was really lost this time. Finally, I saw the door she was talking about. There was a gold plaque that said TO FOURTH FLOOR with arrows pointing up. Relieved, I reached out to open it.

Next thing I knew, I was falling forward, with nothing but vast darkness underneath me. I held on to the door handle, but I was losing my grip fast, and I knew I was about to drop into whatever that void was.

Someone grabbed on to my cloak just in time and yanked me back. We both stumbled and collapsed into a heap on the floor.

I jumped up quickly and looked to see who'd saved me. A mousy little thing with glasses perched on the end of her nose stood up. She wore a Lambana gown, with silver flats poking out beneath it.

She curtsied stiffly, pushed her thin shoulder-length hair behind her ears, and said, "Hello, Your Highness. Um, I heard your conversation back there, and, maybe it's not my place to interfere, but, um, Lady Oscura was lying to you. She sent you to the refuse shaft. It's for waste incineration and experiments gone wrong."

I should have known.

"Lady Oscura doesn't like hapcantos," she added, grimacing. "You know, half-human and half-encanto?"

Oh. I guess I needed to add bigotry to the list of things to deal with in Biringan. That also meant the girl—Lady Oscura—*did* know who I was when she was talking to me like that. And if this girl hadn't been around, what might've happened to me? I felt like such a fool. A fool who almost got incinerated. Was this just a prank, or another attempt on my life?

She pointed to the door. The plaque now read plainly: REFUSE ROOM. DO NOT ENTER.

That's what I got for trusting a bully in magic school. "Thank you," I told her, and I really meant it. "What's your name?"

"Fortunada, Your Highness. From Bagobos." She made a quick curtsy.

"Beautiful name. Also, just call me MJ. How did you know who I was?"

She blushed. "Everyone knows who you are. It's all anyone can talk about—how the princess has returned. Where's your first class? I can help you get there, if you'd like."

Even though I knew, I looked down at the parchment to double-check. Maybe that had been changed somehow, too. "History of Biringan, room 421." Still the same. A small relief.

"Oh, Professor Borromeo. I had her. She's really nice. It's down this way."

I followed Fortunada through the halls. "I like your bracelet," I said. It was gold, with luminescent pearls and sparkling diamonds. Didn't really match with her understated vibe, though.

"Thank you." She touched it. "It belonged to my grandmother."

That explained it. "It's beautiful."

"It was a gift from her brother," Fortunada said, almost as an aside. She pointed to a door in front of us. "Here it is."

On the complete opposite end from where I'd been sent, of course. "See you around," I told her. "And thanks for saving me."

She waved her hand shyly and hurried away, her hair falling back over her face.

Class had already begun. I felt bad because that meant Fortunada was late for hers, too. Hopefully I didn't get her in trouble or anything.

"Princess, we were getting worried about you," Professor Borromeo said as I walked into the room. "Please, have a seat." She held her hand out at the empty desks. There weren't many other students—maybe half a dozen. The desks were large and sturdy, made of the same shiny, knotted wood as so many other things around the school, and the chairs were big and comfortable.

As I sat, I looked to my right and saw the girl who sent me to the refuse room. Lady Oscura herself. She smirked at me ever so slightly.

"Coronation plans delay you this morning? I'm sure it's well under way by now, with so little time to spare," Professor Borromeo said.

Lady Oscura squirmed in her seat and looked away. I could've ratted her out. Instead, I said, "Yes, I'm so sorry to keep you waiting. It won't happen again."

"Quite all right." There was a book the size of an old dictionary on the desk in front of her. She flipped it open and said, "Now that we're all here, we can begin. Please open your texts to page one."

I watched everyone pull a book from a shelf under their desk. I reached under my own and found a deckle-edged, brown leather tome with gold-foiled letters embossed on the front: BIRINGAN: A HISTORY.

Lady Oscura leaned into the girl next to her. "Of course we have to review for her," she whispered. "We all know this already."

Professor Borromeo began reading from the intro: "Nobody knows exactly when the fairy realms were founded, but we know it predates the human world by at least several hundred thousand years . . ." I knew all that, along with the fact that Biringan was only one of the fairy realms. There were others—Avalon, of course, as well as Valhalla, Narnia, the Grey Havens, and Jade Mountain, just to name a few.

I shouldn't have tuned out the lecture, but I couldn't help it. I figured I could always read the book later. At the moment I was too distracted by Lady Oscura and her attempted prank. Too angry, really. The entire class I thought of ways to get back at her. I could prank her back, but I didn't know enough about this world yet to pull that off. I could confront her. Or I could pretend nothing ever happened. That one didn't sound too appealing when all I wanted was to get back at her, but it would probably annoy her the most, since a reaction was exactly what she wanted.

I got my chance the next hour when I arrived at room 1123 for Pagkahari at Paggalang (Royal Etiquette and Governance), this time with some directions assistance from Professor Borromeo.

Lady Oscura was sitting right up front alongside a tall, impossibly handsome boy in matching Court of Sigbin regalia. She had her hands clasped delicately in her lap, back straight against the chair, her perfection on display for all to see. I caught her companion's eye as I walked to an empty desk, though I quickly looked away.

"Do you smell something?" she asked him. She'd obviously been waiting for that moment.

"No, actually, I don't," he responded.

Lady Oscura tried to look at me discreetly without turning her head, as if I wouldn't notice. "Are you sure?" she pressed. "It's something . . . earthy. Almost like . . . trash?"

"Quite sure," he said. He raised an eyebrow. "Why?"

She crossed her arms. Her foot began to tap. On the inside, I was laughing. Her little scheme to embarrass me was falling flat.

Another student walked in. She had Chinese features, with pale skin and dark eyes. Most of the encantos in Biringan had the same features as their human counterparts in the Philippines—a mix of Filipino, Chinese, and Spanish heritage. Her hair was up in a braided bun, and she wore the pink-and-green Lambana robes. I noticed the hem was stained and fraying, and some of the seams were coming undone. She plopped down in the seat next to me, out of breath. "Phew!" she exclaimed. "Didn't think I was going to make it." She looked at me. "Oh, hey! You're the newbie. King Vivencio's daughter."

I nodded. "That's me."

She held out her hand. "I'm Phoenix Xing. But people I like call me Nix."

I shook her hand. It was nice to be treated somewhat normally after the last couple days. "I'm MJ," I told her. "Your name sounds really familiar."

"So. Is it true you're half-human?" she asked.

I hesitated. After what Fortunada said before, I wasn't sure how to answer that. In those few short seconds since we met, I already wanted Nix to like me. I liked her casual, no-nonsense style right away. "Yes," I said. If she wasn't going to like me for that, then she wasn't going to be a good friend anyway.

"Yeah, me too," she said, like it was no big deal. "I lived in the human world until last year." She lowered her voice and leaned closer. "It's bananas, though, right? All of this?"

I nodded emphatically. "Totally."

"I'll help you out." She winked. "Us hapas, or hapcantos, have to have each other's backs." She gestured at Lady Oscura with her pen. "Especially with those types. I didn't even know girls like that existed anymore. Didn't she hear bullying is out of style?"

"She tried to send me to the refuse room," I told Nix. Her eyes widened.

At that, an elderly man with a long white beard glided into the room.

"Here comes Gandalf," Nix whispered to me. I stifled a laugh, but it snuck out as a snort. Lady Oscura turned and curled her lip at me.

The professor stood at the front of the room and surveyed us. It seemed like he didn't like what he saw. Aside from the Court of Sigbin menace and her boyfriend, there were me, Nix, and a few other students from the various courts.

"You have found yourself enrolled in Pagkahari at Paggalang, an exclusive course of study only for court heirs and future rulers that replaces your former second-hour classes. If that is not you, please exit quietly." He waited a second. No one stood. He grunted. "Excellent. In that case, we can begin. My name, as most of you know, is Professor Manatubay. It is not 'Manatubay.' Nor is it 'Prof.' It is 'Professor Manatubay.' Now that we've established that I am your instructor and not your friend, we can move on to our first line of business: You are all expected to come prepared to work on a daily basis. Our first unit will focus exclusively on those skills which are of utmost benefit in light of the impending coronation of our new queen."

Everyone looked at me again. I smiled weakly and shrugged. I was not used to being the center of attention like this. I was no one in the human realm—forever the new kid, always out of place. Here, I was a princess, but mostly I felt like a fraud.

At least I managed to stay awake this time, not because Professor Manatubay was catering to me, but because of Nix's entertaining commentary, which she slipped across our desks on tiny pieces of paper. *He's actually older than Gandalf, I think,* said one, and the next was a hastily drawn sketch of Lady Oscura and the boy she was next to, with a leash around his neck. Underneath his portrait Nix had written *Sir Lucas the Loyal.* So that was her boyfriend's name: Lucas.

Professor Manatubay snatched the paper off Nix's desk. "What is this?" He stared at it. "Mocking our classmates, are we? Is that conduct worthy of royalty?"

"But, sir, Amador tried to kill the princess," Nix said sweetly.

A series of gasps erupted around the room. Even Professor Manatubay was shocked. He stammered before managing to say, "Don't make baseless accusations against—"

"It's not baseless," Nix insisted. "She sent the princess to the refuse room."

Professor Manatubay looked at Lady Oscura, who had her hand over her heart and her mouth hanging open. "What is the meaning of this?" he asked her.

"Professor, I, for one, am floored. *Of course* I wouldn't do something like that. It was a simple mistake. Why would I want to hurt our princess?" She locked eyes with me. I refused to look away first.

The professor stepped between us. "There will be no more non-sense like this at our school. Is that understood?"

He glanced around while everyone murmured, "Yes."

"Good," he continued. "Perhaps it needs to be reiterated: Biringan faces an uncertain future. These are dire times. We must all play our part in keeping the realm in balance, or else everyone suffers. I will not tolerate destructive behavior unbecoming of our future rulers. Each of you carries great responsibility; do not squander it. Or you squander us all."

Everyone remained silent while he walked back to the front of the room, crumpling Nix's drawing along the way.

AT THE END of class, Nix asked me where I was going next, so she could give me real directions. I pulled out the parchment again. "By the way, what do we do in the afternoon?"

"Oh. We leave after lunch."

"Really?" I was stunned. School here was only a half day?

"I know, right? Isn't it great? When I got here and found out about the short school day, I was so excited. And for real, kind of mad that I didn't get here earlier."

It was definitely a perk. One of the few so far without strings attached. "Is there somewhere else—a library, maybe—where I could go during lunch? Like, if I have something I need to do."

"There is," she said slowly. "You know, I have to meet with my adviser today. But if you want, meet me at lunch tomorrow, and we'll sit together, okay? Unless you have other plans already," she added quickly.

"Yeah, no. I . . . don't know anyone."

"Say no more. I'll see you tomorrow." She waved as she took off down the hallway.

That had never happened to me before. On my first day at a new school, I might have managed to make a friend.

8

EVEN THOUGH IT was a month away, coronation preparation was already in full swing. On the way home from the academy, I saw horses pulling carts full of giant flowerpots and pallets of lumber. There were workers trimming trees and planting new flowers. Everywhere I looked, it seemed like the citizens of Biringan were eagerly anticipating their new queen. It seemed a bit much, but then I remembered all the lead-up to the British king's coronation back home. Maybe royal protocol was the same across all the worlds.

With a start, I realized I was going to disappoint everyone in Biringan if I didn't figure out my magic soon. *No, far worse than disappoint them,* I reminded myself. They were sure to be devastated. The whole realm hung in the balance until the new ruler was crowned.

When I returned to the palace, I headed straight to my private rooms to change out of my uniform. I threw off the robe and flung it over the back of a chair. Underneath I was wearing a simple linen tunic and pants in matching Sirena colors.

I walked into the huge closet—its own room, really—and there were four more matching uniform sets already hanging there.

Another thing to get used to; someone was always in and out of my room. This place didn't feel like home yet. More like a fancy hotel where I was the guest of honor.

I heard the door open and shut. Jinky rushed into the room, out of breath. She found me in the walk-in closet.

"What's wrong?" I asked, alarmed.

After curtsying, she said breathlessly, "Your Highness, apologies for my absence; I was tending to your afternoon meal in the kitchen, and there was a slight mishap. Had I known you were back—"

"Jinky," I interrupted. "It's fine! Don't worry about it. I thought something bad happened."

She looked relieved. "I should have been here before you. And I will be, going forward. Is there anything I can do for you, Your Highness? Would you like me to bring your merienda now?"

There was something I wanted to ask her, but I didn't want to be too obvious about it. "Actually, yes, I'd love my afternoon tea. How did you know? Must be your talent, huh?" I cringed internally. Real smooth.

Luckily, she didn't seem to notice how awkward I was. She beamed. "In fact, my talent is sweetening tea leaves, Your Highness. It's very minor, but it comes in handy."

"Oh, wow, that's cool. How did you find it?" Yeah, I was not winning any awards for subtlety.

She scrunched her nose. "I'm not sure it's something you can find, at least not intentionally. It comes naturally—like yours, yes?"

Definitely had to steer away from this direction. While I tried to think of what to say, she added, "I suppose many find their talent when they don't expect it."

That was it. I needed to give myself space for quiet, to let it reveal itself organically. I couldn't force it. And the best place to do that was right outside my window—the gardens. All I had to do was get there alone, and it would happen.

Then she blurted out, "I am enjoying our conversation, Your Highness, only, I'm supposed to take your school robes every day for cleaning."

"Oh!" I took it off the back of the chair and handed it to her. It wasn't dirty, in my opinion, but I didn't want to give her any more strife about doing her job. She held it draped over her open arms.

"I'll return shortly, Your Highness," she said, curtsying.

This was my chance. "Actually, I was thinking about taking a walk in the gardens before my afternoon tea. So if you get back and I'm not here . . ."

"Oh, of course. I will inform the guards."

"Uh. Do you have to?" I was hoping to have some real alone time, not alone time being shadowed by a bunch of people in armor. That would make me self-conscious.

She looked terribly conflicted. "I suppose not," she said slowly. "If that's what you want. Though Don Elias will be furious with me."

I didn't want to get her in trouble, but I didn't want to be followed around either. "No one even has to know that I told you where I'm going. If there's a problem, I'll say I decided while you were bringing the clothes to the laundry."

That satisfied her. I headed out of my rooms to go find the exit nearest to the gardens. The hall was silent. The only noise was way off in the distance, a dim hum of voices traveling up from the main foyer and the faint clang of guards' swords as they did their rounds. At least I'd hear them coming.

From what I could remember, the doors that led to the garden were in the receiving room two floors below my chambers. I decided to use the nearest servant stairwell as a shortcut, though Jinky and Ayo would probably have a heart attack if they knew.

I hesitated, listening for anyone walking, but it was completely silent. So I crept down the steps. At the bottom, I entered the hall, then hurried through the long space, dodging all the heavy furniture.

Nobody bothered me the whole way. I went through the glass doors, then took the stone path that curved all the way around the fenced gardens. Along the edges of the palace grounds, I could see guards patrolling, so far away that they looked like little toys, heads bobbing as they walked. When I got to the white iron gate, I slipped inside without opening it all the way and shut it softly behind me.

Beyond the fence, the scene looked like what I pictured when reading *The Secret Garden* years ago. It looked wild and unkempt, except there were no weeds anywhere, only lush green shrubs and bright, full blooms, and the path itself was neatly edged.

Yes, this was the best place to allow my magic to reveal itself.

There were two white benches near the entrance area, and a few feet ahead, the path split in two. A wooden sign indicated that the rest of the garden was to the left and the hedge maze was to the right.

I wasn't exactly sure what I was supposed to do, so I decided to wander in the hedge maze for a bit. Also the best way to avoid being seen, I figured.

For a while, it was just me and the chirping of nearby birds, the occasional chipmunk peeking at me before running away. I ran my hand along the scratchy bushes that made up the walls of the maze and imagined I was a goddess from a Greek myth exploring her kingdom.

I waited to feel something.

Any minute now.

I closed my eyes. Tried to clear my head and listen only to the sounds around me. Maybe the natural environment, the place of my ancestors, would inspire something to stir within.

Nothing.

Frustrated, I walked farther into the maze. I worried I might get lost, but then again, maybe that would actually help. I'd have to use magic to find my way out.

I took turns randomly, until I wasn't sure which way led back to the exit.

As I headed around another corner, deeper into the maze, I heard a noise. Something moving in the bushes. I held back, making myself as flat against the shrub wall as possible. There was a slight tap of feet against the ground, and then it stopped.

I peeked around the corner. There were two girls, huddled together, whispering. Judging by their gray-and-white dresses, they were palace maids, from either the kitchens or laundry. Why come all the way out here? It could be a secret tryst, but it didn't seem like that. I strained to hear what they were saying. Not because I was being nosy—well, a little bit—but because I wanted to know if they were talking about me.

Their heads turned. I flattened myself back and held my breath, certain they'd heard me.

I tried to peer through gaps in the bush; I could only see parts of them. One led the other to a bench. Good, they didn't know I was there.

"Did you hear what Marikit said? She was the one who found him," I heard one of them say. "She said it wasn't natural."

No, their conversation wasn't about me. They were gossiping about something far more interesting. I inched as far forward as possible without giving myself away.

The other voice added, "I told you. It was the same as the other one."

"Did you hear about the note he left?"

"What note?"

"Supposedly the king was writing a note when he died."

"If you ask me, it was dark magic that got him. He was cursed!"

"But all the witches were banished—"

A branch crunched and snapped in the distance. The maids went silent. I was as worried as they were—someone could be sneaking up on me or them. Then one of them said, "Ay! Hali na!"

Their skirts swished as they hurried away. Within seconds, I did the same, making a hasty exit back the way I came.

LATER THAT NIGHT, I was sitting at the marble vanity in my suite while Jinky brushed my hair to wrap it up in a bun for the night. I didn't want to mention anything about what I'd heard earlier in the garden and get anyone in trouble, so instead I asked casually, "Jinky, what do you know about the king's death?"

At that, Jinky nearly dropped the heavy gold hairbrush she was holding. "I know nothing, Your Highness," she said, hand still shaking.

I turned in the chair and faced her, putting my hand over Jinky's. "It's okay," I assured her. "I've heard things . . . and I'm just wondering if you have, too."

Jinky stood very still and looked at the ground. "I'm sorry—I know nothing."

"I know they say he died of a heart attack, but I don't think that's the truth?" I pushed. I hadn't wanted to feed information to Jinky, hoping she would say that herself, but this was the only way I was going to get her to feel safe confiding whatever she knew.

Jinky looked at me then. "No, it isn't," she said.

"What do you know?" I asked her, perhaps a bit too excitedly.

Jinky pulled her hand away, fearful again. "I misspoke," she said, shaking her head. "I was confused."

"Trust me," I pleaded. "I'm not trying to trick you into saying something that will get you into trouble—I really want to know. He was my father."

After a few beats of silence, Jinky sighed and nodded. "All right. All I know is that there are many who say the king did not die peacefully, though none can say for sure. Very few were allowed to see the king's body. Those who did have been tight-lipped." She stopped speaking but seemed to have more still to say. She opened her mouth, closed it, opened it again. "If I betray a confidence . . ."

"I swear to you," I promised, grabbing her hands again. "I will never tell a soul."

Jinky looked around as if someone might be listening. She lowered her voice. "Many fear there was a conspiracy, that dark magic was used. Some say one of the other great houses was involved. But from which court, none can agree. I've heard that Don Elias knows there might have been foul play but is trying to keep things quiet to maintain order. And the palace maid who was tasked with cleaning the scene—she said there was evidence. Of something nefarious."

"What evidence? What was it?"

"I don't know," Jinky said. "The maid was let go from the Court of Sirena's service. Though I must tell you, there are rumors that she was done away with."

I absorbed this information and pressed further. "I heard that when he died, he was writing a note of some kind?"

Jinky looked me straight in the eye. "I heard the same."

That made my heart skip. "Would you do something for me, Jinky?"

"Anything, Your Highness."

"Would you try to find this note—if there is one? And tell any of the other maids to look as well."

Jinky looked dubious, but she said, "I will do my best."

9

"CLASS!" PROFESSOR BORROMEO was frustrated. She never raised her voice like that. "It would behoove you all to pay attention, particularly in light of recent events. Perhaps you believe the past doesn't matter, when in fact, history is where we find the future."

It wasn't our fault. All the commotion outside made it really hard to hear, let alone concentrate. There was a crew of nunos, small little mountain elves, installing posts all along the drive, and our room, which happened to be facing the front of the building, had a clear view of the scene down below. Apparently, *every* road in Biringan City—the main capital of Biringan—would be lined with lights and flowers for an entire month following the ceremony, not just the main ones. The plans kept growing. So now, instead of a week of feasting and celebrating, the coronation would also include endless parades and parties and "general revelry," as Elias put it. He said the people would need the release after so much worry. Also, until I arrived, the weather had been terrible, and now that it was sunny again, people wanted to celebrate.

I was set to become queen in three weeks and three days. And still no magic to be found.

Little did people know their big party was actually going to be more like a funeral.

No offense to Professor Borromeo, but ancient history was hardly my main concern right now. I was worried about my mother. Elias's patianaks had found her in a local hospital after almost a week of searching. She was injured but stable. I wanted to go to her immediately, but Elias said I had to wait. He had sent encantos to keep watch over her while she recovered. But for her safety, there would be no communication between us in the meantime. Elias hoped he could bring her back in time for my coronation. Still, I worried.

I tried to focus on the lecture. Professor Borromeo had picked up steam. "As you all learned in your earliest lessons, once upon a time, there was no separation between encantos—magickind—and humankind. For thousands of years, we lived together in the same world with a shared purpose: to be stewards of the universe.

"Until the humans decided they wanted to elevate themselves over all other creatures. To subjugate nature. Harness the bounty of the land for their own gain. But the encantos protested, trying, vainly, to convince them that none could own or control the moon and stars, the sand and seas. Cooperation was the only way. If nature was out of balance, nothing good would come of it. Encantos are one with nature; our kings and queens kept the balance, ensuring that the seasons cycled as they should, that the planets remained aligned.

"Thus, the wars began," she continued. "Humans attacked first; they went after any who stood in their way, and encantos fought back, only adding to the death and destruction. As the fighting dragged on, the diwata in charge of the circle of life was distracted, and as predicted, nature began to spin out of control. There were hurricanes, floods, famine. Eventually, magickind fled to the farthest parts of the world to escape the disasters and avoid doing any more harm, lest everything cease to exist entirely. In Biringan, the entrance to the city was closed off, leaving humans outside of it. Over time, Biringan grew to become four distinct kingdoms.

"Meanwhile, in the human realm, diwatas and those of higher power are remembered as gods, and encantos as mythical creatures, although these days most humans don't believe we exist at all. We've been trying to repair the damage from those wars ever since."

I ZONED OUT through the rest of my classes. Just before lunch, Professor Rosas, the tiny, seemingly timid Hayop at Halaman instructor from the Court of Lambana, was droning on and on about the various types of noxious vegetation in each region, dependent on environment, and which have gone extinct over time—or, in the case of poisonous ones, been purposely eradicated. I was supposed to be taking notes, but once again, my mind was wandering.

Who would want to kill my father, and why? The most obvious answer was to take the throne, though that still brought me right back to who. I didn't know enough about the politics of the courts to even come up with a suspect.

I had to find that note the maids were talking about.

"Before I let you go, children, remember the next test will cover the past four sections of the text, from page 206 through 808."

My head snapped up. A test, covering six hundred pages? Everyone around me stood to leave. I raised my hand.

Professor Rosas looked at me. "Yes, Princess?"

"May I get an extension for the test?"

Her answer surprised me. "Why would you?"

I thought it was obvious. "Well, I wasn't even here when most of that was covered."

"And yet your coronation will not be delayed, will it? If you're to take on such responsibility, I recommend you do whatever it takes to prove you're prepared. You must know the land if you are to rule it, yes?" She smiled at me over her glasses.

I was beginning to understand that the Court of Lambana only seemed passive on the surface. I smiled back. "Of course," I said. I'll just add that to the list. Reading, studying, coronation plans, figure out what happened to my father, oh, and find my elusive magic, which I may not even have. Sure. No problem.

"I'LL HELP YOU with Rosas," Nix promised at lunch. "I was one of her star students, even though she gave me a hard time when I first got here, too. She just has high expectations."

I tapped my finger against the table. "Can I ask you something?" I hoped it wasn't a sensitive issue.

"Anything."

"Do you . . . do you have a talent? Ayo asked me what mine is, and . . ."

"Oh, my magic? I think I can make even the most wilted flowers bloom. And once I healed a dying bird." She shrugged. "Not really sure yet how it works. I just know I can do it."

"Cool," I said, feeling worse. I wished I hadn't asked. No wonder Professor Rosas liked her so much.

"Why, what's yours?" She looked at me, read something in my expression, and changed course. "If you don't know how to control it yet, don't worry. I figured mine out by accident. Lots of people need practice."

I didn't believe that, but I appreciated her attempt at making me feel better. I was tempted to tell her the truth. That I probably didn't have one at all. But what if she told someone? Not maliciously, but she did have trouble censoring herself.

"Once, when I was a kid, this house plant was dying, and I felt sorry for it. That's it—I just felt sorry for it. And by the next day, it was thriving. Like, it wasn't drooping, it wasn't browning, it even looked like it had grown overnight. I thought it was just the sunshine coming in the window. I mean, it is always sunny in San Diego . . ."

San Diego, California. Something from that last morning I was home came back to me. I sat up straight and leaned forward. "Wait a minute—I heard about you. You're the missing girl." The news article. *Phoenix Xing was last seen leaving school a year ago . . .*

"Heh. Yep, that's me," Nix said uneasily. "Heh." She picked at one of the gaping seams of her robe.

"No way! But if your parents brought you here, why were you reported missing—"

"I don't know," she cut in. "That is weird." She flipped open her agenda book. "Hey, when's the coronation again? I get an invite to the Coronation Eve Ball, right?"

Strange. She was touchy about the subject, but I let it go. I didn't want to push, since I barely knew her and wanted to keep my one friend.

"Of course," I told her. Agenda book . . . that reminded me, I had a big-deal council meeting coming up. Tomorrow? Or the next day? Maybe if I actually used mine instead of forgetting it every day, I would feel more organized. Nix always seemed to be on top of everything.

"What about Amador and Lucas? Are they going, too?"

I shrugged. "I'm sure they're invited. Her parents are from the highest-ranking house in the Court of Sigbin and everything."

"Yeah, true, plus Lucas's dad used to work for the Court of Sirena," said Nix.

"Excuse me?"

"You didn't know that?"

"No." I had studied the family trees of the great houses of each court, but I had missed that detail.

"Yeah, his dad was commander of the Royal Guard."

"How do *you* know that?"

"No one pays attention to me. I listen. And I read. That's all it takes. Everything's out there. Not like it's a big secret."

I looked over at Lucas and Amador's table. They were laughing, sharing some private joke, probably at someone else's expense. I couldn't imagine how Lucas had ended up in the Court of Sigbin if his father had been working for mine. "So, then, is his dad with the Sigbin Court now?"

Nix wasn't listening to me; she was busy putting her books away. "Huh?" Nix asked, with a shake of her head. "His dad? No, he's not."

AFTER LUNCH, NIX and I agreed to meet up again soon. I offered Nix a ride, but she had to pick something up in town, so she headed out the back door, and I went to find my obnoxious carriage ride out front.

Following a few wrong turns in the halls, I ended up lost again. I found myself in yet another completely unfamiliar wing of the school, probably reserved for the more advanced botany courses because, scattered all over the hall, there were potted plants in various states of growth. I leaned down to read a handwritten sign stuck into the dirt next to one of the seedlings: *Touch me not, for if you do, I'm sure to rot.* And another: *If this plant you should touch, the poor wee thing will turn to muck.*

I heard voices. Familiar voices. Amador and Lucas. They were nearby—and getting closer. I ducked down next to a tall ficus. WEEPING FIG, the label said.

Lucas stopped in front of Amador and turned to her. I could see their feet from my hiding spot. Lucas's boots were black with blue stitching. "Remember, she's just a hapcanto, and half sirena of all things," she said, emphasizing each word. "You better back me up."

Lucas whispered back, "We have different ideas. But you make it sound like I'm against you. I'm not."

"I hope so," Amador said, shuffling her feet. "I'm counting on you."

"Yeah, yeah," he replied, irritated. "I know what you want me to do."

They began walking again, deep in hushed conversation about their scheme, whatever it was. Unfortunately, as hard as I tried, I couldn't hear another word of it. I waited until their footsteps faded before I scurried away in the opposite direction, heart racing. If they were talking about hapcantos, they had to be plotting against me. I had to get out of here. I wasn't safe anywhere. I had to leave Biringan!

Then a wave of fury swept through me. I definitely wasn't going to let two spoiled, entitled, social-climbing schemers like Amador and Lucas scare me into handing over my birthright, or fleeing my ancestral world. I had as much of a right to be here as they did. No one was going to bully the rightful queen.

I found my way out by following the direction they'd taken, got into my awaiting carriage, and chewed on what I'd heard on the way back to the palace. I wished I had a phone, some way to message Nix about what was going on.

When I arrived back at my room, Elias was waiting. "We were getting worried about you, Princess. You're late."

"I realized I'd left a book in class," I lied.

"Well, no matter; here you are just in time. Jinky will see you're dressed, and then I'll escort you downstairs."

"For . . . ?" I asked, confused.

"Why, the meeting, of course," he said incredulously. "It's very important. Your first official political engagement is with the Court of Sigbin. It's in your agenda."

I let out an involuntary groan. Elias looked scandalized. His eyes widened. "Princess, this is a serious matter."

"I understand," I said. "Remind me, what is this meeting about, again?"

"It's a formal introduction. For the purpose of future alliances, to build rapport."

I almost told him what I'd overheard earlier, but I kept it to myself.

"Would you prefer the courtiers arrive with you or before you?" he asked me.

"I don't think any courtiers will be necessary," I said firmly.

Simple was better. More fuss would just complicate everything and take away from the purpose. A simple meeting with representatives of the Court of Sigbin. On my turf. Not a big deal.

He hesitated for a long time. "Yes, Your Highness." He nodded, then left.

I couldn't wait until I was crowned and of age, so I wouldn't need a guardian keeping tabs on me all the time like I was a baby. Elias was only looking out for me, but I could look out for myself.

JINKY WANTED ME to wear a very formal pale-pink terno, but the stiff peaked butterfly sleeves and brocade fabric on the gown seemed way too much for a simple meeting. I dug around in the closet until I found just the right thing. A white silk blouse with short sleeves and a pair of sleek red pants and a matching red scarf. I held them up for Jinky. "These are perfect!" Simplicity. Yes, that was the remedy for how overwhelmed I was.

She cringed. "That's a katipunero outfit! It's for working in the garden!"

"No, trust me, these are perfect for a meeting." I wanted to look powerful, not like a doll. Anyway, being queen meant making my own decisions.

An hour later, Elias and Jinky accompanied me down to the grand hall. I was going to nail my first official engagement.

I took a deep breath as the doors opened in front of me.

10

NOTHING COULD HAVE prepared me for what I saw.

"I thought this was a standard meeting," I hissed at Elias, trying to smile politely at the same time.

He shrugged, as if saying, *I told you so.*

The room was full of visiting courtiers and their guards from Sigbin, dressed in their best from head to toe. They all looked me up and down. I tugged at my stupid blouse. Jinky was right. I should have worn the gown.

Yep, totally nailed it, MJ. Good job. I decided the best thing I could do was act like I was underdressed on purpose. Like nothing was wrong.

I strolled in with my head high. Despite what I felt earlier about Elias, I was glad he was there now. He pulled out a heavy, high-backed golden chair for me. I sat and waited for the rest of the Sigbin courtiers to arrive. Jinky took her place behind me. I had no idea what to do. Looked like I was going to have to wing it.

After a few minutes the door opened, and a man in a beautifully embroidered barong Tagalog walked in. He didn't look directly at me.

His mouth opened, and a booming, deep voice rang out. "May

I introduce the grand duchess of the Court of Sigbin, Lady Amador Oscura, alongside her most esteemed knight, Sir Lucas Invierno, datu of Mount Makiling." He stepped aside.

Of course. I was here to meet *them*. I should've known. Actually, I probably *would've* known if I'd read the agenda. Fine. Lesson learned. Again.

After a fashionable pause, Amador and Lucas strode in, arm in arm. As much as I didn't want to admit it, they were even more intimidating out of their school uniforms. Everything about her was flawless, from the complicated braided updo in her dark, blue-highlighted hair (and the frosty diamond tiara perched on top of it) to her shimmering, icy-blue, floor-length Maria Clara dress. Even Lucas was perfect—all cut-glass cheekbones and dark hair that fell into his eyes, the colorful malong draped over his shoulder a perfect match to her dress.

Though this was not a casual situation—or at least, I imagined two nobles from rival courts having their first official meeting was not a casual thing—I sensed a certain amount of humor about him, in regard to the entire scenario. His inky dark eyes were playful, and he had a slight smirk at the corner of his mouth.

I stood and wondered if I should bow. Or curtsy or something. I made some kind of awkward movement in between the two, unsure what to do, but then I noticed Elias put his hand out slightly at his side to indicate I should not. I pretended I was fixing my shoe instead. One gaffe narrowly avoided. I was a little embarrassed that I almost genuflected to a lesser-ranking noble. I wasn't a subject of the Court of Sigbin. I was the queen of the Court of Sirena, or about to be, and I needed to get used to it.

"Please, have a seat," I offered, opening my hand toward the plush chairs across from me. Amador, or rather, the duchess—this was an official occasion after all—curtsied while Sir Lucas bowed, and then they stepped forward in unison and swept into the seats as if they were gliding. Once seated, they exchanged a loaded look. I pretended not to notice and moved on, though I wasn't sure what I was supposed to say now. "Pleased to meet you," I began. *You idiot, you already know them!* "Meet you here," I said, hoping that covered my mistake. "I'm happy to welcome you to the Court of Sirena." That sounded good.

"What do you think of it so far, Princess?" Lucas responded. "Has it been long since you last visited?"

I felt like there was some kind of insult behind the question. "Since I was but a toddler," I told him honestly.

"Ah," he said, as if he didn't already know my entire life story. I had no doubt that I was the subject of all the latest gossip throughout the four kingdoms. Then it occurred to me: "visited." Insinuating that I didn't actually belong.

"No loss," Amador quipped.

Lucas jumped in. "On your part, she means." He forced a chuckle. "Because, well, it's just that, the Court of Sirena is known for—well, it's not me saying this, mind you, I'm only telling you what is commonly known—"

"Lucas is always honest. Some people can't handle it, but I, for one, prefer the truth," Amador said with a smirk.

"As do I," I told her. I hoped that sounded like the threat that it was. Maybe I felt intimidated when they walked in, but I was never going to let her know that. At least not on purpose.

"Then you won't mind my saying, frankly, the inhabitants of the Court of Sirena are known to be rather, let's just say, well . . ." He feigned reluctance. *"Simple."* He practically whispered it, as if he didn't want to say it. Some of the Lambana courtiers stifled laughs.

So this was what they were talking about earlier. Amador had put him up to this. I decided to play innocent and almost bat my eyelashes a little bit. Fight fire with fire. "Oh? What do they mean by that?"

"You know," he said, waving his hand around like he was trying to catch a word. He hesitated before speaking. "Rustic. Provincial."

"Ignorant," Amador happily chimed in. "Some would even say dirty. Or, you know, *fishy*." She smiled as if she had made a clever pun.

"Oh, I see, is that because my people came from the sea?" I exclaimed, as if they'd enlightened me. "But I suppose that's better than, say, what the Court of Sigbin is known for?"

"And what would that be?" Amador sneered.

"Chaotic, disorderly, arrogant, spoiled, and useless?" I smiled and let my words hang in the air.

I felt triumphant, but Elias's eyes were wide with horror. Some of the courtiers were scowling.

Amador's lips pursed, and her eyes narrowed. "In any case," she said, quickly changing the subject, "we've come to discuss the relationship between our two courts, haven't we?"

"That's my understanding," I answered.

She went right in. "As you must know by now, there was a treaty signed by our ancestors many years ago, uniting the kingdoms and vesting the leadership in the Court of Sirena. However, I'm sure you'll agree that the terms of that treaty have become untenable. In fact, I've been told that you only fulfilled the agreement under great duress. And there's no reason for you to suffer if we all want the same thing." She smiled widely at me.

"And what is that, Duchess? That we all want, I mean," I asked her.

"Please, call me Amador." She flashed me another empty smile, then leaned forward a little bit and lowered her voice, as if we were having a private tête-à-tête. "You're not equipped for this, Princess. It's so obvious. And you shouldn't have to be. No one should be forced to do something they don't want to do." She glanced around and lowered her voice even more. "If we nullify the old agreement, you can have your life back. I understand you left your mother behind. I'm sure you miss her. Biringan will still be safe. Everything is solved."

"And then what?" I asked her, not bothering to be quiet. "Who would take my place?"

"As princess of the Court of Sirena, or—"

"As the heir to the throne of all of Biringan," I corrected her. I didn't appreciate being manipulated or treated like I was clueless. Even if she was right about how I hadn't wanted to come there, she was wrong if she thought I was going to let her call the shots and boss me around.

"Oh, that won't be a problem," she assured me. "There's always someone ready to take it on."

"And I suppose you intend that person to be you and your insurgents?"

The courtiers in the room gasped in shock. Elias was glaring at me. Warning me. He was suspicious of the Court of Sigbin, but as he explained, not enough to warrant any official accusation.

"Are you accusing us of treason?" Amador said with steel in her voice.

I had to back down. Or else I was in danger of openly declaring war. "You said it, not me," I said sweetly.

She shrugged slowly, as if she was just now considering it. "Of course not. We are loyal to the Court of Sirena, as we always have been. I was only saying that if you chose to vacate your position, someone else could fill it."

"You, I assume."

"Perhaps. Perhaps not. All depends on how it shakes out." She flashed me yet another broad, phony smile.

"I'll take it under consideration," I told her. That was diplomatic, right? "In the meantime, I intend to do what my father wanted of me. After all, we don't have the luxury of playing games, Amador." *Cut off the discussion while you're ahead.* "If there's nothing else . . ."

Amador and Lucas looked stunned at my dismissal. At least they knew how to take a hint. "Well, then," she said, the indignation rising in her tone. "I understand you're in a strange place without the first clue about how anything works or who you are dealing with, so we'll leave you to get some rest. For now. You *clearly* need it." She stood up and pulled her skirts around her to straighten them out. Lucas stood as well next to her. I smiled up at them with my hands clasped on the table.

"I look forward to seeing you at the council meeting," she said before twirling around and heading for the exit, Lucas at her heels, just as Nix had drawn the first day. As she reached the door, she added, "I suggest you come prepared."

11

"OH! GOOD MORNING, Your Highness." Jinky curtsied and placed the breakfast tray on the bedside table. "You're already awake." She handed me my cup of champorado.

"Thank you," I said, taking the chocolate rice porridge from her. "Yes, I'm really looking forward to formally meeting the council." More like, I was energized by rage at everything that happened the day before. In fact, it kept me up half the night, tossing and turning, various plans running through my head. I was also nervous. I tried to tamp down the flutters in my stomach. *Reveal no weakness*, I reminded myself. No time for that. I was on a mission. I wasn't going to have another disaster like that one. I wasn't going to be dressed like a katipunero this time.

While I sipped on the hot chocolate, Jinky put my hair up in one of her elaborate designs. When she was done, we went to the wardrobe to choose a dress. I intended to make an entrance. "Casual" had been a huge mistake, one I didn't intend to repeat. I had to command attention. Project authority. I pulled out the most beautiful baro't saya I found in my closet, a deep-purple-and-gold A-line satin gown with a high, jeweled collar that matched the gems on the bodice and at the edges of the pointy, peaked sleeves, which came with a lace-trimmed silk shawl that would drape elegantly over my shoulders.

My garments made me feel older. Like a queen, not a princess. Exactly what I wanted. I spun a bit in the mirror to watch how the skirt twirled and settled around me.

"Ay! Ang ganda!" Jinky said. She stood back and smiled. She was wearing her favorite dress, too, a light-yellow-and-white empire-waist gown with short butterfly sleeves and matching gloves. It suited her perfectly.

"Thank you. You look gorgeous, too!" Inside, I thought, *Yes, let's stun them.* If I was afraid of my own power, others would take advantage of that vulnerability. "Could you please request every available guard to escort us? And the two best to escort me personally? Actually, make it four. Two to march behind me and one for each side. And I'd like them all to carry their swords."

Jinky looked surprised but immediately left to gather the extra security. Another power play on my part. I wanted to send the message that I was not only well protected, but also willing to use force if necessary.

Once I was ready and the guards were gathered outside my room, we walked down to the front atrium, where two calesas waited. One for me and Jinky, and one for my additional security detail. Elias also rode with us.

"This is the only council meeting until the coronation," he said on the way over. "It is quite likely they'll have something to say about how we're handling it."

"Like what?" I asked.

He shrugged. "Someone always takes issue with something. The scale of the affair. Which of their representatives are included.

Who knows what they'll come up with? There may even be real trouble like yesterday. That was unwise, Princess."

"As you've told me a hundred times since yesterday's meeting," I sighed. "I promise, I won't do it again."

The Council of the Courts met in a building past the Market District, right in the center of the four kingdoms—a massive glass dome, probably the size of a city block, that reflected the sky. I did my best to maintain a poker face, as if I saw that type of thing every day in boring, human California. *Show no vulnerability*, I reminded myself. I had to hold this realm together.

The road circled all the way around the entire building. Where it split from the main avenue, it was paved with silver stones that twinkled like diamonds.

As we got closer, I looked out the window and saw that the stones weren't silver, as they'd appeared from a distance, but glass or crystal—or maybe even actual diamonds. I wouldn't have been surprised if they were. However, in line with my personal oath, I was not going to play the ingenue and ask.

The carriage pulled into the circle. There were other vehicles in front of us, carrying representatives from each of the kingdoms. I watched as the occupants emerged and paraded down the wide, deep steps that led into the building. I was glad I went all out on my outfit choice that morning. They were dressed to impress, too—in the most lavish malong capes and jeweled ternos, form-fitting all-white ensembles next to head-to-toe black. There was a councilor in traditional datu costume, a multicolored short jacket with matching trousers, with no shirt underneath, a curved sword at his hip.

I was relieved that I was the only one wearing dark purple and gold. Perhaps as in the human realm during medieval times, purple was only worn by royalty.

Finally, it was our turn to pull up to the front entrance. Elias stepped out first and offered his hand to Jinky, then me. The attendees who were congregating near the doors all turned to watch as I got out of the coach, my dress shimmering and flowing around me.

The other carriages had all pulled away, so the entire drive up to the council was full with my security detail, outfitted in their formal white uniforms.

I nodded politely at the curious onlookers as we climbed the steps—slowly. No rushing in as if I was intimidated. Some of the attendees returned the favor and nodded back; others simply stared, even open-mouthed, gawking at the display. It was their first look at the new princess, so I wasn't offended or all that surprised. It helped that I felt great, too. I knew their staring wasn't because I was making some kind of faux pas.

Once we reached the top, we entered through a round door that had to be fifteen feet tall. It was held open by Biringan City guards, a special battalion meant to keep the peace between kingdoms during events like these. That seemed to be the theme everywhere I went—lots of guards. Rather than make me feel safe, it was putting me more on edge. If such a place needed so many neutral guards, there was a lot of danger present, and to me, a real utopia wouldn't require that. Again, I was glad I made the right choices for that day—I definitely met the mood with my personal security detail.

Inside, there was a large round room, brightly lit thanks to the glass dome. I looked up—the glass was nearly invisible; the clear sky loomed over us as if there was no roof at all. Meanwhile, all around, groups of people stood together like they did outside, talking, some of them holding drinks. It felt like a fantasy courthouse. There was even a horse inside, for some reason. And then I saw it stand up on its hind legs and walk, like a human, over to speak with a man wearing a dark-red floor-length gown. Elias saw me staring. He leaned down and said, "Tikbalang. Harmless, mostly. They emerge from the woods of Biringan for the council meetings, but otherwise, we hardly see them."

"Would you like something to drink?" A servant with a gold tray popped up next to me.

"Sure," I said. I picked a tall narrow glass from the tray. When he walked away, I sniffed it as inconspicuously as I could.

"It's only lavender calamansi," Elias whispered to me.

"I knew that," I said. He laughed softly. I took a sip. "Oh, wow." I couldn't help saying it. "This is really good."

"Biringan calamansi juice is the best," Elias said. "Better than lemonade."

I sipped some more. "You're not kidding."

He looked confused. "No, I'm quite serious."

"Your Highness," Jinky said, gently touching my arm, "I think they're about to begin." She nodded toward the groups starting to migrate into one of the smaller doorways on the right.

"Welp. Here we go." Reluctantly, I set my calamansi juice on the nearest table. I didn't think walking in with a sweaty glass in my hand would create the glamorous entrance I was hoping for.

Elias went in first, then Jinky, and finally it was my turn. Standing alongside two guards with the rest behind us, I took a huge, deep breath, waited a beat, then stepped inside.

And it worked just as I'd hoped. Talking stopped when I came in.

The room was set up like an ancient stadium. In the center there was a massive round table for the head of each court, surrounded by riser seating, all carved out of stone. Each court had its own section, so the effect was similar to a sporting event because so many in the audience wore their faction's official colors.

But there weren't tons of onlookers—and the few who were present were comfortably spread out. I glanced over at the Court of Sirena, which was already occupied by members of the court, most of whom I hadn't even met yet but had shown up for me. There were also rows of guards who walked in before me, standing. Once the rest marched in, the entire section would be full.

I smiled at the thought.

As I stepped inside and began my procession down the aisle to the center, there were some barely concealed scowls and dirty looks shot my way. There was also plenty of the opposite—smiles and head nods encouraging me on. I did get a sense that if I was going to take the throne as planned, I was going to have to win some naysayers over. Otherwise, there would be a lot of resistance, particularly from the Court of Sigbin. None of them appeared friendly—it was all smirks and glares from that set. Amador regarded me coolly. I was surprised to find Lucas was not with her.

Once the heads of court were seated and the Court of Sirena guards took their places, a leader—I wasn't sure of her name or title or even which court she belonged to—banged a large, old-fashioned gavel and declared that the 846th Biannual Biringan Meeting of the Councils had begun.

"Baroness Tanginaw of the Court of Sigbin?" the council leader called out.

"Here," came the reply. The baroness wore a Maria Clara dress and a jeweled comb made of mother-of-pearl.

"Sir Dorado of the Court of Tikbalang?" the council leader called next. Another answer in the affirmative, from a knight wearing a tribal mask over his face.

"Duchess Siria Prado, Court of Lambana?" A woman in a simple camisa, with a matching pañuelo over her shoulders, nodded.

I was glad for the roll because I learned who was who. I made it a point to repeat each name in my head so I'd remember if I needed to address them. A few of them stood out easily, though: The one in the datu outfit was Joaquin Valeria, a representative of the Court of Tikbalang. The couple clad in contrasting white and black were from the Court of Lambana—Lord and Lady Camangayan.

"First call to order," the Biringan master of ceremonies announced. She didn't even need a microphone or anything—her voice carried clearly through the entire room. "For the establishment of unrestricted travel ways in the common areas of Biringan. Initial call. Those in favor, say aye."

A series of ayes popped up across the room. I looked at Elias. He nodded slightly. I joined the chorus with one aye.

"All those opposed?"

One squeaky nay rose from somewhere around the table. It looked like it came from an empty chair, but then I saw that the little voice was actually coming from the creature standing on the table.

"Bibao Court opposes," the master of ceremonies announced for the record. I hadn't even heard a Bibao Court in the introductions.

"Why?" I whispered to Elias.

"They oppose every motion, unless all others oppose, in which case they vote in favor."

"Why?"

"They're an opposition court. Technically they aren't even recognized." Bibaos were ordinary spirits, household sprites.

I didn't have time to get more clarity on that. We were on to the next thing. The master of ceremonies made another announcement: "Open house session. Any court that wishes to raise an issue, your concern can now be heard. One councilor from your court should stand and wait to be called upon."

Around the table, a few began to rise. The MC—of course they didn't call her that, but I couldn't help it—took her time looking them over before raising her finger and pointing to one. "The gentleman from the Court of Tikbalang may have the floor," she announced. The others sat, a couple groaning that they'd have to wait a while longer.

The datu cleared his throat. He had to be nearly seven feet tall, and though he was lean, he exuded physical strength. "Tikbalang challenges the succession of the princess of the Court of Sirena."

Loud voices broke out around the room. Some clapping. People began shouting their own opinions at the speaker, as if that was going to contribute anything. As for me, I sat there, stunned. He was talking about me. And judging by the response, quite a few agreed with him. "The king should have passed the line of succession to someone worthy when he had the chance," someone yelled.

Maybe they were *all* insurgents? Was this a trap?

A woman with short white hair and a silver terno, also from Tikbalang, stood up. "The Court of Sirena has monopolized the throne for far too long."

And then a member of the Court of Lambana, a winged man wearing an embroidered robe, responded, "We all know the agreement, and it has worked thus far."

"But she is a stranger to our land! And a hapcanto!"

"What is going on?" I asked Elias. "Is this a coup?"

Elias stood abruptly without acknowledging what I said. "The Court of Sirena objects to this disrespectful statement!" he declared. "The line of succession is not up for debate!"

People began shouting and arguing again. I didn't like this. Not at all. I looked behind me; the guards were on alert, their weapons within reach, scanning the room for threats. I was worried for my safety, sure, but even worse than that, I felt betrayed. I'd been led to believe I had to be there, that I was wanted there. Maybe not by everyone—Amador and Lucas came to mind—but I certainly had not expected to be roundly rejected by all four kingdoms.

Almost like they heard my thoughts about my hostile classmates, another man in a malong scarf stood up. "The Court of Sigbin concurs with the Court of Tikbalang." There was some clapping.

Elias sat down, defeated.

"This is not good," I said to him.

"No, no, it is not," he said.

"Did you know about this?" I asked him.

"There is always strife when the throne is vacated. So, to answer your question, yes, I knew there was some discontent. Someone will always try their luck and make a claim. But did I expect this level of—" He gestured at the chaos. "No."

The Tikbalang representative spoke up again. "We assert that the princess of Sirena is, in actuality, not the one true heir." A hush fell over the room. I noticed that, though they'd all been talking about me, none of them would actually look at me. When I came in, they all stared, and now they acted like I wasn't even there. He continued, "The princess of Sirena is ineligible to rule, due to her well-documented and easily verified status as hapcanto." Lots of murmurs of agreement now. "She cannot rule above us as she is half-human."

Elias stood again. "If I may," he said. The noise continued.

"The Court of Sirena is recognized," the MC shouted over the din. She banged the gavel. The voices finally stopped.

Elias cleared his throat. "King Vivencio Basilio Rodriguez was the widely accepted one true king of Biringan as established by the succession laid out in the ancient treaty of the kingdoms."

He paused. No one dissented. He went on: "The princess is his legitimate and true daughter. Therefore, she is the one true heir. There is no clause in the treaty stating both parents must be encantos." Now there was some dissent. The voices rose again. Elias raised his hand to quiet them. Shockingly, they listened this time.

"It is established by tradition," someone shouted. The Court of Sigbin representative stood up to challenge Elias.

"Tradition does not supersede the treaty," Elias told him.

"According to whom?" the Sigbin rep responded. The two men stared each other down.

Elias straightened his shoulders. "What I hear you saying is that you wish to go to war."

The councilor from Sigbin smirked. "We at Sigbin have been accused of this twice now. And yet it seems that the Court of Sirena is eager to fan the flames of discontent and ignite conflict rather than do the right thing and stand aside."

"You speak nonsense," Elias said. His face was red, almost purple, with fury. I was shocked to see him that way—he'd been so even-tempered all the time, even when I was being a pain. "If you are being honest, then you are not qualified to hold that seat, because everyone is aware of the terms of the treaty. The princess returned home when summoned, as she was obliged to do, because even in the human world she could understand the importance of her role. She did not ignore her responsibility to her ancestral seat. She is here to fulfill her duty. And now you stand there and deny it."

"If King Vivencio had been so concerned about his descendants, he would not have married a human."

"Once more, there is no clause prohibiting a legitimate-born child of the king from inheriting, no matter their status . . ."

The councilor from Sigbin pointedly ignored Elias. "So it seems to me, King Vivencio already broke the treaty with his marriage to a human female and by siring a half-breed and leaving no rightful successor. Thus, we are *already* poised for war." He looked around for supporters. "Are we not?"

Some agreed; most stayed silent. Even if they didn't exactly love me, they didn't want to go to war. Only those who are convinced they'd benefit ever do.

A gray-haired woman in lime green stood.

"The Court of Lambana gets the floor," the MC shouted, gavel banging again.

"My fellow encantos," she said. Elias and the Sigbin councilor both sat down. This woman must have had a lot of clout—everyone stopped talking and gave her their full attention. "The facts are these: It is true that Biringan tradition suggests no one aside from a full-blood encanto shall sit on the throne." I deflated at that. I thought *someone* would be on my side.

The old woman went on: "It is also true, however, that the treaty, which was signed by the rulers of all houses, says absolutely nothing about this tradition. And tradition is *not* law. Don Elias of the Court of Sirena is correct; King Vivencio's daughter is the one true heir as established in the treaty, and if we wish to avoid war, famine, and widespread suffering—which it seems we all do, barring, perhaps, the Court of Sigbin." She glared at the clearly irritated councilor. "We must follow the treaty. The princess will demonstrate her viability at the coronation ceremony and be crowned queen." She sat down, and the MC slammed the gavel once more.

That shut everyone up. There was no more disagreement, even from the discontented Court of Sigbin. I was the one true heir, and I would take the throne. The meeting was adjourned.

I tried to remain poised and calm amidst the animated chatter all around me and feel better after the Court of Lambana's support, except her confidence actually made me feel a lot worse.

I had to find a way to fake my magic somehow. Otherwise . . .

12

I WOKE TO Jinky shaking my shoulder. "Your Highness," she yelled in my ear. "Wake up. You're going to be late."

I groaned and turned away from her, dragging the fluffy blanket over my head.

Jinky persisted. "Princess, please, you're going to be late for your classes."

I had no intention of showing my face at BANA after what happened at the council meeting. They'd all heard about it by now, no doubt. "I'm sick," I lied, my voice muffled by the bedding. I forced a phony cough.

Jinky tsked at me. "You're perfectly fine, and you have exam review today." Then she added with forced cheer, "Wouldn't want you to miss something so important."

I groaned again, but I knew she was right. Not about the exam—I definitely wouldn't have minded missing that—just that I needed to go. The real test was whether I could withstand this kind of opposition. Raise my head up high and show my face to people like Amador. I couldn't allow them to keep me from the throne. My pride was at stake, too. I wasn't gonna let them win.

I was taking that throne one way or another.

* * *

ON THE WAY to school, I saw lights going up on the street poles and purple banners being lifted. In the grassy common areas, more nuno workers were busy erecting scaffolding and bleachers for the parade audience. Ayo said invitations for the Coronation Eve Ball were going out with the messenger that afternoon. It was all happening so soon.

Then I noticed something, way off in the distance, beyond the Paulanan Mountains. Dark clouds. A gathering storm.

I yanked the window curtain shut and sat back against the seat.

At least my classmates had finally gotten used to me being around. Most of them had stopped staring when I arrived every morning and switched over to either total indifference or—though it was embarrassing to admit—fawning admiration.

A trio of Sirena first-years ran up to me as I approached the front doors. "Hi, Princess. My name's Darna," one of them introduced herself, while her two friends looked too scared to speak.

"We wanted to give you this as a token of our loyalty," Darna said, bowing before handing me a beribboned box. "They're polvoron cookies. We made them ourselves."

"Oh, how nice!" I said. "My favorite."

Darna and her friends beamed. She continued: "We're all writers for the *BANA Bulletin*. We know you're really busy and everything, but we were wondering if maybe you'd be interested in joining?"

"Oh, cool! I don't think I can take on any more right now with the coronation and everything, though." I did feel sorta bad turning them down; they were being so nice. There was just no extra time. I was running on empty as it was.

"Right, of course," she said sheepishly. "I'm sorry."

"No, don't apologize. I appreciate the invite. I'll get back to you when things calm down?"

Her face lit up. "Sure! That's great." She handed me a copy of their latest issue before they walked away. I glanced over it as I walked inside and noticed a headline, *What Can the Crown Princess Do for BANA?*, at the bottom of the front page, alongside photos of three students and their responses. One was "One uniform for all students. Why are we divided by where we come from?"

As soon as I walked in, another Sirena tapped me on the shoulder and handed me a piece of paper. "Your Highness, we're having a bonfire at Lake Reyna, if you want to come—"

"The princess can't come to your bonfire." Fortunada walked up.

The guy slinked away.

"First-years," she said. "They don't get it." I noticed she'd ditched the glasses and added a ring to her daily ensemble. It matched her heirloom bracelet, with a huge pearl surrounded by diamonds.

"It doesn't bother me," I said. "I'm glad they like me, to be honest."

"I'm only concerned they're interested in social perks and not friendship," she said. "I'm trying to look out for you."

"That's very nice of you"—*it wasn't*—"but it's all good."

"Sorry." She cringed. "Now you're mad at me."

"No, not at all!" I heard the bells chiming. "Shoot, I don't want to be late. I'll see you around, Fortunada."

"See you around," she said. She stood and watched me until I disappeared around the corner.

In history, Professor Borromeo called on me first thing. "Princess, tell us about Biringan's break from the human world."

Luckily, I'd paid attention last time. "A war broke out because humans and encantos did not agree about how to treat the land," I said. "Afterward, humans lost touch with magic. Their knowledge of the enchanted ones faded over time, aside from myth."

Amador raised her hand primly. As soon as Professor Borromeo acknowledged her, she looked right at me and said, "The split ushered in an age of darkness and ignorance in the human realm." She'd repeated that directly from the text, putting forth the now-familiar story that Biringan was a utopian paradise while the human world was a mess. It was so one-sided. Impulsively, I raised my hand.

"Princess?" Professor Borromeo called on me, somewhat surprised that I'd volunteered to ask a question after how quiet and reluctant I'd been up to that point. "Do you have a comment?" she asked.

"It's just that—" I paused, realizing there was no way for me to talk about my mother without giving away too much about my private life, so I changed tack. "Aren't encantos guilty of some of the same atrocities as humans?"

If my classmates were drowsing off before, they weren't now. The air in the room changed completely. Everyone perked up, probably curious how the professor would respond to such an inflammatory question. A couple of them shook their heads in disgust. Most of them stared at me, in shock. I knew it was a provocative thing to say. I didn't know it would be quite so shocking to everyone, though.

I looked at Professor Borromeo, expecting to see anger or disappointment. Instead, she looked excited. "Let's explore what the princess said, shall we?" She began pacing around the room. "What do you all think? Are we as guilty as the humans?"

"No," someone said from the back of the room. He was sitting back with his arms crossed, defensive. "That's ridiculous."

Then another voice piped up. "She has a point. We have war just as the humans do; we have murder. And what about the humans who can't leave our world? The black rice, for example."

"Nobody actually 'tricks' any human into eating the black rice. That's absurd," someone added.

"Yes, they do," another said. "One of the shopkeepers in town, her father was human, and he was fooled into eating the black rice, and he was stuck here forever."

"None of the shopkeepers are hapcantos," someone scoffed.

"Class! Please remember to raise your hands before speaking." Professor Borromeo tried, hopelessly, to rein everyone in and maintain some kind of decorum. But no one seemed to hear her. They were all turned in their seats, interrupting one another.

"They have to stay because we need to protect ourselves. They shouldn't rejoin humanity knowing we exist and jeopardize our safety!" someone called out, at the same time as another said, "Don't tell me you believe we kidnap humans against their will. They're trespassers. They *want* to be here. They eat the rice on purpose so we can't kick them out." To that, the youngest in the class, a small girl who usually sat in the corner desk, nervously twisting the ends of her hair, said, "I don't think that's fair."

The arguments took up the rest of the class time. I don't think we ever came anywhere near an agreement. I wasn't even sure what I thought anymore—having seen both worlds now, I could safely say neither one was entirely innocent or guilty. When we were dismissed, Professor Borromeo stopped me on my way out the door. "I just wanted to tell you . . ." she began. I felt like I was about to be reprimanded. But then she continued, "I really appreciate your thought-provoking contribution today. It really started a lively discussion."

"Oh, thanks," I said.

"I hope you'll continue to pose difficult questions," Professor Borromeo called after me as I walked out the door.

I got to my next class, Pagkahari at Paggalang, before Amador and Lucas. A relief. I hated walking in while they stared at me, Amador inevitably whispering something rude to him while he smirked and doodled on his parchment. I was able to get situated before they sauntered in. Amador tried to stare me down, but I pretended like I didn't even notice she was there, focusing on reviewing my notes instead. She made lots of noise and let out her shrillest giggle in an attempt to make me look up. It didn't work. Then Nix arrived and took the seat next to mine, saving me from any more of Amador's pathetic theatrics.

"Hey," Nix said cheerfully. "So. Are you ready for our official royal training?"

"You know it."

"They'll turn us into *proper señoritas* one of these days."

"I sure hope not. I kind of enjoy being a teenage dirtbag."

Nix laughed. Amador got quiet all of a sudden. I sneaked a glance at her. She was digging through the glittery tote she always carried at school, as if she was super intent on finding something lost at the bottom. But really, she was trying to eavesdrop on our conversation.

Professor Manatubay cleared his throat at the front of the room. I hadn't even noticed him until then. We all stopped what we were doing and sat up straight in our desks. He had that effect on people. "Today we are going to practice proper etiquette when meeting with emissaries from other courts." There was a barely detectable collective groan. He ignored it (or didn't notice) and went on: "We'll work through a series of scenarios in pairs." Amador nudged Lucas, indicating they'd work together. Professor Manatubay did not see that, though. "I've taken the liberty of choosing your partners already, to better portray real-life situations."

Amador made a pouty face. I was surprised she didn't stomp her feet, too.

"Once I call your names, please find your partner." He started going through a list. I listened as the small class was paired off, dismayed as the names quickly dwindled. "Phoenix, you'll work with Amador. Lucas, you'll work with the princess." Figured. Nix and I exchanged a look.

Neither of our assigned partners made a move to join us, so Nix and I stood and went to the front of the room, taking the two desks behind them. Amador turned around and smiled at Nix. "Let's make this as painless as possible, shall we?"

"That's totally up to you," Nix said, giving her an equally fake smile in return. Amador didn't understand that Nix was insulting her.

Lucas still had his back turned to me. He was putting the final touches on one of his drawings. I tried to take a peek at it without being too obvious, expecting something stereotypically masculine, like a video game character or whatever the equivalent might be in Biringan. Instead, I was surprised to see a detailed floral pattern, a vine of sampaguita flowers. He dropped the quill and turned around to face me. I looked down at my own notes. Hopefully he didn't notice I'd been looking.

"Let's sit in the back," he said.

"Oh, okay." I was surprised he wanted to be separated from his precious Amador. He got up, and I followed his lead. Amador watched us, a protest forming on her lips, and was stopped by the professor's watchful eye.

We stood side by side near two desks. Professor Manatubay announced the assignment. "Imagine that you and your partner are both heirs of rival houses. It doesn't matter which two. You meet for an official dinner at a neutral location. In other words, this is a social event, not a political event. When you arrive, you find your seat, as indicated by the place cards on the table. To your dismay, you are sitting next to your sworn enemy." I couldn't help but notice he looked directly at me when he said that. "To show contempt could be interpreted as an act of hostility. How will you behave? Proceed in three . . . two . . . one."

Lucas and I looked at each other. Now what? Neither of us seemed to know who was supposed to make the first move.

"If I'm not mistaken, you outrank me," he pointed out.

"Right," I said. "I knew that."

He smiled out of the corner of his mouth. Like he was saying, *Sure you did.* I hated how stupid he made me feel. How defensive. "Therefore," he went on, "if we're in an official social situation, I'm supposed to genuflect." He bowed deeply to me. It made me uncomfortable, despite the fact that everyone else in the room was doing the same thing. I noticed Professor Manatubay making his rounds, watching everyone. He looked over at me and Lucas. I had to play along if I wanted credit for the activity.

I curtsied slightly and nodded to Lucas. "Pleased to make your acquaintance, Sir Lucas," I said.

He pulled out my chair. "Princess," he said, gesturing that I should sit.

So gallant. I couldn't help but notice how his eyes crinkled when he smiled, and the dark swoop of his hair over his brow. *Ew, stop it*, I thought. *He's dating that skank who probably sent the insurgents to kill you.* "Thank you," I said as coldly as I could, with my nose in the air. I sat at the desk; he took his seat, too. Professor Manatubay approached, so I had to think of something polite to say to Lucas. "Are you having a terribly rainy season in the, um, in the Court of Sigbin?"

"Actually, we've had some beautiful days. You should come and see it sometime." Lucas had a twinkle in his eye. As much as I hated him, I had to admit, he knew how to be charming.

"I don't venture out of my kingdom very often," I replied. Professor Manatubay loomed over us.

"Understandable. You must be very busy. Hope you're able to get out and enjoy this lovely weather, at least."

"I try to walk in the gardens every night." I wasn't even sure why I said that. I didn't actually get to walk in the gardens in the evening, though I did want to. I felt like I had revealed something about myself somehow or worse, like I'd extended an invitation.

Professor Manatubay must have been satisfied with our progress because he moved on from us and went to hover over Amador and Nix, who appeared to be completely ignoring each other.

"Ah, yes. I've had the privilege of visiting the exquisite Court of Sirena gardens," Lucas said. "They were a favorite of mine as a child."

I had no idea how to respond. I suddenly had an image of little Lucas running around in the place I now called home, making memories long before I ever knew it existed—having a childhood that could have been mine. What if we had grown up together? Would I be his Amador now? Did I want to be?

Ew, why did I keep thinking like that?

He was staring at me, waiting. I shook my head to rid myself of the thoughts. Confusion crossed over his face briefly. "Uh, yes, they are amazing. Quite spectacular," I added, trying to sound fancy. I needed to change the subject, away from the weather and our backyards. "How are your parents doing?" Mundane enough.

Lucas pulled back, brow furrowed. He looked down at the desk and began tapping his fingers on it. "Wow. That was pretty low," he said. "Even for you."

"Excuse me?" I was totally taken aback.

"You didn't have to bring my parents into this," he said sternly. "I don't know what your problem is with me—"

"Excuse me?" I repeated, nearly shouting. The partners at the nearest desk turned their heads toward us. I lowered my voice. "I have no idea what you're talking about. I'm just playing along with this stupid game."

"Oh, please," he snarled at me. "As if you don't know that my parents are dead."

I felt like I was hit in the gut. "Oh! Lucas, I swear I didn't." I wanted to crawl under the table. I was so embarrassed. "I wouldn't have said something like that if I knew. I mean, my dad just died."

"You didn't even know your father," Lucas shot back. "You only showed up to claim your inheritance. My mom died when I was born, and when my dad died last year, he was all I had."

"Wow," I exclaimed. "You don't even know me. You know

nothing about me, in fact. Less than nothing." I was tempted to bring up my mother and how she was still in the hospital, clinging to life, but I didn't owe him that piece of me. "But you *should* know that I'm only here because I was *forced* to be here in order to avoid a war with your stupid, stuck-up court."

The room was silent. Every single person, including Professor Manatubay, was staring at us. Lucas was red in the face and looked like he wanted to punch something.

"Told you," Amador said to Lucas from across the room.

Told him what? Before I could ask, Professor Manatubay put his hands in the air and shouted, "Enough!"

Lucas and I turned away from each other and sat forward with our arms crossed. I kind of felt like punching something, too. I had no intention of starting a fight or hurting Lucas, no matter how much I disliked him.

"I'll see you after class," Professor Manatubay said to me. "As for the rest of you, the exercise is complete. Gather your things and prepare to be dismissed."

Minutes later, once everyone had left the room, the professor approached me. Before he could say anything, I said, "I didn't know about Lucas's parents."

"Maybe you didn't; maybe you did," he said, infuriating me further. "However, it doesn't matter. Your role as ruler of the Court of Sirena includes knowing everything about everyone and navigating a minefield of possible blunders gracefully."

"I just got here," I said. It wasn't fair. I was always expected to adjust to new places, new people, new rules.

"Yes, you did," he said. "And now that you're here, what *have* you done?"

I didn't answer him. He was being hard on me, and to say I didn't appreciate it was an understatement. I had enough on my plate already, learning about this place, adjusting to their rules, trying to prove myself worthy of the throne. I'd done a lot, as far as I was concerned.

"You're dismissed," he said. "Think about what I've said."

I got up and left the room without another word. Yeah, I'd think about what he said. *I think it's ridiculous.*

My other classes were, thankfully, uneventful. No one seemed to know what happened that morning, but it was only a matter of time before I became the academy's main villain. The new girl, who thinks she's just going to waltz in and claim the throne, decided to take a shot at poor orphaned Lucas. Great. That would help my already precarious social standing. Gossip like that was too juicy, and the situation so easy and satisfying to judge. One more example of how ethereal teenage beings weren't all that different from their human counterparts.

I was relieved when it was finally time for lunch. The best thing about BANA was the cafeteria. We sat at formal, round tables, and there was no line for food. Instead, all the dishes magically appeared, steaming hot and delicious, as soon as we sat down. Today was grill day—chicken inasal, pork barbecue, with heaps of garlic rice and vinegary achara. My mouth watered.

As soon as we started eating, I expected Nix to ask me about what happened. Instead, she said, "What do you say, after school, we go explore the city?"

I wanted to, for sure. I needed to forget about the unpleasantness this morning that I had caused. I would never hurt anyone deliberately. The only question was how to get there without an entourage following me around. "Not sure how I'd get away," I told her.

"Easy. Tell them we're staying after to study, and to pick you up later. Once they're gone, we'll walk into town and get back in time for them to pick you up."

I couldn't see why not. And more than anything, it felt good to think about doing something normal. "Okay," I agreed with a shrug.

"Yay!" Nix clapped her hands. "I've been dying to check out some of the new boutiques. You won't believe the stuff they have here. Makes Rodeo Drive look like a discount mart."

Nix gushed about every shop she'd been to in the main Market District, in the downtown district of Biringan, and how much better everything was than at home, especially the food. "If you think this is good," she said, motioning to the stew and halo-halo I was drooling over, "wait until you try the food in town. I'll bring you to the lumpia vendor, oh my god. To die for."

An hour later, having done exactly as she'd advised, we were on our way to town in a hired carriage. I wasn't even bothered by the ongoing coronation activity that surrounded us. I was too giddy with freedom and the promise of friendship, something I'd been without for such a long time. I even forgot the entire drama with Lucas. Along the way, Nix told me all about the different places she'd explored on her own before I arrived in Biringan. Her excitement was contagious. "And we have to stop at Doña Ximena's, you will not *believe* the cloaks she makes. She also has the best shoes. For jewelry, we have to go to Kumikinang. The owner is also half-human, like us."

Up ahead, around a bend in the road that led into the hills, a row of buildings emerged before the entire town opened up in front of us. I don't know what I was expecting—a medieval-style village, maybe—but it was better and stranger, in every way, than I could have imagined. Like the palace, the buildings were all cut out of the surrounding stone. Except they weren't glittery like the geode surface of the castle. They were grittier, rougher, gray and brown and black streaked with white. The shop fronts had huge windows and smooth wood doors in a variety of shapes—no plain rectangles here. The doors had unique iron handles, too. In the shop windows, the displays moved around, featuring a parade of wares sort of like a commercial. There were carts selling food, with smoke rising from them, and a mix of savory and sweet scents filled the air. People walked in and out of the buildings, in long coats almost like the ones we wore to school, and there were also more fairies like the ones I'd seen the other day. But then I noticed more creatures, like a kapre with sharp fangs and large, leathery wings. He didn't look friendly. There were also a few encantos in partial animal transformation. A feline pilipit and a wolf of some kind. I'd heard there were shape-shifters but, so far, hadn't actually met any.

Nix laughed. "Your mouth is hanging open," she said.

I shut it. "Sorry."

"Anyway, where do you want to go first?"

I couldn't possibly choose. "Up to you."

"I was hoping you'd say that!" She grabbed my hand and dragged me faster along the road. A carriage rumbled by. The man driving raised his hat to us. I waved with my free hand.

"Don't do that!" Nix reprimanded me. "He'll think you're flagging him down."

She pulled me toward a shoe store. In the window, boots in different heights—with no heel and high heels and everything in between, and even toe styles from square to round to pointy—swirled around.

When we walked inside, I was shocked. Instead of shelves full of shoes, there were only two pairs on display: plain black boots and a pair of flats. I didn't see a salesperson anywhere.

"Watch this." Nix walked over to a full-length mirror. "Come here," she said.

I went and looked in the mirror. I saw our reflections staring back.

"Now grab whichever footwear you need and bring them here."

I didn't need (or like) either one, but I grabbed the flats and went back to the mirror.

"Look down," Nix said.

The flats were on my feet. "Whoa!"

"What's your favorite color?" she asked.

Before the word made it from my brain to my mouth, the shoes turned purple. I started laughing. "That's wild!" I moved my feet around, and in my reflection the shoes did, too.

"Do you like stiletto heels?" Nix asked.

Not necessarily, but I pictured them on my feet, and they appeared in the mirror.

"I could do this all day," I said, admiring my reflection.

A fairy walked out of the back room. I noticed her taking in Nix's shabby school robes before she even noticed who I was.

"Let's go to the hat shop," Nix said abruptly. She took the shoes from me and put them back on the shelf, then dragged me out the door and down the street, past shape-shifters—manananggals who were flying around without their lower halves, and a group of what looked like male sirenas, judging by the gills and shimmering scales on their necks, who were walking on land for a change.

"Berberoka," Nix whispered in my ear. Swamp creatures who drowned the unsuspecting. "Steer clear."

A couple seconds later, she pointed at a shop. The sign in the window said ALTHEA'S APOTHECARY.

"Althea is my friend," Nix told me. "If you ever need anything, go to her. Or summon her to the palace. She makes house calls."

We stopped and cupped our hands over the glass to peek in the window. There were two women standing side by side with their backs to us, looking at a display of herbs and bottled liquids. One had wavy salt-and-pepper gray hair all the way down her back and wore a long, brightly colored cotton skirt. She reminded me of an old hippie from back home. The other was holding a baby.

"That's Althea," Nix said, motioning to the gray-haired hippie.

Althea put her arm around the mother, who appeared to be crying by the way her shoulders were shaking. I noticed she was cradling the baby in her arms. Then Althea walked around to the other side of the display, picked up one of the bottles, and wrapped it up in brown paper. She closed it with some twine and held it out to the mother, who seemed to be protesting taking the package. But Althea insisted and the mother accepted, thanking her profusely.

"I told you she was nice. She helps people whether they can afford it or not. Like me," she said as we entered the store.

"You?"

Nix shrugged. "Not all of us can live in the palace."

I thought of her frayed uniform and felt abashed that I had

never offered to help. I never thought she needed any—she was so confident and self-contained. "Oh, Nix . . . if you ever need anything . . . I'm so sorry . . ."

Nix laughed and dismissed my concern. "It's fine, I'm fine! Mostly thanks to Althea, who helped me get settled here."

The mother with the baby turned around to leave, so we moved on before they caught us watching them. Althea noticed Nix, though, and greeted her warmly. "How are you, sweetheart?" she asked.

"I'm okay," Nix replied, beaming.

Althea smiled. "You figured out that spell that was giving you trouble?"

Nix laughed. "Yeah, I was pronouncing it wrong." She turned and introduced me. "This is my friend MJ."

Althea bowed. "It's good to have you back, Princess."

I still wasn't used to people bowing to me, so I bowed back. "Thank you."

The old healer scrutinized my face. "You have her eyes. Your mother's. She was a good friend to me."

I flushed with pleasure to know someone who knew her. "Did you? When she lived here?"

Althea nodded.

I wanted to ask more questions, but Nix was already out the door. I followed reluctantly, thinking I would have time to talk to Althea in the future. Even though my mother taught me its history, she never spoke much of her time in Biringan.

On our right, there was a tavern or restaurant of some kind, the busiest place I'd seen so far. It was similar to our school cafeteria—lots of glass tables of customers being served huge plates of food.

But there was also a bar, cut from quartz, where people stood around talking and drinking from mugs and teacups and tall, skinny glasses. Maybe we could stop in there, get something to drink. I was starting to feel like I needed to tell someone about my talent, or lack thereof. And maybe this was a good opportunity to confide my secret to Nix. She might have some ideas, either to help me discover my power or at least how to fake it.

"Wait!" I shouted, yanking Nix back a couple steps.

She looked alarmed. "What is it?"

I didn't answer. I leaned against the front window, gazing inside. Way in the back of the tavern, I saw *him*. I was right. It was Lucas.

He was having a heated argument with someone—no, multiple someones. A group of men—who all appeared to be human—stood across from him, fists clenched, one of them yelling back at him.

Suddenly, Lucas drew his arm back and punched one of the men right in the face. Nix and I both gasped, watching as Lucas pummeled the men one right after the other, throwing one of them up against the bar, where he hit his head and crumpled to the floor. Another bent forward, holding his belly, after Lucas kicked him square in the stomach.

"Let's go," I told Nix. I'd seen enough. As if I hadn't hated Lucas already, now he was starting fights in taverns and beating people up. *Vulnerable human beings* who might even have been prisoners in this realm.

13

WHEN I GOT back to my room, Jinky hurried up to me, out of breath. "Your Highness," she said, bowing her head. "May I speak to you, in private?" She was wringing her hands and glanced around as if she was afraid someone was listening or watching.

"Of course," I said carefully. I wasn't sure I even wanted to hear what she had to say right then. There was so much I needed to process about the day already. "Can I ask what this is about?" Maybe it could wait.

She shook her head, her eyes wide.

"Okay." I reminded myself that the queen should know everything that was going on around her. Just like holding my head high and showing my face when I'd rather hide under the covers, I had to get used to being available for crises when I'd rather not.

Jinky closed and locked the door as soon as we entered the room. Unusual. Then she began checking behind the curtains, under the bed, in the closet. I stood there and watched her flit frantically around the room for a couple of minutes before finally asking her what was going on.

"Lambanas!" she exclaimed, pointing a finger in the air as if she'd just had an epiphany. Then she ran to the plants in the corner and began pulling the leaves aside to look for the tiny creatures.

"Jinky! Please tell me what is going on!" I was starting to get worried. Maybe there was a direct threat I needed to be aware of. I had an awful thought: Maybe I'd seen something I wasn't supposed to that afternoon in town, and now Lucas was angry, especially after how I'd upset him in class.

She started walking back to me, still looking all over the room, even picking up pieces of paper on the desk and looking under them. When she got close, she began whispering, "Okay, I don't think anyone—or anything—is here."

"How would there be? I can't take another second of this. What happened? Does this have something to do with Lucas?"

"Sir Lucas?" Jinky shook her head. "No. I'm sorry, Your Highness, but you'll understand my caution in just a moment, once I tell you what I learned this morning." She walked over to one of the rattan peacock chairs and motioned for me to sit down.

Leaning forward, she whispered, "On my way to the kitchens today, when I was bringing your tray down, I overheard some of the maids and pages discussing how the king was found."

"And?"

"Do you recall the circumstances of King Vivencio's death?"

"He was found in his office. He'd been up late into the night, and they claim he overworked himself into a heart attack." Now that I said it that way, it didn't seem as suspicious as it had the first time Elias told me it was a "natural death." That happens all the time. Particularly to stressed-out, burnt-out people.

"Well, what I heard is that he was found first thing in the morning, slumped over his desk, the writing quill still clasped in his hand. The door was locked." Nothing Jinky said so far was news to me. And I was still failing to hear the suspicious part. Then she came out with it: "The only strange thing was what he had written right before he died."

"You found the letter!"

"Yes! Well, one of the other maids did. Only, it wasn't a letter, exactly." She pulled a folded piece of parchment from her apron pocket and handed it to me.

I opened it eagerly, careful not to tear it.

The letter turned out to be a few hastily penned words:

Temo was right. It's time to tell her the truth—

A large inkblot covered the rest.

My stomach lurched. *Tell her the truth.* Tell who? Me? My mother? Someone else? And tell her the truth about what? Who was Temo, and what was he right about? "Where was this found?"

Jinky shrugged. "I don't know. I'm not even sure which maid found it. None will speak of it. And I'd be afraid to inquire any further. If the note was missing at first, it means that someone didn't want it to be found. Someone who has something to hide."

I nodded. "You're right. Don't ask." I read the note again. "Do you know anyone in the palace named Temo?"

Jinky shook her head. I almost blurted out the next thought, but I kept it to myself. I trusted Jinky, but that didn't mean she wouldn't tell someone else in her confidence. I was going to have to get into the king's chambers and do some investigating myself.

"Thank you for this. Listen, I think we both need to clear our heads. You can have the rest of the evening off." I had to distract

Jinky if I was going to get into the king's chamber without anyone knowing.

She looked at me like I'd sprouted wings.

"Take a long, hot bath, maybe?" I suggested. "Read a book?"

"Why are you trying to get rid of me, Princess?" she asked, her eyes squinted.

"I'm not," I protested. "It's just that you're always doing so much for me, and I don't need anything right now. There's nothing we can do about the letter presently, so you should take some time for yourself for once. Use my bathtub; it's amazing. And then you're right there if I need you."

She still looked suspicious, but she also looked tempted. "I mean it," I continued. "In fact, I order you. I'm just going to read in bed. I had a long day, and I want to stop thinking about my father's death. We can think about this tomorrow. It's not going anywhere."

"Princess, this is such a generous offer. I can't thank you enough for your kindness . . ." she said.

"It's nothing! Take your time." I picked up a random book and plopped onto my bed with it. *Ensiklopedya ng Hayop at Halaman.* "Homework," I said, pointing to the book.

Jinky disappeared into the bathroom. I waited until I heard the water running and could smell the bubble bath wafting out from the steamy room. She began singing. I recognized the song or, at least, the melody of it. My mother used to hum it to me when I was very small. All that time it was a Biringan lullaby. Now it made sense why I never heard it anywhere else.

I had to go before I got distracted by nostalgia. Jinky wouldn't be in there for long. I stuck the note inside the book and left it on the nightstand.

"Temo was right.

It's time to tell her the truth."

About what?

What was my father hiding? And from whom?

Who is Temo?

The next problem was the guards. There was no good way around them. I could cause a distraction somehow, make them run toward it and away from here. But that could backfire, put the palace on alert, and then I'd be followed even more closely.

My other idea was . . . I didn't have another one. I flopped down onto an oversized armchair and leaned my head back onto Jinky's cloak, which was slung over the back of it. I was running out of time. This just wasn't going to happen, at least not tonight.

Tell her the truth.

No, it had to happen. I wasn't going to sleep until I looked for myself. I needed a better plan.

The water shut off. Jinky called out, "Are you sure you don't mind me here?"

"Not at all," I called back at the door. "Like I said, take your time."

The water turned back on. I sighed and rubbed my face with my hands.

I needed a disguise.

I looked back at the door.

Before wasting another second, I grabbed Jinky's cloak, threw it on, put the hood up over my head, and started for the door to the hallway. There was a tray sitting on a marble console table near the entryway. I picked that up and brought it with me so I looked like I was busy.

Heart racing, I opened the chamber door and stepped out into the hallway. As expected, two guards stood outside. I kept my head down and held the tray as if I was on my way to fetch something from the kitchens.

"Hey," one of the guards said.

I stopped but didn't look at him. I kept my eyes on the ground in front of me, afraid he could see how nervous I was by how hard I was breathing.

"Bring me back a pastry, would ya?" he asked.

I nodded and continued on my way, faster this time, convinced they'd notice I was almost running and come after me. But they didn't. I was home free once I made it to the stairwell.

The king's chambers were in the opposite wing. I'd have to go up the stairs, then all the way across to the other side. There was no way Jinky would be in the bath for that long. But I just had to see it through. *Ask forgiveness, not permission.* I'd heard that phrase somewhere.

First I needed the key. The king's chambers were always locked.

Ayo was in charge of almost everything, from staff to schedules, so he absolutely, definitely had keys to all the rooms in the palace. Hopefully he kept the keys in his office, off the kitchens. I knew his schedule; he was in the dining room organizing dinner service. I had a little time before then.

I scurried up the stairs and all the way down the halls, barely able to breathe but not willing to stop either. I found Ayo's keys hanging on a hook and sneaked out of the office, through the kitchens, and bounded up the stairs that led to the king's chambers. I was careful to keep as quiet as possible. If anyone was alerted, it'd be hard to explain what I was doing there.

Finally, I turned down the King's Hall. I'd made it.

Portraits of Biringan's former rulers lined the walls. Making my way down the hall, I noticed how the kings' and queens' clothes changed over time. The older portraits had much more elaborate headdresses and necklaces, along with warrior masks.

It struck me that these were all my great-great—et cetera—grandparents. The last portrait was of my father. I stopped to look at it more closely. It didn't look like the photos I'd seen. In the painting, he was serious, stern, and looking off into the distance, wearing a regal barong Tagalog and a crown of palm leaves. Next to him was another king, who looked a lot like my father, only older, with white hair and a beard. King Paolo IV, according to the plaque. There was another of King Paolo with a woman who looked like him. At first I thought it was his wife, but the placard named her as his sister.

There was no time to examine the paintings further. I'd already taken too long. I continued to the chamber door and checked back down the passageway behind me. No one was there, and I heard no one approaching. So I took out the key ring.

Next problem: Which key? None were labeled, but they were all different—gold and brass and silver, light and hefty, plain and decorative. I looked at the doorknob. It was made to look like a shiny silver sirena, her pose resembling those mermaids on the front of pirate ships. Her tail made up the curve of the door handle. I looked back at the keys. The head of one of the larger silver keys matched the sirena's tail.

I slid it into the lock. It fit perfectly. One quick turn—and *click*. Unlocked.

I put the key ring back in the cloak pocket and turned the knob. It creaked a bit. I paused; it sounded so loud. But all was still behind me. I pushed the door open and stepped inside. Silent as a tomb. I could hear my own breathing. I found a torch on the wall and lit it so I could see.

I made my way across the room, careful not to knock anything over or bump into something. With my luck, one of the giant vases would crash to the ground and draw the attention of about a hundred guards. The king's grand desk sat right in the middle of the room, still strewn with papers and writing utensils. There was a high-backed gold chair behind it, and two comfortable sitting chairs in front of it, for guests. There was another table by the window to the right, and on the left, another group of seats, which looked like they were made from wooden branches, arranged around a large round table that seemed to be made from the trunk of a massive, ancient tree.

There were tapestries woven with gold and silver thread hanging on the walls, each representing important events in Biringan's history. The one on the wall behind the king's desk depicted his coronation. Then I realized the one to its left, where an older king with white hair stood next to a young prince, was of my father and grandfather, whose portraits I'd just seen. And finally, on the tapestry to the right, I saw my father as king with a baby on his lap. Me.

I had no idea this existed. All this time, he had this hanging in the room where he conducted so much official business. He looked at that every single day. He never forgot me. Me. His daughter.

Tell her the truth.

If I was reluctant before, or felt like I just didn't belong there, something clicked into place right then. This was not only where I belonged, it was my destiny. And my responsibility.

Still awed, I crept to the desk. Another thing occurred to me: This was where he was found. Sitting right there at that desk. In that chair. It sent a shiver down my arms.

Something crunched under my shoe. I looked down and gasped, jumping back. Some kind of beetle. Gross.

Then, to my horror, I saw them—tons of them. Beetles. Dead beetles. Some living ones crawling among them. All over the floor around the desk. And on the desk. They were also on the windowsill.

No wonder nobody wanted to come in here. This was an infestation. I heard a sound then, of the door opening. Someone was coming inside! Frantic, I looked around for somewhere to hide.

The only place was under the desk. With the bugs.

Still, braving some dead beetles was preferable to facing off with whoever was about to catch me snooping around in here.

I hurried behind the desk and crouched beneath it, conjuring all my inner strength to ignore the crunching beetles under my feet and the fact that the bottom of my dress was spread out all over them. It was hard not to gag. I put my hand over my mouth and tried to keep my breathing quiet.

Footsteps entered the room.

I held my breath. If I lost any control whatsoever, I'd probably give myself away. My heart was pounding so hard I was sure the intruder could also hear it.

The person stepped cautiously, slowly. One creak at a time, a dull thud against the old wood plank floor. A crunch.

Please leave, just go away, I prayed silently. What did they want? Didn't they realize that no one was here? Unless they'd seen me come in and waited for the right moment to ambush me, all alone . . .

The steps were coming around to the other side of the room. I pushed my body as deep into the desk as I could.

I saw the boots. Black. With dark blue stitching.

It couldn't be. It had to be someone else, even someone else from the Court of Sigbin, with the same boots.

The boots turned the opposite direction, and I saw the custom stitching on the heel, a looping letter *L*.

Lucas.

14

"**YOU LOOK AS** if you're running a fever, Princess!" Jinky had come to wake me up the next morning. For once in my life, I wasn't faking. I'd actually made myself sick.

"Stay in bed today," she said. "I'll go and fetch you some pandesal. And I'll ask the healer to come see you."

I nodded weakly. It was just as well. Hiding seemed like a reasonable solution to all my problems, in particular to facing Lucas after what I'd witnessed the night before. I wasn't ready.

I welcomed the opportunity to rest, though without internet or even trashy daytime television, a day home from school was not a whole lot of fun. All I had were my schoolbooks and a window to sit at and watch palace staff go about their business—an endless procession of food deliveries and bolts of fabric and slatted crates filled with who knew what—baffling in their sheer volume. I wondered when their activities would end, how much more they could possibly do. Or maybe I was just irritated because it was a nonstop reminder of impending disaster, like the gathering storm over the mountains, which not only hadn't gone away but was getting bigger.

Because of course, three weeks before the coronation, I still had no clue what my talent was. Maybe I had no magical ability and should just let the Court of Sigbin take the throne.

So I stayed away from the windows, too. The view was only making me feel sicker.

I thought about going to the library to see if I could find more about the beetles—or maybe even tips for magicless mortals on how to pull an enchanted scepter from a chest. But I didn't want to draw any attention in case someone decided I was well enough to have another impromptu fitting or to answer another question about flowers. Medium pink or dark pink? Which type of filler flowers did I prefer?

Althea, the healer who was Nix's friend, arrived. She gave me some black tea, like my mother used to do, and explained that sometimes encanto food and the air in Biringan are hard on the human nervous system. Maybe I just needed some time to adjust to living here. She instantly made me feel better and made me miss my own mother. Taking her advice, I slept through lunchtime and into the afternoon.

After I woke up, I read from the Hayop at Halaman text and finished an essay a week ahead of time. Then I heard Jinky out in the hall. She'd gone down to the kitchens to get our afternoon merienda of fried bananas in sugar.

I wrapped my robe around me as I opened the door. "Jinky, could you ask if there's any—" A surge of fear and anger shot through me when I saw the face on the other side. "What are you doing here?"

Lucas looked like he was trying to run away, but he'd been busted. "Oh, hey," he said sheepishly, raising his hand in a slight wave.

"I said, what are you doing here?" I demanded, a little more stridently than was warranted perhaps, since he didn't know that I had seen him in my father's office the night before. Plus, it was irritating being so close to him; he was so annoyingly good-looking, and I couldn't help but notice how long his lashes were. Ugh.

He looked around helplessly, as if someone might help him. "I was . . ."

But I didn't let him finish. "Lurking around my room?" I accused. "Is that it? Like you lurk around my father's?"

To my surprise, he began to walk away. He didn't even try to answer me.

"Wait! Where are you going?" I called after him. "Lucas! Get back here!"

He only walked faster, almost tripping over his own feet.

"You better keep running, then! And stay away from here!" I yelled, feeling a bit foolish after having just told him to come back. "Guards!" I shouted. "Guards!"

His footsteps faded down the hall and around the corner.

In anger, I'd been bold, but now that the immediate surprise had passed and he was out of sight, I realized I was shaking, from my hands to my feet. I felt kind of weak, like I needed to sit down.

Lucas had been in my father's rooms, and now he was outside my door, when I was alone. When confronted, he'd offered no explanation; he just ran away. Staying home hadn't protected me. I was foolish for letting him get away. In my panic, I wasn't thinking straight.

I clutched my dressing gown tighter around me, as if that would shield me. "Jinky?" I called out. She should be nearby. I shouted again, louder this time: "Jinky!" And where were the guards? How long could a shift change take? Had they allowed Lucas to walk right up to my door? If so, that meant anybody could take advantage of that window. Something would have to be done about this. They were always around to stop me from doing things I wanted to do but not around when I needed them to be.

Then I noticed it. My blood ran cold. A crack in the stone wall, something moving around it. Many somethings.

The same ones I'd seen all over the king's desk and window.

Black beetles.

A FEW DAYS after Lucas's unexplained visit, I invited Nix over to the palace for merienda. The afternoon snack was by far my favorite meal of the day. "By the way," I said as casually as I could, "what do you think about Lucas?" Since we were both transplants from the human world, I trusted her opinion. It was a relief to have someone who understood me, who saw this world through eyes similar to mine. Not that I was going to tell her everything just yet.

"I guess he's cute," Nix replied, shrugging. "Not my type, even though he's the reigning Arnis champion in all four kingdoms, two years in a row."

She didn't need to remind me. Anytime his name came up at school, it was like, "Sir Lucas Invierno, youngest knight to ever win the all-realm martial arts tourney." With the way everyone strained to watch him when he walked by, I was surprised there weren't more neck injuries at school. It was kind of nauseating. Not that I totally blamed them. He really was so handsome, if you could get past the whole egomaniac thing.

Nix added, "Amador drags his currency down some, though."

Then she did a double take, smacking her hand against the table and leaning forward. "Wait! You *like* him?"

"No." I shook my head vigorously. "Of course not! That's not what I meant. Like, do you think he's dangerous?" The answer should have been obvious, except I kept thinking that maybe he had a valid reason to be in the palace. His father did use to work there. Which meant the guards knew him. Maybe he came in to get something that had belonged to his dad? It was a stretch, but better than the alternative.

Nix pondered that. "Dangerous . . . ?" Her voice trailed off. "He's friends with Amador, so."

My stomach flipped. "So that's a *yes*?"

"Well, I would've maybe said no before, but after the other day, I'm not so sure."

"What happened the other day?" I asked, fighting to keep my tone casual. *The other day* could mean when he'd crept around in the king's chamber, right before lurking around mine.

She shook her head. "It could be nothing." She took a sip of her drink. "If it's nothing, you didn't hear anything from me." She pointed a perfect pink nail in my direction. "But if it's *not* nothing, remember I'm the one who told you."

"Of course," I promised, holding up my hand to vow.

Nix leaned forward. "All right," she began. "I was going to the market in town, looking for some more of that fabric I found last week. The one with the tiny roses?"

I nodded. Nix liked to tell stories with a million tangents. But if I hurried her through, she might rush to get to the point and leave out crucial details. And anything might be relevant, even if she didn't think so. I had to let her do her thing.

"I was looking through the bolts, and I couldn't find the right one. So I asked the vendor if she had any more or if what I'd bought was the last of it. Because I want a bag to match the skirt I'm making. And while I was waiting for her to check, I got bored, so I happened to turn around, and then I saw him."

"Lucas?"

"No, this creepy-looking guy I'd never seen before. He was just sort of standing around. Not shopping. More like he was waiting for someone. Or looking for someone to rob. Well, that someone was not going to be me, so I kept my eye on him. And if I hadn't, I would have missed who he was there to meet."

"Who? Lucas?"

"No." She waved her hand as if to say Lucas wasn't important. "Another shady-looking guy. The second guy walked up to him, and they looked like they were conspiring."

"And then what?" I asked hopefully.

She shook her head. "First the fabric woman came back and said she didn't have any more. I asked if they were going to get any more, and she didn't know, so I thanked her, and I decided to go check the other fabric merchant on the other side of the market. When I turned to go, I noticed that the two men were gone. I forgot about them and went to find out about the fabric. And you are not going to believe this."

"What?" I had a feeling she was finally getting to the interesting part.

"The other fabric merchant had one single half bolt of the rose fabric left! Isn't that amazing?"

"Yes," I said, pretending not to be disappointed. "It was meant to be."

Nix nodded enthusiastically. "It was!" She drank from her tea-cup. "This is really good," she said.

"It is," I agreed. "The cook uses a rare cinnamon for the champorado."

"I need to get some," Nix said. "Can you find out where it's from?"

I nodded. "Sure. So then what happened?" I asked. I was getting really antsy.

"Oh! Right. Well, I'm getting the matching bag made as we speak."

"With Lucas," I pushed.

"Oh, right. I saw him talking to the creepy guy."

"Which one?"

"Both of them at first, I think. I saw the second guy walking away from Lucas and the other one. After I went to the second fabric merchant, I took the long way around the other side of the market, which I never do, but I was in a good mood, and I wanted to shop some more. If I hadn't done that, I wouldn't have seen them."

"Did he see you?"

She shook her head again. "I don't think so. He was deep in conversation."

"Okay, so you saw Lucas talking to the creepy men. Why did you think they were shady?" There had to be more evidence of Lucas being nefarious than that.

"For one thing, they kept looking over their shoulders, like they were afraid of getting caught. They were watching everybody who walked by. And one of them kept putting his hand on his sword, as if he was preparing to use it. They were also dirty, like they hadn't showered in a long time, and they just looked mean."

"Do you think they were insurgents? And that he was conspiring with them?" If Mr. Two-Time Youngest Arnis Champion of the Four Kingdoms meant to take me out, I doubted he would risk his own life or reputation. He'd do anything for his kingdom, though. Like hire an assassin to kill the king in his palace? And if that was the case, then perhaps he was hiring them to do another job. To take out another royal rival. Me.

Elias's investigation had generated no real leads so far, and he was more than frustrated about it. Although he did say that once I was crowned and imbued with all the power of Biringan, there would be nothing more to worry about. Once I was queen, I could kill people with a word. The prospect was a little daunting, to say the least.

But for now, if no one was going to actually protect me, I would do it myself. "What do you say we go look for them? Those men Lucas was talking to? And find out what this is all about?" I asked her. I started getting up from my seat.

Nix put down her drink and blinked at me. "That sounds extremely reckless and dangerous." A huge smile broke out on her face. "I'm in."

15

NIX AND I decided we would borrow some of Jinky's clothes and head to the market to see if we could find these shady characters. Jinky wasn't due back to check on me until dinnertime. The main precaution we had to take was avoiding her on our way out of the palace so that the guards wouldn't be sent to shadow me. Luckily, that wasn't a problem. I was getting pretty good at sneaking around the hallways.

"We'll have to hurry," I told Nix as we descended the servant staircase that would lead us down to the main floor. "They're always keeping tabs on where I am."

Nix was an ideal co-conspirator. She went along with everything I said, no questions asked and without hesitation. She led us with confidence through doors and sharp turns, almost like she knew the palace better than I did.

She grabbed a basket and hooked it in the crook of her arm. "Can't shop without a basket," she whispered.

After a few minutes of lurking through the back halls, we burst out the rear doors and scurried off through the gardens. A few times, we had to flatten ourselves against the hedges and wait for guards to pass, then we ran, giggling, until we needed to hide again.

Finally, we escaped from the palace grounds to the main road. We kept our hoods up and our faces down, walking slower, worried about drawing too much attention. "If anyone asks, we're just two kitchen girls going to buy herbs," Nix said.

I nodded. "But what are we going to do if we can't find those guys?"

Nix shrugged. "Then we'll buy some cake and go home. I call that a win-win."

Everywhere I looked, there were calesas and carts, their wheels shaking against the stone roads, alongside clacking hooves and drivers shouting at one another for getting in the way or not going fast enough. The royal armorer sat outside her workshop, polishing formal chest plates that the guards would wear for the coronation festivities. There were ribbons hung over every window, hoping to entice the crowds that would descend on the town square during the celebration to step inside their shops. Villagers crowded the walkways, stopping to admire pottery and scarves or ducking in and out of shops, the bells on their doors constantly tinkling.

The scent of bread and roasted vegetables wafted from a tavern nearby. We'd left all our food uneaten at the palace. "Let's eat," I told Nix and grabbed on to the sleeve of her cloak, pulling her playfully toward the enticing aroma.

"They have the *best* empanadas," Nix said, pointing to one of the taverns up ahead.

My stomach growled. "All right, let's go there, then," I said, steering to the right. We crossed the street, dodging horses, and pushed open the door. It tinkled, then slammed shut behind us, making me jump a little. The inside was much quieter than the streets outdoors but had its own ambience—silver mugs slamming down on thick wooden tables, utensils scraping against pottery, the constant din of voices deep in conversation, occasionally shouting over one another. I couldn't hear most of what they were saying, except I did catch some of one particularly loud man's strong opinions—about me. "You better hope she's up to it. Or you can kiss your backside goodbye" and "Do I need to remind you there is no king right now? And never mind now, we're lookin' at the foreseeable future!"

Luckily, nobody paid any attention to us. I kept my hood up just in case.

Nix grabbed a seat at a table in front of the window. "We can watch for *you-know-who*," she whispered.

"Right, good idea." We sat down and waited for someone to come over. I scanned the streets outside, looking for anyone who fit the description of the men Lucas was talking to, but I didn't see any. Nix was right, though; even if we didn't find them, the outing was worth it.

A dwende appeared at the table. "Good afternoon. And what will you be drinking?" he asked.

"Tsokolate, please," I said.

Nix chimed in. "And empanadas for both of us."

He walked away without another word, and we went back to staring out the window.

Soon, cups and plates piled with puffy, savory treats were being laid in front of me, but I'd stopped paying attention to what was happening directly around me. I'd spotted someone on the other side of the road, a black-clad head bobbing in the crowd.

"Nix," I said, trying to hold down my excitement. "Is that one of them?"

"Where?" She turned and gazed out the window with me.

I pointed. "When that carriage passes, you'll see him."

She shook her head; I felt deflated. "That's not one of them," she said. "Hmmm . . . He looks like he might know them, though." She picked up one of the pastries and took a bite.

I did the same. "Oh my god, this is amazing." The crust was buttery and crisp and filled with a thick paste of cheese and vegetables. Better than anything I ever had back in the human world.

"I told you! Makes being here worth it," Nix said, then suddenly leaned closer to the window. "Wait, hold on. I think it is one of the guys I saw."

"Should we go over there?" I asked, even if I kind of hoped she'd say no. This was the second merienda we hadn't finished. But she was up and heading out the door before I could stop her. I took out some coins and left them on the table.

Nix was already prepared to cross the street when I caught up to her. "Hey! Wait for me."

"I'm not ditching you," she said. Her head swayed back and forth, watching for a break in the traffic. "Just wanted to make sure one of us got there before he left." She tugged on my sleeve. "Come on." We dodged horses and calesas, almost getting run over by a farmer's cart, until our feet were planted firmly on the other side.

"That was harrowing," I said.

"He's still there," Nix said. "Let's hurry."

We dashed down the street, swerving around slow walkers. Right before we reached the flower stand, we slowed down. "Here," Nix said, tilting her head toward the bookshop next to us. There were tables out front, covered in old books. She began leafing through one of them, looking up at the suspicious man from beneath her hood. I followed suit. The nearest book was huge, like a coffee-table book but hundreds of pages long. The cover was plain brown leather. I opened it and read the title: *Spells and Incantations: A Forbidden History*. I wondered if there was anything about the beetles in here. I flipped to the back, but there was no index. So I paged through it randomly instead. If the entries were in any sort of order, I couldn't make sense of it. There were some about potions and poisons, coercion spells, love spells—nothing about beetles or bugs.

Nix grabbed me again. "He's on the move."

We followed the man a little farther up the street, past the flower stand, a fabric shop, and a rug seller. He didn't stop walking until he reached the spice merchant. We jerked to a halt and started examining the rugs.

"These are very expensive," an old woman said to us. "If you want something more affordable, they're on the other side."

"Just browsing, thanks," Nix said. We walked away while the woman glared at us.

We were going straight to the spice cart. "What are we doing? Do we have a plan?" I whispered. The possible insurgent was only a few feet away from us now. And he didn't look particularly friendly.

She nudged me gently in his direction.

"Why me?" I asked. Now, all of a sudden, Nix lost her nerve?

"You're right," she said. "This was a bad idea." She retreated a few steps and turned as if she was going back to the palace.

This time, I grabbed her by the cloak. "Oh, no," I said. "We didn't come all this way for nothing." I was still reluctant, but I tried to feel brave. Nix was looking at me, encouraging me to go ahead. Counting on me to lead the way. I figured if I was going to get any respect as queen, I needed to prove I deserved it. No one would approve of a leader who couldn't even start a conversation with a random guy in the market, no matter how sketchy he looked.

I took a deep breath and started walking toward him before I could talk myself out of it again. Nix followed me. "Here's that cinnamon I was telling you about," I told her.

"Oh, wow, yes," she said, picking up a small jar. She smelled it. "Ah, yes. *Wonderful* indeed," she said in a weirdly formal voice. I felt like slapping my hand to my face. It was obvious we were up to something. The spice merchant gave us a withering look. "I'll take this one," I told him, yanking the jar from Nix's hands.

The old man nodded. "Twenty gold crowns."

"I left my money at home," Nix whispered to me.

I took the coins from my skirt pocket and handed them to him. The shady guy was still looking the other way, but I could tell his ear was perked and he was listening to us. At that point I knew for sure he'd noticed us following him.

I stepped closer, as if I was also inspecting the cardamom pods. I watched his hand inch closer to the knife on his belt. I felt a lump in my throat and belly at the same time.

"Sir!" The word escaped my mouth louder than I'd thought. "Any idea what Sir Lucas was talking to your friends about?" I cringed a little at my candor. It was too late to backtrack now.

"Why don't you ask him yourself?" he replied without looking directly at me.

Aha! So this man did know Lucas! I was trying to formulate a reply when Nix stepped forward, indignant. "What's that supposed to mean?" she said. I held my arm out in front of her so she wouldn't get any closer to him. He scoffed at her advance. True, she could hardly threaten a fly, but I was more worried about what he might do to her than vice versa.

"Look," he said, putting his hands up, as if to say he wanted nothing to do with this. "Like I told him, I don't run in certain circles anymore."

"Maybe not," I challenged him. "But you must know what they were talking about."

"I wish I could help you," he said. "However, I'm afraid I cannot."

As if I believed that. "Maybe you could," I blurted out. I hesitated, unsure I should say what I was thinking, because it could backfire. He could use it against me in multiple ways. But I decided there was no better way to figure out if he was telling the truth.

His face was blank. I was hoping for some type of clue—like maybe he'd seem really interested in what I was about to say, or even totally bored. But he was neither. He just stared at me. Somehow that was more unnerving than either of the other options. "I was wondering if you could help me get back home. You know, *outside* of Biringan." Maybe I was missing home. But I thought if anyone would be able to travel through realms undercover, it would be a sketchy guy like him.

He shook his head. "I already told your noble friend. He's got the wrong guy. I don't deal in human trafficking anymore. My hands are clean. He has no reason to come after me."

"Huh?"

"Listen, I don't want to end up bloodied on the side of the road, okay?" he growled.

I thought about how I'd seen Lucas beating up some men the other day—human men. Hold on. Maybe they *weren't* human? Maybe they were encanto? What if he was beating up *traffickers*? Was that what he'd been doing?

"Sir Lucas is after human traffickers?"

The man blinked at me. "I don't know why he cares so much about what happens to humans. Stupid, if you ask me. I told him I don't know who's bringing them in and keeping them here, but it's not me. I don't trade in torture and kidnapping."

I tried to keep my face as neutral as his was, though I felt like I was failing. Nix definitely was not keeping a poker face. She looked outraged and terrified at the same time.

"Right, I'll make sure he knows—" I began. Nix grabbed my arm and started pulling me away. I resisted, and she let up. But she was super antsy. She looked at me, raised her eyebrows, and glanced back toward the palace, as if saying, *Let's go.*

"Of course, Your Highness," he said, bowing with a flourish. He rose with a smirk on his face.

I froze. It took me a few seconds to think up a reply. "What did you call me?" I feigned ignorance.

He raised his cap, bowed again, then turned and walked away.

"I knew it, I knew it," Nix said.

"You knew that he knew who I am?"

"No," she admitted. "I knew something was wrong."

"No matter," I said, thinking of what he'd told me about how Lucas cared about the humans trapped in Biringan and how he'd been beating up people responsible for their misery.

16

"I THINK WE'RE going to make it in time—don't worry," Nix assured me when we were back on the road. I nodded, breathing heavily. We were nearly to the grounds. The sun was going orange already. But as long as we could get back into the palace the way we got out, we'd be fine. We'd sneak up into my chambers, and no one would ever know, just like the other day.

Because if the sun set and the princess wasn't around, they'd send out the entire royal army. My ruse would be over. I'd never be left unsupervised again, that was for sure. No more secret outings. No more tiny tastes of freedom.

We walked briskly down the road, nearly running at times, constantly looking around to make sure no one witnessed us, should it be an issue later. At one point, we heard a horse approaching, so we ducked into some wildflower bushes and waited for the rider to pass. It was a good thing, too, because I recognized him as one of the page boys in the palace.

The outer gardens beyond the gates looked gorgeous at night, as if the rising moon was enhancing all the colors somehow. Or even like the flowers were glowing from deep inside. I wanted to stop and explore, but Nix was rushing ahead. She turned and saw me standing, out of breath. "Come on," she urged. "You can rest later."

I hurried to catch up. "The gardens are so strange at night," I said to her. "The flowers should be harder to see, but they're almost brighter?" The little discoveries about the differences between the human world and the fairy one were never-ending.

The lampposts blinked to life, their faint light illuminating our path. Nightfall was nearly upon us now. The world was quieting, a hush falling over everything. All I could hear was my own breathing, labored from so much running, our feet on the gravelly path, and water streaming over the falls into the outer garden lake.

"Aren't your parents going to worry about you?" I asked Nix. Then I heard a loud splash. "Wait." I slowed down. "What was that?"

Nix turned around to face me. "I'm not sure," she said.

"A fish?"

She shook her head. "No—whatever that was, it was way too big to be a fish. And that's basically a pond, too small for big creatures."

We listened for a moment. It was quiet again, just the normal sound of the waterfall. But then, more splashing. Not one big thunk into the water as before, but more like something continuously hitting the water. "Someone's swimming," I said.

"They shouldn't be. This is palace property, even if it's beyond the gates." Nix looked angry again. This time she didn't hold it in. Arms pumping at her sides, she charged directly through the trees at the water.

"Nix, don't worry about it," I tried—though not very hard, admittedly. Because I was curious, too.

"Go back to the palace," Nix called over her shoulder. She disappeared around the bend.

I knew I should've gone back right away, but I wanted to know who was there and make sure Nix was okay. Plus, if I was going to get busted for sneaking out, I preferred not to get busted alone.

"Oh, it's just you," I heard Nix say.

I let out a huge breath, relieved. Whoever it was, Nix knew them. No threat.

I followed into the trees right after Nix. There was a shirtless boy standing in the water. He wiped the wet hair back from his face.

Lucas.

"What are you doing here?" I yelled at him for the second time in a week. I wasn't afraid of him anymore, but I was suspicious of him.

"Yeah, what are you doing here?" Nix echoed me. "This isn't your pond."

"There's no good swimming in the Court of Sigbin," he said, and even had the nerve to smile. He began to walk out of the water. All he was wearing was a pair of soaking wet breeches that hung so dangerously low, his hip bones jutted out. I had to turn my head away. Out of the corner of my eye, I could tell he was looking at me and still smiling. Enjoying my embarrassment, I guess.

He slipped a dry shirt over his head. I looked back at him, though I was still a little flustered. The fabric stuck to his wet skin, on his corded stomach muscles. I focused on the ground instead, trying to get the image out of my head. "Well, since you're here, are you finally going to tell me what you were doing outside my room?" I demanded.

"Wasn't it obvious? I was paying an official visit to the soon-to-be queen of Biringan on behalf of the Court of Sigbin to issue an apology," he said. "But I could tell you weren't in the mood to see me."

"An apology for what?" I asked.

He had the temerity to blush, and then I remembered that he had practically called me stupid in front of his entire court and mine. *Simple. Provincial.* Amador had put him up to it, but he was the one who had insulted me.

"Oh," I said, taken aback. "Right."

He bowed his head. "Please accept my apology."

I dismissed it with a wave of my hand. "A convenient excuse. You were obviously sneaking around! I saw you!"

"Can someone please explain what's going on here?" Nix asked, looking from me to Lucas in confusion.

"Saw me? Where?" he asked, furrowing his brow.

"In my father's office! Don't pretend you weren't there!" I accused.

"Um, as much as I'm enjoying this conversation, we need to go," Nix interrupted. "Like, now." She pointed to the sky. It was super dark.

Lucas was frowning. He seemed to want to say something, but Nix was pulling my arm. "Come on!"

He picked up his coat and boots and made to leave. But I wouldn't let him. "You're coming with us! We aren't done here," I said haughtily.

Nix looked at me pleadingly. "Um, we're going to get in trouble if we don't get back in time and—"

I cut her off, mortified. "No one is in trouble," I manifested.

"We're just late for dinner. Lucas, you're coming with, because I'm not done questioning you." There was no reason he couldn't just take off, so I added, "It's not optional. If you don't comply, I'm sending the Royal Guard to arrest you for attempted regicide!" He needed to understand I wasn't playing around.

Nix shifted uncomfortably. "Um, Princess—"

I shot her a look that silenced her immediately.

Lucas folded his arms across his chest. "Attempted regicide? What in the great blue sky are you talking about?"

"Spying on the Court of Sirena and being at the palace without permission," I snapped.

He stepped toward me. I fell back. "For your information," he said, jaw clenched and face red, "I've always had permission to be here—from your father, in fact. But I guess you don't know that, since you don't know anything at all about Biringan except that you want to rule it."

"Both of you, please!" Nix was desperate now. "Enough! We have to go!" She pleaded with Lucas, "Just come with us."

"Fine," he said. He pulled his boots on and shrugged on his coat. "I wouldn't want Her Royal Highness to sic her goons on me."

The three of us walked the rest of the way to the palace, Lucas in front so I could keep my eye on him. All the way I battled with worrying about what he was up to and whether I was about to lose all my freedom on top of it.

As we walked through the gate and up the path to the palace, we saw there were people swarming everywhere: guards, staff, and a crowd of onlookers. The front doors were wide open, which was never the case once the sun went down. Whatever was happening seemed like a lot more than Jinky discovering that I was missing for dinner.

"What's going on?" I asked out loud, even though I knew neither Nix nor Lucas could answer.

Both of them were silent. Suddenly, Lucas held his arm out to block me.

"What are you doing?" I asked, indignant.

"Wait," he said. "We don't know what this is about."

"I'm about to be queen," I said. "I have every right to—"

"*Shhh.*" Lucas held his finger to his lips.

"How dare—" But I didn't get to finish.

"Stay here," Lucas said, darting off back into the woods. As much as I didn't like him telling me what to do, I had to admit to myself that he was right. I had no idea what I was walking into.

"Did he just use that as an excuse to take off?" I asked Nix.

"I don't think so," she said. "I kind of believe him."

"What do you mean?"

"I don't think he's lying to us. I think he did just want to swim. And I think he meant his apology."

"Nix." I closed my eyes and rubbed my face with my hands. "I saw him in my father's chamber. Then I caught him outside my door. He might not be lying about wanting a swim, and maybe he feels bad about insulting me at the council meeting, but I'm pretty sure he hasn't told us the truth about why he's always around here. Unless you think I'm the one who's lying?"

"No, of course not. I believe that you saw him there. But I don't think he was doing anything to hurt you."

"Then what was he doing?"

She shrugged. She wrapped her arms around herself and shifted her feet. "I don't know. I thought he sounded sincere. Like, really surprised you accused him of trying to kill you. I mean, when you think about it, why would he want to do that? It seems a little far-fetched, don't you think? He is a knight, after all, and made his vows. All I know is, I've been going to school with him for a year, and, yeah, he's way too into himself, and his girlfriend is a stuck-up brat, but . . ."

"But I'm not a killer," Lucas said.

Both Nix and I jumped about a mile into the air. "You scared me!" she shouted. I didn't say anything, but my heart was racing. I wondered how much he'd heard.

"And by the way, Amador's not my girlfriend. She just wants everyone to think she is," he added.

Oh, he'd heard a lot, then.

Lucas stepped up close to me. I sucked in my breath and stared him down, annoyed to notice his dark eyes had glints of gold in them. Did he have to be so beautiful? And so close to me? "Listen," he said, gripping both of my forearms with his strong hands. "I did not harm your father. And I don't want to harm you. I'm sorry for what happened at the meeting of our courts. It was wrong of me. I don't share those views. I regret what I said, and I hope you accept my apology."

We looked into each other's eyes for a few seconds. His hands were warm; I could feel the heat of his touch through the thin fabric of my sleeves.

"Please?" he asked, then let go of me.

I felt cold suddenly without his touch, and as much as I hated to admit it, in my heart, I agreed with Nix. I believed him. There was something desperately sincere in his tone, and while he might have been a pawn of Amador's, I didn't take him to be cruel.

"Fine, apology accepted." I relented, then quickly changed the subject. "So did you find out what's happening at the palace?"

He shook his head. "I couldn't get close enough. But . . ." He craned his neck to look farther down the road to the palace. "No one else seems to be coming. With all the commotion, we could probably just appear in the crowd without anyone questioning where we came from."

"They've probably been looking for me already. Maybe that's what it is. Someone noticed I was missing." I was in deep trouble. I'd never escape again after this.

"Okay." Lucas was contemplating something. "In that case, no big deal. We'll say we were exploring the gardens, lost track of time, got turned around in the maze."

"You don't think they already looked there?" I asked.

"Sure, but there are all sorts of coves and hidden spots. It's certainly possible to go unnoticed."

With the stress of the moment, I didn't think to question why or how he knew that, or else I would've been suspicious of him again.

The three of us agreed to the same story—Lucas wanted to discuss relations between our courts, Nix tagged along as a chaperone, we got lost walking in the gardens, and we finally found our way out. Reasonable enough. It could work. Everyone in Biringan trusted and respected Lucas, even outside of the Court of Sigbin, so they'd believe it if he said so. Whether they *should* trust him was another story.

We waited for the right moment, when no one was paying

attention to what was going on beyond the gates and slipped right into the crowds as nonchalantly as possible. We walked casually to the entrance, where guards tried to stop us.

"Hold on, there!" One of them held out his staff across the walkway, blocking our path, then lifted it within seconds. "My apologies, Your Highness, he said, bowing. He was flustered. "I didn't know it was you."

"It's okay," I said. "You're just doing your job."

His shoulders relaxed, and he bowed again.

"What's with the commotion?" I asked the guard.

"I wish I could tell you," he answered. "But I don't know. I've only been told to stand watch."

I thanked him, and we continued for the door. As we stepped inside, Lucas leaned toward me and whispered, "You shouldn't show weakness like that."

I stopped abruptly and snapped at him: "Do *not* tell me what to do." My jaw was clenched tight. "How did I possibly 'show weakness'?"

"Oh, relax," he said, downplaying my anger. That only made me madder. He stepped closer to me and whispered again. "All I'm saying is you never truly know what's going on with anyone here—who they might have a deal with, who they might trade information with, whether they're involved with the insurgency. If you act like you don't know what's going on, they could take advantage."

I cut him off. "Fine, got it." He did have a point, as much as it pained me to admit it. I also wasn't going to forget the reason I'd been out tonight to begin with. "The same goes for you. Who knows what's going on with you?"

He leaned back and looked me up and down. "Exactly" is the

only thing he said before continuing to walk into the palace. I was annoyed all over again—what did that mean? He wasn't even going to deny that he was up to something now that he got me to do what he wanted. Maybe I wasn't using him to get back into the palace—maybe he was using me.

"Wait," I said, stopping again. This was very strange. No one had rushed up to me, asking where I was. People were still gathered at the edges of the castle foyer, whispering in groups, guards flanking every single door, their eyes darting around the room on high alert.

Lucas seemed to catch on to what I was thinking at the same time. For a second he seemed a bit annoyed that I was standing there again, but then he looked around, then back at me, and raised his eyebrows. "Something's wrong."

He charged forward again. Nix and I followed him. "Are you okay?" I asked her. She had been awfully quiet for a while. She didn't look great either.

"Yes, I'm fine," she assured me. She swallowed.

"Are you sure? Because you don't look fine." Her hands were shaking.

"Can you tell me if—if anyone looks like they're from Jade Mountain?" she asked.

I was confused. "Jade Mountain? The Chinese fairy realm?"

She nodded.

"No—I don't think so."

Nix looked relieved, and I wondered what that was about—why she would be so concerned if there were encantos from Jade Mountain in Biringan.

Lucas pushed through the only closed doors we'd seen so far—to the tearoom. There, we found a crowd of guards and nobles, and a few palace staffers crouched in a circle, surrounding something.

"Can someone tell me what exactly is going on here?" I shouted. All heads turned to me. A few people in the crowd stepped aside, revealing what everybody was staring down at.

There, on the floor, was a body.

17

A WOMAN WAS crouched over the body, rocking back and forth. Judging by her face, she was my mother's age; she had dark-gray hair, long, in two thick braids, one over each shoulder, and she wore a yellow scarf on her head. Tears were streaming down her cheeks.

"That's the healer," Nix whispered to me. I looked at her quizzically. "Remember, the healer from the market? Althea? My friend?"

"Oh! Yes." I remembered her kindness when I wasn't feeling well. Her warm, soft hands on my brow.

More people were pushing into the room by the second.

All I could see was the other person's legs and the green ballet flats they wore on their feet; their upper body was obscured by the healer. The shoes looked really familiar—I couldn't quite place them, though I knew I'd seen them somewhere before.

"Don't come any closer, Your Highness," one of the guards warned me.

I opened my mouth to ask what was going on. Lucas beat me to it. "Someone needs to inform the princess about what's going on, immediately," he insisted.

No one answered. They all looked at one another, waiting to

see who was going to talk. The healer, Althea, rose from the floor. She stood and looked down at the body, wiped her eyes. "It's useless to ask them," she said, gesturing at everyone else gathered in the room. "They have not the answers you seek."

I stared at the body on the floor. I recognized her right away— it was Marikit Baluyot, one of the page girls I saw almost every day. She delivered letters and packages from town throughout the palace. The image would never leave me. Her mouth was set in a silent scream, bloodshot eyes staring off into nowhere. Her hands were up near her face, as if she'd been trying to shield it.

I did everything I could to avoid looking by the healer's feet, to the face of the girl who just days before I'd seen running around the palace, perfectly healthy, with no idea of the horrible fate that was about to befall her. "What happened?" I asked.

"It's not the what, so much as the why. And the who," Althea replied. I was getting tired of opaque answers and was about to say so when she began speaking again, this time with actual information. "She's been taking lessons from me to become a healer in her own right. Everything was fine. Then she started to convulse." She closed her eyes and took a deep breath before opening them again. "It's been a very long time since I've seen that."

"Seen what, exactly?" I nudged. I felt for her; I did. But if the girl had been assaulted somehow or poisoned, we needed to know and quickly. There could be a murderer in the palace. Maybe in this very room.

"Darkness," she whispered. "A darkness that comes for us all."

My stomach lurched. I could tell Lucas and Nix exchanged a look.

"What do you mean?" I demanded. Why was this girl dead? Why was Althea so spooked? What had she seen?

"The darkness is all around us." Althea shuddered. "It comes out of the walls."

Lucas stepped forward. "All right, the princess has heard enough. Let's not upset her any more." Then he looked to one of the guards. "Please escort Althea to the library so an investigator can speak with her."

The healer nodded and allowed the guard to take her arm and lead her out of the room.

I wondered whether Lucas was trying to be helpful or to control the situation. I looked over at him. Handsome, self-assured, calm. Innocent? Nix said she believed him, that he didn't mean any harm to me. I believed that, too, but just because he didn't mean *me* any harm didn't mean he wasn't dangerous. I wondered if, before swimming in the gardens, Lucas could've killed the girl. He knew his way around the palace, after all. But why would he do something like that? He'd said it himself—he wasn't a killer. Or was he?

The guard commander stepped over to me. "Your Highness," she said with a curt bow. "Can I speak to you privately?"

"Yes, of course," I said. I looked around. There were people everywhere. One of the adjoining rooms would probably be emptier. We went in there, and she closed the door behind us. She was in charge, since Elias had left that morning, still bent on rooting out the leader of the insurgents. Another lead had taken him all the way to the Paulanan Mountains, on the far reaches of the island.

"We are preparing to arrest the healer Althea," the commander said solemnly.

I was taken aback. "Why do you believe she's responsible?" I asked.

She blinked at my question but, to her credit, didn't break her professional demeanor. "She was alone in the room with the victim when it happened. There are no other suspects. She is the only one who could have done it. According to the kitchen staff, she was with the victim for more than an hour, and the page was perfectly healthy before then."

"Did she explain why she was here?"

"She claims she was summoned to the palace by the victim. That a letter arrived at the apothecary, asking for urgent assistance."

"Did she produce the letter?"

"According to the suspect, she left it behind in her haste."

I shook my head at *suspect*. "Althea had no reason to do this. And even if she did, why here, in such a public way? She could have done it some other time and been long gone."

"Maybe that was part of her ruse. To make it appear so obvious that she wasn't covering up, to confuse an investigation."

"Maybe. It's always possible," I conceded. I didn't have any concrete evidence, of course, but I just didn't think Althea was responsible. Much the same way Nix just didn't believe Lucas had anything to do with my father's death.

"Regardless, Your Highness, I think the best course of action is to put the entire palace into lockdown immediately. I've already notified all stations."

"If that's what you think is best," I told her. She was the security expert. Privately, though, I wasn't sure I liked the idea of being locked inside with a possible assassin on the loose.

"And if you're correct and Althea is not the culprit, all the more reason to institute a lockdown. The perpetrator could be anywhere."

I nodded. She was right about that.

"I'll escort you to your room personally, then," she said.

Admittedly, I was relieved to leave that gory scene. As we headed out the door, another guard stepped alongside us with Lucas in tow. "So, are you being escorted to a 'safe room,' too?" I asked him as we walked.

"A bit flippant under the circumstances, no?" he replied.

He was insufferable. "If I took everything in my life too seriously, I wouldn't be able to cope."

"Being a princess is *quite* demanding," he muttered.

"For your information, Sir Lucas," I hissed back at him, trying to keep my voice low so the guards ahead of us wouldn't hear, "my life has been anything but regal, and I didn't ask for any of this, nor did I particularly want it."

He had the nerve to roll his eyes.

"Well, lucky for you, I'll be locked up in my chambers until the killer is captured, so you won't have to deal with me," I told him. I looked around. "Where's Nix?"

"I don't know. I assume she went home while you were talking to the commander."

I hoped Nix wasn't too shaken by the scene and was able to get home safely. I'd have to ask her about why she was so afraid of encantos from Jade Mountain. We didn't get many foreigners from other realms—a few Avalonians here and there once in a while, or someone lost on the way to El Dorado.

"Here we are," the guard commander announced. I was so busy shooting daggers out of my eyes at Lucas that I nearly ran into the guard when he stopped in front of me. We were standing in front of one of the guest suites.

"I guess this is you," I told Lucas.

The commander opened the doors and walked inside. Lucas and the guard followed. I was being left alone in the hall. The guard noticed I wasn't with them and turned around. "Your Highness," he said, indicating I should go with them. I wasn't sure why I needed to be present for this, but I went along anyway.

It was one of the nicer suites, with a spacious sitting room but no balcony, making it harder to get in or out. A solid choice, I thought. After all, there was still a possibility that Lucas was the one behind all this, or at least had something to do with it.

"Hope this will suffice," the commander said to me.

"I'm sure he'll be very comfortable here," I said, looking at Lucas. I couldn't help but rejoice a tiny bit over his unfortunate circumstances.

The commander looked at me, confused. "And you as well, of course."

"Me?" It was my turn to look puzzled. And embarrassed. Now Lucas was smirking at *me*.

"Yes, you will both be staying here."

"What about my rooms?" I asked, voice edging on shrill. I felt a bit panicked at the idea of being locked in this space with . . . *him*.

She shook her head. "I'm afraid there was an incident in the queen's wing. Your safety is paramount while we secure the scene and investigate."

"What kind of incident?" I demanded.

"It appears as if the lock was damaged and the outer chamber, the receiving room, was breached. Someone managed to riffle through the desk and some files. Until we know the full extent of the situation and find the perpetrator, alternate lodgings have been arranged."

Someone had broken into my rooms? Was I not safe anywhere?

Lucas plopped into a chair and crossed his ankle over his knee. "Get comfortable, Princess. We might be here awhile."

Obnoxious man. This was unbearable. While I was thinking of something sarcastic to say back, the commander stepped in between us. "I'll have two guards stationed at the door at all times. If anything happens outside this room"—she looked at both of us, one at a time—"*or* inside, security will be at the ready. Sir Lucas has been tasked to protect you, as our highest-ranking knight of the realm."

Oh.

"I've got this, Commander," Lucas said with a smile. "The princess will be completely safe with me."

The commander nodded. "In that case, I better return to the others. We'll have the palace secured and the perpetrator apprehended as soon as possible." She bowed and left the room. The door shut firmly behind her. I heard a loud click from the lock as it was bolted.

We were locked in here together?

"So," Lucas said, grinning, "do you play cards?"

"I'd prefer to go to sleep, if you don't mind," I told him as I pulled my cape around me and walked (rather haughtily) into the adjoining bedroom. Out of the corner of my eye, I caught him shrugging, as if he didn't care, yet I thought I detected some disappointment on his face. I almost felt a little bad for him. Almost.

He was still irksome and egotistical and shady, and I didn't want to be anywhere near him, let alone locked up in that tiny suite together. Whether he had blood on his hands or not—and admittedly, I was beginning to believe he couldn't have been the killer— he was still my enemy.

18

I WOKE UP in a strange room, totally disoriented, face stuck to the pillow with drool. I didn't even remember falling asleep, let alone in my clothes. It took a few seconds for the events of the previous night to come back to me. When they did, I groaned out loud. I was locked in a guest suite with the most annoying guy I knew. Speaking of, I wondered what he was doing, so I got out of bed, crept over to the door, and cracked it open. There was no sound, and I didn't see him anywhere. I opened it more but still didn't spot him. My heart soared. We must have been cleared to leave while I was still asleep. I walked out and went to open the main door.

It was locked. I knocked on it, then called out, "Hello?"

"It's a bit early for all that shouting," a groggy voice mumbled behind me.

I spun around. "Oh my god. I thought you were gone." Lucas was sprawled on the big chair where he'd been sitting the night before, his arm thrown over his eyes. I must have missed him when I walked by.

He sat up slowly, cringing while rubbing his neck. "Remind me to ask for a pillow tonight." His hair was tousled, and of course it made him look even more charming and boyish.

"Oh, don't worry. That won't be necessary. Not a chance I'm staying in here another whole night."

He looked up at me, his eyes still not fully awake, and smiled. "Then I guess you better hope they capture the killer."

I didn't have anything to say to that. I stood there for a few seconds, arms crossed, a million thoughts running through my head at once. I wanted out of there, first of all. Then I wanted something to eat. And I wanted to know who killed the page.

For lack of anything else to do, I went and sat in the chair across from him. "They think Althea, the healer, did it," I said. Might as well address the one issue I could at the moment. "What do you think?"

He shrugged. "Maybe she did."

"Do you really think so?" I couldn't believe he thought she'd be a suspect.

"No, but that doesn't mean she didn't."

He had a point. "I don't know much about healers," I said. *Or anything at all.* "Do they . . ." I cleared my throat. I wasn't sure I should go there, but I'd already started, so might as well. "Do they use bugs? Like beetles?"

Lucas leaned forward, resting his chin on his hands. "Hmmm. Healers might use leeches, but bugs aren't usually a healer's choice of murder weapon."

"What is?"

"Poison, usually. Beetles require magic. Healers don't have that."

"Why not?"

He regarded me with what seemed like curiosity. "You're really new to Biringan, aren't you?"

I didn't answer, which was answer enough.

He sighed. "Healers are always human."

I was confused. "What do you mean? Althea's human?"

"Yeah. They aren't diwata like you. They aren't even hapcanto. They're entirely human."

I didn't like what that insinuated. "So she's a prisoner here?" Then what was said in class about Biringan trapping humans to remain here was true. I felt a little sick.

"In a sense," he conceded. "Like the others, she came here willingly. At least at first. And then, though she was forbidden, she gave in to temptation and ate the black rice."

"Right," I said, remembering that conversation in Professor Borromeo's class.

Lucas nodded.

"Why healers?"

"For a time, healers were recruited from the human world because they had knowledge we did not. Their illnesses had contaminated our world, and we were powerless against them. We needed their healers. After a while, we learned their ways and didn't need them anymore. Some of them returned, and some of them stayed—by choice or because the rules dictated it."

Althea said she had known my mother. My mom was a nurse back home. I wondered if Althea had been one, too, and if she'd bonded over this with my mother. Somehow, I struggled to believe that Althea would deliberately hurt anyone. I had seen firsthand how kind she was to her patients, and she had been there for Nix when she needed someone. Although if she was trapped here, maybe she was driven mad and initiated a killing spree. "But you said healers don't use beetles."

"They don't. It's not their way. They aren't mambabarangs."

I must have looked confused, because then he said, "You don't know what that is either?"

"I mean, I've heard of them, but I haven't met one." I recalled that Elias had asked that of the patianaks when they brought me to him. If there had been a mambabarang among them.

"Hope you never do. A mambabarang is a dark witch. One who deals in the black arts. Evil magic. They were expelled from Biringan when their coven was discovered. They'd been using dolls to curse their enemies or anyone they considered an enemy—mostly innocent people who were unfortunate enough to cross their path. Their mistake was going after a lady of the Court of Tikbalang. That sparked an investigation across the realm, until they were rooted out."

"Could Althea be one, and we just don't know?"

"Highly unlikely, as humans don't have any magical powers."

"Yeah, you keep saying that." I wasn't sure what to think. "And what about you? Do you know any dark magic?"

Lucas laughed, so loudly I felt a little insulted. "No, Princess, I don't work with dark magic. My talent lies elsewhere." He waggled his eyebrows, and I wanted to hit him, except he looked so silly I laughed.

He beamed. "So she does have a sense of humor after all."

I chortled. "Shut up."

For a moment I wished I knew what my talent was as clearly as he knew his. But I got back to the issue directly at hand. "Then what about the beetles in the king's chamber?"

"What about them?"

So he was going to be difficult. "I told you. I know you were there," I said. "I saw you."

"Then that means you were there, too. How do I know the beetles weren't *your* doing?" He sounded serious, but the smile on the edges of his mouth told another story.

"Because I wasn't even here when my father died! And this is my palace. You seem to forget that." Whether he was teasing me or not, I didn't like it. This wasn't a joke to me.

He put his hands up in front of him. "Whoa. Point taken."

"Are you going to explain yourself? Or keep messing with me? I want to know what you were doing in the king's rooms. And what were you really doing outside *my* room?"

Lucas took a deep breath. "Investigating."

"Investigating? You expect me to believe that?"

"You can believe it or not believe it. It's the only truth I have, however."

"Investigating what, then?"

He hesitated, as if he was unsure of whether to trust me. The irony. At last, he said, "The beetles. I suspect your father was the victim of some long-forgotten curse." He sighed, and for a moment I saw something in his face—something real, like grief and fear, behind his cocky façade. Something vulnerable. Lucas was scared.

A curse. It was the same thing I'd overheard the maids saying in the garden, that the king had been cursed by dark magic. But I wanted to know what he knew. "What kind of curse?"

Lucas shrugged. "I'm not sure. That's what I'm trying to figure out."

I didn't want to believe him, yet I did. I felt he was being truthful. One thing still didn't make sense to me, though. "Why were you creeping around outside my room, then?"

"Same reason. I had been trying to find the source of the bugs.

That led me up to the queen's wing. I had to get the guards away so they wouldn't catch on to what I was doing. I didn't want anyone to know, in case any one of them may be the culprit. I lured them away with a tray of treats from the Court of Sigbin. They absolutely love the coconut pandan cake our chef makes—"

"Okay, but what did you find?" I was anxious to get as much information as I could now that we were finally laying it all out on the table.

"Not much. I found the beetles, of course. But not their origin. It appears they're not in your rooms—at least not yet. I'm glad we're having this conversation, actually, even if it isn't under ideal circumstances. I was trying to think of a way to let you know, but it's kind of hard when . . ."

"When we hate each other?" I finished for him.

"Ouch. I didn't know you had such strong feelings for me." His face lit up with a rakish grin.

I couldn't help but laugh once more, but I was also blushing. God, why did he have to be so attractive? Was I so basic I was falling for him, too, like every starry-eyed first-year at BANA?

Neither of us spoke for a minute after that. I was trying to process everything and figure out where to go from there. Lucas was just as lost in his thoughts as I was.

"Penny for your thoughts," I offered.

This time it was his turn to blush. Huh. Was he thinking about me? And if he was, how would I feel about it? Somehow, I knew I wouldn't be as dismissive of it as I had been just the other day. I think I would maybe even welcome it? It was strange to think that last night I still considered him my enemy, but by this morning we were almost friends.

The silence was getting awkward, so I thought it was a good time to ask him more questions. "By the way," I said, "who were the two men you were talking to in town?"

That one genuinely surprised him. "How'd you know about that?"

"Let's just say I have my sources. Aren't they smugglers?"

He looked down at the ground and clasped his hands together. I knew I had him this time. "I didn't realize I was being spied on," he said, as if he had any right to be upset about that after the discussion we just had.

"Then we're even," I pointed out.

He raised an eyebrow. "Yes, they were smugglers," he admitted.

"I knew it." Vindication. "How can you work with them? They bring humans into Biringan to be enslaved!"

Lucas's eyes blazed. "For your information, I have personally tracked down and imprisoned anyone who would hurt or harm humans."

It was exactly as the shady man had said—Lucas cared about the humans in Biringan. He wasn't involved in exploiting them. I was mollified and grateful for the confirmation. But I still needed to know his reasons.

"Why, then? Are you trying to make some extra money on the side? Or what?"

"No. Those guys I talked to don't deal with human trafficking. They mostly run a black market of stolen goods from the human world—some encantos can't live without their iPhones. You'd be surprised how many here love them. Oh, yes, I know all about 'technology.' Anyway, I was trying to get some information about the beetles. Smugglers tend to know about things that are illegal or illicit in the kingdom. But all they could tell me was that they originate in the Sombra Woods. Look, the fact is, we're on the same side, Princess," Lucas insisted. "Neither of us wants to see anyone else get hurt. Especially if we're dealing with regicide here. The page's murder was probably a threat. A warning to the future queen." He looked straight at me.

"So how do we find out who's behind it? We need a plan. Elias's investigation hasn't been very fruitful."

Lucas leaned forward and clapped his hands together. "All right, finally something I'm good at. Okay, here's the deal. We need to know for sure what happened to the page. How did she die? Was she poisoned? Was she strangled? Stabbed? It makes a difference. Then we find out who had a chance to do it. A list of suspects."

"It's not Althea. It's too easy. I think she's being framed. Like you said, healers don't have magic. And the beetles—whatever they are—they're definitely dark magic, right?"

Lucas nodded. "Yeah, that's what I think. So, if we want to prove Althea isn't guilty, we need to figure out who is."

"I could ask around, but what if the killer is in with the guards? It happens. I mean, what better way to control the investigation?"

Lucas agreed. "That's why we're not even going to ask them. As soon as they let us out of here, we're going down to the morgue."

19

"WE'VE SECURED THE person responsible, Your Highness, so I'm pleased to let you know it is now safe for us to release you and let Sir Lucas off his post."

Lucas and I looked at each other.

"May I ask who it is, Commander?" I said.

"We've arrested the healer." She looked quite proud about it, too. "She was apprehended attempting to escape the premises."

No! They've arrested the wrong person. Althea is a kind soul. This is nothing but a trumped-up charge. I had to put a stop to this. "Are you sure? I don't think—"

Lucas interrupted me. "Thank you, Commander." He turned to me. "Don't worry, Your Highness. The threat is contained." He shook the commander's hand. "Thanks for your work."

The commander bowed again. "If that's all, we have more to attend to."

"Yes, thank you," Lucas said, directing the guards toward the door. Once they were out, he shut it behind them.

"Why did you do that?" I asked him.

"Because if you convince them to let Althea go, then they'll lock us up in here again while they search for someone else. If you actually want to help her, the best thing we can do is go investigate ourselves."

I hated how much sense he was making. I sighed. "Fine."

Lucas stuck his head out the door, then shut it again. "They're gone. Let's go."

We walked out as casually as possible. As we passed the guards, Lucas said loudly, "Wow, I'm famished. What do you say we grab something before we go into town?"

"Sounds good," I said, a bit too cheerfully. I cringed at how fake I sounded. But the guards didn't even look in our direction.

Once we were out of their sight, we relaxed and began walking faster. "How far is it?" I asked him. I assumed we needed to go into town or at least close.

"One floor beneath the cellar," he said.

I stopped walking. "What? Like, in the palace?"

He turned around. "Yes—where did you think it was?"

"I don't know, somewhere else? Not here!" Sneaking into a dungeon morgue in the darkness while a killer was on the loose was absolutely not my idea of a good time. "I don't know if I can do this."

"Sure you can. Come on." Lucas took my hand and pulled me along. At first, I was going to pull away, outraged that he'd grabbed it. Except I didn't mind as much as I thought I should. It did make me feel safer. Besides, there was no point to my objection. It wasn't like there was another option available to us.

We descended the stairs to the cellar. It was cold down there, the coldest I'd experienced in Biringan so far. There were rows and rows of jarred fruits and vegetables lining the walls. I shivered. "Should have warned me. I would've changed into something warmer."

"You'll get used to it." Lucas led me farther into the darkness, past the stored food and then stacks of wooden crates. It got so dark that I started knocking into things.

"Careful," he whispered.

"I'm trying," I replied. There could be anything lurking in the darkness. Despite how I felt about Lucas, I grabbed on and stuck as close to him as I possibly could. I held his hand tighter, and he squeezed back. It gave me butterflies, and I wondered if he felt them, too.

Lucas stopped. I heard a door open, then saw dim light on the other side. He walked ahead. "Watch where you're going," he warned me. We walked down a few shaky wooden steps.

The light came from sconces lit on the stone walls. "Where are we?" Wherever it was, it was even more ancient than the other parts of the palace, I could tell. It looked like we were in a cave, almost.

"The catacombs beneath the palace," he said. "That's an old access door. No one uses it anymore. The main door is that way"— he pointed to the right—"but is heavily guarded."

"How did you know about that door?"

"I do my homework" was all he said. He started to the left. The passage dipped down as we went. We were heading deeper into the ground.

We were approaching a door. It looked like it was about a thousand years old, made from wide planks of splintering wood held together with iron straps. I yanked back and wrapped my arms around myself. "I don't think I can go in there. Do we both need to go? I could stay here and keep watch."

"You'll be fine."

"What if we get caught?"

"We won't; I promise. No one is coming down here at this hour."

"Unless they're up to no good."

"In which case, I'll take care of it." His jaw clenched, and the glint in his eyes made him look sexy and dangerous. I felt a thrill at that, to know how strong he was, how capable and how fearless.

"I'm not really scared," I said, trying to believe that was true. I was frightened—I never liked dark places or things that went bump in the night—but I didn't want to be a coward.

"Let's go, then," he said. He had his hand on the door. I fought the urge to yell, "Stop!" or to run back the way we came. Before I even had a chance, he'd already opened it and slipped into the room. I gathered my strength, held my breath—because didn't bodies stink?—and followed him.

Unlike what I'd seen on TV, there weren't any corpses lying around in the open. I exhaled. That was a relief. "Oh, so this is it?" I asked.

Lucas laughed. "No, not yet." He pushed open another door and waved for me to follow him back into the darkness.

"*These* are the ancient catacombs," he explained. "The deeper we go into the mountain, the older the tombs. They say if you make it through the entire maze, you'll reach the final resting place of the very first Biringan monarch, Queen Felicidad, who ruled over all four kingdoms, long before they were divided in the Endless Wars."

"The first ruler was a queen?"

"Yes, and she was a great warrior, too. She unified the Biringan kingdoms after the split from the human realm."

"Huh. Cool. Have you ever seen her tomb?"

"No one has. Anyone who's tried either gave up and came back or was never seen again."

I gulped. That meant, somewhere deep in the mountain catacombs, there were other dead bodies of those who had gotten lost underground . . . I shook off the thought; it was too morbid.

"Doesn't mean we didn't try. It's a common game growing up here—dare your friends to find the first queen."

So that was actually how he knew about this place.

While we were talking, Lucas had been shining his light into the holes in the walls.

"No one's buried here anymore, but the rituals are still performed in the sacred space. The mages purify the burial ground before the funeral."

"Wow. I feel like I don't know anything."

"Well, how could you? You grew up over there." The way he said "over there" suggested he didn't think much of the human realm. Before I got defensive, he added, "I can lend you some books if you'd like. They're the kind of thing children read when they are starting to learn our history, but perhaps . . ."

"Yes," I said gratefully. I wish I'd thought of that before. "That would be great, actually."

"I think I found her," he said. He stuck his head a little farther into an opening in the wall, then pulled back quickly. "That's definitely the page girl." His hands were trembling, but he tried to hide whatever had spooked him by laughing about it. "Guess I wasn't prepared for that."

"What is it?"

He put up a hand to stop me, looking very serious all of a

sudden. "Wait." He bent over with his hands on his knees and took some deep breaths.

"Oh my god, will you just tell me?" I began walking to the spot, and I was about to look when he held his arm out in front of me. He held his light right at the opening.

"Don't get too close," he warned.

I crept toward the light. There wasn't anything to see. I shook my head. "I can't . . ."

"Here. But I'm not going any closer to the body." He held the light deeper in the crevice. I leaned in. And then I saw it: her feet and legs, then the rest of her body and her face, partially veiled by the darkness, and something moving. My throat constricted because, at first, I thought her lips were moving, and then I realized that wasn't it at all—it was a beetle. So many of them. Crawling out of her nose. Of her ears. Of her mouth. They were everywhere.

I screamed and jumped back, nearly knocking Lucas over. I put my hand over my mouth, eyes wide with fear. "She was cursed!"

He nodded. "Yeah, that's a curse, all right. We should leave now." The fact that Lucas was freaked out freaked *me* out even more.

"I agree," I said. Now I was the one shaking. "So it *was* a mambabarang. Who can it be?" I murmured, more to myself than anything.

"We can talk about it later. Right now, we need to leave."

We hurried back through the corridors that had brought us there. All the way, I felt like something was right behind me, about to grab me or crawl on me. I clung to Lucas the way I once held on to my mother the first and only time she ever took me to a haunted house.

Just as we were about to burst through the door back into the palace, Lucas stopped. "Wait," he whispered.

"What is it?"

He put his finger to his lips. My heart was pounding in my ears. Then I heard it, too; someone was in the other room. Multiple people. Their heavy footsteps were echoing against the walls. I heard the slight clang of metal. I wanted to ask Lucas: guards or insurgents? But I was afraid to speak and give us away.

"No one here," a voice in the room said.

"They *were* here," said another.

"Where'd they go, then?" the first asked.

There was a moment of silence. The first voice spoke again. "You think? I don't know why they would go in there. I don't even want to go in there." Quiet again. Then boots against the floor, this time softer. They were trying to sneak up on us.

We moved back into the corridor more. Lucas put his light out. "They're going to open the door," I whispered.

"Yes, I'm quite aware," Lucas hissed.

This was where my high school experiences were finally helpful. Three schools ago, couples were getting busted in an old storage closet behind the driver's ed classrooms on a daily basis. "If they come in here, you're going to kiss me," I said.

Lucas whipped his head around to look at me. "What?"

"Trust me. They'll think we just came in here for some alone time."

"I can't, Princess. You don't understand. I have my honor to uphold."

"Don't worry about your honor right now," I told him. "This is just to save our behinds." The strangers were right on the other side of the door, mere feet away. We could hide in the darkness, but that would only work if they didn't shine a light inside or start searching the catacombs. We couldn't run, either, because they'd hear us.

The door began to open. Without another thought, I leaned back against the wall and pulled Lucas close to me, smashing my mouth against his. At first, it was just that—a phony, stage-type kiss. Then something changed, and I felt him relax into the real thing. I opened my mouth tentatively, and he breathed into me, and soon all I could think about was how close we were. I could feel his heart pounding against mine. He drew me in closer, and then he was kissing my chin and my neck, soft, sweet kisses that turned urgent and made my head spin. His whole body was wrapped around mine, and I ran my hands through his hair, marveling at its softness. While the rest of him was so hot . . . and hard. Somehow, he'd pinned me against the wall, and it was all I could do not to swoon.

Before I could process what was happening, the light from the other room revealed the two of us locked in a heated embrace.

I looked up as two Royal Guards stepped back. "Your Highness," they said in unison, bowing. One was older, and the other must've been around my age. "Sir Lucas." They bowed.

We immediately released each other. I pretended to be mortified. Lucas, on the other hand, appeared very *genuinely* flustered. His cheeks were bright crimson, and he looked like he was about to break out in a sweat, and he kept his hands in front of him, standing in that formal way soldiers are taught to stand.

"We were just discussing some schoolwork," I said, forcing a nervous laugh. "It's about, um . . ." I turned and looked around me. "Ancient Biringan architecture. And Lucas offered to show me the best example, right here underneath my own palace." I added that last bit on purpose, to remind them who they were talking to.

Lucas cleared his throat. "Yes, all is well. You are dismissed."

"Yes, sir," the older guard said. He nudged the other one. "We're going." They began to leave, but then he turned back. "Not to be rude, Your Highness, but it's probably best to return upstairs."

"Oh yes, of course," I said quickly. "We're right behind you." If I stayed in his good graces, maybe he wouldn't mention this to anyone. "If it's all right, um, I'm sorry, I haven't memorized everyone's names yet."

"It's Briel, Your Highness."

"Briel, I hope you don't mind me saying, but I'm very pleased with the good work you and all the other Court of Sirena sentries are doing."

Briel's face glowed; there was even a flush to his cheeks. "It's our pleasure, Your Highness."

I glanced over at Lucas. He was staring at me, smiling like he'd found new respect for me. He nodded and mouthed, "Nice."

I shrugged, as if to say, *No big deal*, then I thought of how much I'd enjoyed our ruse and the way I'd pulled him right up to me, and I looked away, hurrying to catch up to the guards.

20

ONCE ELIAS RETURNED, I would talk to him about how they had wrongly arrested Althea, but he was still a few days away. In the meantime, she was being held in the dungeons. I was worried about her, and so had no patience when Amador glared at me harder than usual as I walked into class the next day. *Great.* Lucas must have told her what happened between us in the catacombs, then. I looked around but didn't see him anywhere. I remembered how he'd murmured in my ear after he'd kissed my neck. "I've been wanting to do this," he'd whispered. Just the memory of it twisted my stomach into delicious knots. I wondered if I would ever kiss him again. If he'd been wanting to kiss me, then it meant he wanted to kiss me again, right? But I had to stop daydreaming.

Professor Manatubay wasn't there yet. I sat at my desk and took out a few pieces of parchment and an ink pen, doing my best to keep from looking at Amador or acknowledging her. I had already successfully avoided her in history class earlier.

She got up from her seat and sauntered over to the desk in front of mine. She sat down, facing me, and leaned over my desk. "Stay away from Lucas," she snarled in a low voice.

My heart was racing, but I refused to look at her, pretending

I was intensely focused on finding my notes while needlessly shuffling my papers around. "Who are you? His keeper?" I sneered. "I'll do as I please."

Amador didn't say anything for a few seconds. She looked me up and down, obviously searching for a retort, then leaned even closer. "We were betrothed as children, you know," she finally blurted out, still a hushed whisper. For once, she actually sounded sincere. She looked around, but our classmates were all absorbed in their own conversations, paying no attention to us whatsoever. "We are engaged to be married."

"In that case, congratulations," I told her. I tried to be nonchalant, like I didn't care, but inside I was shocked. Betrothed as children? It seemed so medieval. Then again, I supposed Biringan wasn't the modern world.

"I assumed you didn't know." She shifted in the seat. "Don't say anything, though. It hasn't been announced."

Does Lucas know? I wondered. He swore she wasn't his girlfriend.

"I'd have to care to tell anyone about it," I snapped. But ugh, I did care. After last night, after that kiss, I didn't find him so annoying anymore. Alas.

She sat back in her seat and flipped her long hair over one shoulder. "Good. I don't want to make Lucas uncomfortable. That's all."

Hmm. I bet he didn't know. I gave her my fakest smile. "I hope that clears the air between us, then," I said without exactly confirming that I'd keep our conversation a secret. I didn't intend on rushing over to Lucas to discuss his engagement to Amador, but I also didn't know whether I might need to use that information at some point. "No reason for us to be enemies," I added. Which was true enough.

"We aren't enemies," she said, taken aback. Then she said, "We just aren't *friends*."

Leave it to Amador to add the insult. Wouldn't want to accidentally say something nice. "Of course not," I said with a huge, disarming smile. "Nobody wants to be *friends*."

She narrowed her eyes at me and said, "Right."

Our professor saved me from any more bickering with my not-enemy-but-not-friend. He shuffled up the aisle between us, bringing with him the stench of musky cologne and something like cigars. Incense, actually. Amador slid out of the chair and returned to her own. Professor Manatubay made it to the front of the room, where he clung to the lectern and looked at the ten of us over the top of his glasses. He waited a few more seconds before saying in a booming voice, "Today we are exploring the effect of the moon's phases on Earth magic and how that pertains to political relations between realms."

There was a slight commotion at the back of the room. We all turned to look, and there was Lucas, flustered and rushing to get into his seat.

"Sorry," he muttered, slightly out of breath. The top buttons of his shirt were undone, so that his dark brown skin contrasted against the white linen.

"We'll discuss your tardiness once class has ended," Professor Manatubay told him. "As I was saying, the phases of Earth's moon do, indeed, have an effect on the power derived from an individual spell cast, insofar as it is . . ."

Lucas was never late for class. I wanted to ask him what

happened, but not with Amador around. She was facing him with a quizzical look. Out of the corner of my eye, I noticed him shake his head at her.

I tried to pay attention to the lecture, but I was distracted by what was going on with Lucas and Amador, what Lucas and I discovered in the morgue, and what happened between the two of us there. There was also the not inconsequential fact that there was a killer somewhere in the palace. A mambabarang, no less. A dark witch. But who?

As soon as the professor closed his notes and dismissed us, I gathered my things, shoved them in my bag, and tried to leave without any more drama.

"Princess," Amador called after me.

What now? I turned around. Lucas was taking his time, fidgeting with his books, and not looking me in the eye. I felt snubbed, and suddenly furious. I turned to Amador. "Sorry, I have to get to class. Nice talking to you earlier," I said. I wasn't going to let her think the future queen was at her beck and call. Before she could say anything else, I turned on my heel and walked off.

21

WHILE THE QUESTION of who the mambabarang was remained unsolved, the next few days were uneventful for me. By contrast, the palace staff was firing on all cylinders, preparing for the coronation, which was now only thirteen days away.

"Today we have a special guest instructor," Professor Manatubay announced. On cue, the classroom door opened, and an older, stern-looking woman marched in. She wore charcoal-gray wool from head to toe, her only jewelry an onyx brooch; had silvery-white hair bobbed severely at her chin; and was very small, not even five feet, and slim, too. Within seconds it was obvious she was not to be messed with.

"Ah, here she is now," Professor Manatubay exclaimed, beaming. Possibly the first (and only) time I ever saw him look genuinely pleased. "Class, may I introduce Doña Immaculada, our most respected royal instructor. She has likely tutored many of your parents and possibly even your grandparents in their own Pagkahari at Paggalang courses."

The woman stood perfectly straight, with her heavily wrinkled yet flawlessly manicured hands clasped delicately in front of her. "Hello, children."

Professor Manatubay looked expectantly at us. We all mumbled greetings politely but half-heartedly, except for Amador, who was sitting with her back flush against the chair and her hands folded primly on top of her desk, in a perfect mirror of our new teacher. She projected her snooty voice above everyone else's: "Nice to meet you, Doña Immaculada."

Usually, that got Amador lots of brownie points with teachers, but to her credit, Doña Immaculada didn't fawn over the goody-goody act. She barely glanced at Amador. For that, I liked her already.

However, that brief respect changed as soon as she announced our task. "I'm here, by Professor Manatubay's invitation, to assist you in your journey to proper royal etiquette. As you know, we are two weeks away from a very important coronation." She glanced at me pointedly. "Something none of you have yet experienced. There are certain expectations which must be met, should you desire the respect and esteem of your people. A royal without manners is a royal without clout and is, therefore, a royal without a court." She walked around the room slowly, stopping in front of each of us and speaking as if she was talking to that person alone. It was pretty intimidating. Kind of felt like she was about to pull out a riding whip and smack our hands with it like an old Victorian schoolmarm. I was so concerned with being under her spotlight that I could hardly pay attention to what she was actually saying.

"Today, for our initial lesson together, I thought we'd do something simple. Something you *all* should already know. This will demonstrate the way we will structure our lessons moving forward." Doña Immaculada stopped in front of me this time. I gulped. She glared down at me when she said, "And let it be known that I may seem like a softie, but I have very, very high expectations."

When she moved on, I exhaled. I wondered if she'd directed that comment to me personally, or whether I just happened to be the one in the line of fire at that point in her spiel.

"And now, if you will, boys on one side of the room, and girls line up on the other, please," Doña Immaculada commanded.

Everyone jumped up to comply right away. I took my time getting out of my seat and making my way across the room to join Nix and Amador and the few other girls in our class, a futile attempt to get Lucas to notice me. When I took my place next to Nix, she whispered to me in a high-pitched imitation of Doña Immaculada, "Girls on one side and boys on the other."

"Doña Immaculada hasn't been introduced to gender theory, I guess," I whispered back. Nix snorted.

Doña Immaculada side-eyed us as she paced between the two lines. "As you've probably guessed by now, today we're going to dance," she said. She clapped her hands together on the word *dance* like this was an amazing treat. A few students followed suit and clapped politely. Doña Immaculada was displeased. "The lot of you will never make great leaders if you are unable to drum up some enthusiasm in the face of adversity." That made everyone straighten up a little bit.

And even if they weren't overly enthused, everyone at least knew what they were doing, having taken dance lessons in the past. I, of course, hadn't. And there was a good chance this dance wasn't going to involve twerking—although I didn't know how to do that either.

Doña Immaculada stood at Professor Manatubay's desk and lifted the lid on a box. Inside I could see the top of a record player. She held the arm over the vinyl album and shouted, "First, the Biringan Court Dance!" Then she dropped the needle, and classical music began to play.

All the students stepped forward and bowed to the person in front of them. I copied them clumsily. Then everyone took a step back, and I did, too. Out of the corner of my mouth, I said to Nix, "How do you know how to do this?"

"Private lessons. First month I was here," she replied. "At least, that's what I called it. Me and a guy at the pub in town."

"Wow," I said, laughing.

"And!" Doña Immaculada's voice boomed throughout the room. "One, two, three. One, two, three. One, two, three!"

Suddenly they were all doing complicated footwork, which I attempted to duplicate (and failed), and then holding their hand out to the person across from them. My partner was the crowned baron from the Court of Tikbalang with goldenrod eyes, who looked like he couldn't be more than ten, despite being at least five years older than that, but took his role more seriously than just about anyone in the class aside from Amador. We touched palms and walked a few steps, then twirled around and switched hands. Meanwhile, Doña Immaculada was counting and shouting things like, "Now switch!"

At once, one line went one way, our line went the other, and then both lines did some kind of crisscrossing until we were fully switched around and standing in front of someone else. "What the hell is going on?" I murmured in Nix's direction. She just laughed again. We repeated the steps, this time with a different partner, and then Doña Immaculada said, "Once more!" and everyone began the weird zigzag.

When we were back in lines again, I was standing face-to-face with Lucas. I looked right at him, but his eyes were focused somewhere over my head. Doña Immaculada began her counting, and then Lucas and I were touching palms—and unlike when I was dancing with the baron, with Lucas I could feel some type of energy, tension, between our hands. I wished he'd look at me, but for some reason he kept looking anywhere but in my direction.

And then, as quickly as it happened, it was over.

For the rest of class, there was no contact between the two of us again.

I never thought I'd be the kind of girl who'd be ghosted after her first kiss—or that her first kiss would be from a boy she was just pretending to kiss. Maybe that was what he thought, that it was just pretend. I was the one who'd demanded he kiss me, after all.

A FEW HOURS later, after another unremarkable Hayop at Halaman class ended, I rushed down to the cafeteria. Nix was already there at our usual table. "Hey," she said after a while. "You all right? You seem down."

"Do I?" I shrugged.

"Yeah, you've hardly touched your pancit, and I know it's your favorite," she said, twirling the rice noodles with her fork.

I listlessly pushed around the noodles on my plate. She was right; I could hardly taste it. The pressure was getting to me, and I had too much to deal with already. I didn't need to worry about

Lucas and how he felt about me on top of it. I was running out of time to make my magic work. I'd tried meditating in the garden, communing with plants, talking to the horses who pulled my calesa. Nothing. Discovering my talent was more important than anything else, and yet I was obsessing over what was going on with him, playing detective, and wasting valuable time learning ballroom dancing and listening to lectures about things that happened a thousand years ago.

Nix nudged me and asked, "Should we go to town again? We could do some more investigating."

"I can't. After . . . er, what happened, Elias has been watching me like a hawk since he came back. He's not even comfortable with me coming to school anymore. He's got the guards stationed at every entrance as we speak." Plus, I really, really needed to go be alone and deal with this magic thing. The panic had been creeping up in my gut all day long.

"I'll come to you at the palace, then. Or have you already given up on finding the real murderer?"

"I haven't."

"I'll ask Lucas if he wants to come."

"No," I said sharply. Nix was surprised; her mouth froze in the shape of an *O*. I hadn't told her about the kiss. I don't know why. I just wasn't ready to share, plus she would interrogate me about it: *Do you like him? What about him and Amador?* And on and on. I wasn't ready for all that. But I felt bad for getting snippy. "I don't want him reporting everything we do to Amador."

"Good point," Nix said. The awkward moment had quickly passed. She gave me a once-over. "You seem worn out. I'll come by at the end of the week instead."

"Yes, that would be better." *Phew.* Maybe if put my mind to it, I could take care of the main issue, finding my magic, and then I'd be able to focus on the other stuff.

One of BANA's kitchen maids approached our table, carrying a large silver tray with both hands. She set it down in front of us, curtsied to me, and started to walk away.

"Excuse me," I called after her. I pointed to the tray. "I think this is for another table." We hadn't ordered anything.

"Never look a gift horse in the mouth," Nix said to me. She was already picking through the variety of sweets on the tray. "We'll keep it," she told the maid.

I shot her a look. We couldn't eat someone else's food. Nix sat back, a slight pout on the edges of her mouth.

The kitchen maid stepped forward. "No mistake. It was sent for you."

Nix's face perked up.

"Oh, okay," I said, still a bit confused. "Thanks." The maid nodded and started back for the kitchens.

The tray held shiny éclairs, mango cake, and thick, gooey brownies.

"Yum," purred Nix. "I can't choose—they all look so good!"

"It's probably another present from a first-year," I said. Other students in the café took notice of our good fortune as well.

"Maybe it was Lucas. Trying to woo you. Gotta say, this sure beats flowers."

I hated that her joking suggestion made my heart swell for a the briefest second before it came sinking back to reality. "Ha ha, but I doubt it." Though it was interesting, considering what I thought I felt during class. Maybe it could be from him? A girl could hope? I grabbed one of the brownies and took a bite while Nix was still debating which dessert to eat. "You're right," I said with my mouth full. "Amazing."

It tasted familiar, chewier than a typical brownie, *almost like . . .* and then it hit me. As soon as I realized what I was eating, I spit it out into a napkin I was holding and began wiping my lips and tongue with my hand, desperate to get every last speck of it out of my mouth.

"What's wrong?" Nix asked. She set the éclair she was holding on the table.

Once I was satisfied there wasn't anything else I could do to rid my mouth of the toxin, I examined the napkin. I was right. Black rice.

"What is it?" Nix asked again. She looked like she was simultaneously super concerned for me and repulsed by the fact that I just spit chewed-up food out in front of the entire cafeteria.

I fumbled for my glass and took huge gulps of water. Now I had no doubt who sent us the treats. Amador almost got me to eat black rice to trap me in Biringan. I would never be able to return to the human world, never see my mother again. *That evil . . .*

I got up from my seat and looked around the room, trying to find Amador. I spotted her in the back corner, facing the entire room so everyone had a clear view of her, of course. Always on display.

She wouldn't even look in our direction. *Nice try.* She thought that would make her look innocent. I could just imagine how satisfied she was inside. Sitting there knowing what a nasty prank she pulled on me, or nearly did.

Pure rage bubbled up inside of me. So intense I was afraid I would pass out from the pressure of it.

Amador picked up her glass as she laughed haughtily at whatever her friend across the table had said.

I hate you. I hate you, Amador, you nasty . . .

She took a sip of her drink; immediately, her eyes went wide, and she spit out the liquid all over the table. Her friends screeched and flew back, trying to avoid the spray. But it was all over them anyway.

"Ew!" one of them shouted. "What *is* that?"

Amador looked confused, disgusted, then angry. She scanned the cafeteria, then set her eyes directly on me.

I turned and dashed out of the room. Nix stared after me. I felt bad running off from her like that, but I was so sick of everything. Sick of Amador. Sick of Lucas ignoring me. Sick of the games, and the strange rules, and the expectations. I did *not* ask for any of this. I didn't ask to be born a princess, I didn't ask to spend my entire childhood hiding, I didn't ask for any of this!

I ran straight for the front doors, where my calesa would be waiting to take me back to the palace. As soon as I got there, I could pack my stuff—no, forget the stuff. I'd just leave in the middle of the night and go back to the human world, where I belonged. *I need to leave this place,* I kept telling myself, wanting to run away but too heated and upset to think straight.

So I didn't notice someone coming right toward me. We collided.

"I'm so sorry," I said, extra flustered now. "Are you okay?"

"Yes, Your Highness. It's me who is sorry." She pushed the hair back from her face, though she wouldn't look directly up at me. It was Fortunada. Her schoolbag had fallen by her feet when we ran into each other. One of her books, stuffed with tons of paper tabs, was spilling out of it. It was a dark, mossy green with vines stamped in gold on the cover.

"Are you sure you're all right?" I crouched to pick up the bag at the same time as she did.

She cringed and pulled back as if I was about to smack her.

My mouth opened to assure her I had no bad intentions, but without another word, she swooped up the bag and hurried off down the hallway.

I managed to make a mess of everything everywhere I went.

22

A FEW DAYS later, there was a knock on the door. I jumped up to open it. Ayo was supposed to be back with tea and pastries from the kitchen, and I was starving.

But it wasn't Ayo—it was Lucas.

I jumped back in surprise.

"Hey," Lucas said. He looked grim. "May I come in?"

"Uh, sure," I said, grimacing. I wasn't sure what to feel about seeing him—elated? Or wary? Both?

He stepped in, carrying a huge rainbow bouquet of native Biringan wildflowers. "For you," he said.

"Why?" I asked, still a bit stunned to see him here as I took the bouquet. I was almost sure he never wanted to talk to me again after giving me the cold shoulder all week.

He shuffled his feet. "They're a little late, to be honest, and I just wanted to say I'm sorry . . . I should have paid you a call, after."

I froze, still holding the flowers. "After?" I whispered.

"Well, you can't just kiss the princess without a proper courtship, can you?" he grumbled. "I don't have to take Pagkahari at Paggalang to know that." He took a seat on the nearest armchair and immediately put his feet up on the table, like he belonged there. To be honest, I kind of liked that he felt so at home in my rooms.

I peeked at him over the iridescent blooms. "Is that what this is? You're courting me?" I tried to keep my voice steady, but oh, my heart.

He looked up at me and grinned. "Do you want me to?"

Oh, we're playing this game, are we?

"Hmm." I put my hand on my chin like I had to think about it. "I don't know, I mean, it has been almost a week. One could say it's very ungentlemanly," I said as I laid the flowers down on the nearest side table.

Lucas dropped to one knee and put his hands together. "My princess and future queen of the Court of Sirena and all the lands of Biringan, I beg of you, please forgive my foolishness."

"A bit dramatic, don't you think?"

"Not when you've wronged the future queen."

"You make an excellent point." I held out my hand so he could kiss my ring, something I'd secretly wanted to do ever since I saw the Robin Hood movie with the fox as a kid.

He held the ends of my fingers, and brought his lips slowly to my hand, letting his lips graze the skin, sending shocks of electricity all over my body.

In answer, I slowly caressed his cheek with my hand, feeling the rough stubble on his jaw. That was it; he pulled me down so that I was practically straddling him.

"You were too far away," he whispered, pushing my hair out of my face.

"Where have you been all week?" I said softly.

"Waiting" was the reply.

I wondered what that meant, if the betrothal with Amador was real, if it had been keeping him away, or if there were other reasons. But right then, there was no more time for thinking, because this time, he was the one who kissed me. He rolled us over so that I was underneath him, and then he leaned down. "May I?"

"Kiss me, you fool," I murmured.

When he did, I closed my eyes and saw fireworks and felt it all over, too, as his hands cupped my face and under my back, and I did the same, running my hands all over him. I lifted his shirt and touched the muscles on his stomach, making him shiver.

He kissed my neck again, and lower, and who knew how far we would have gone if Ayo hadn't walked in right then, carrying a tray.

"Oh! Excuse me!" The old butler jumped. "I didn't realize you had company, Your Highness. Or else I would have . . ."

Lucas hurriedly rolled away, and both of us sat up, disheveled and red-faced. But somehow, I wasn't embarrassed. I was happy. "Ayo, this is—"

"I know Sir Lucas," Ayo said primly. "Good afternoon, sir."

"I am courting the princess," Lucas explained, motioning to the flowers on the table.

"Ah, I see." Ayo picked them up. "I'm going to get a vase for these," he said, giving Lucas a lingering once-over. "By protocol, sir, if I may. You should ask the princess's guardian for permission before a formal courtship."

"I did," Lucas said.

"You did?" I gasped.

"I sent a note to Elias and just heard back a few moments ago," he said with a smug smile.

So that was what he was waiting for, I realized. He wasn't ignoring me—he was following royal protocol. He had been raised in Biringan, and he knew its rules even if I didn't. Plus, the guards probably alerted Elias to what they had seen in the catacombs.

"Do you need anything else, Your Highness?" Ayo inquired.

"No, thank you," I told him. He made his escape. We were probably making him uncomfortable, since Lucas draped his arm around me once it was clear he had Elias's permission.

I didn't ask Lucas about Amador. If he had Elias's permission to court me, then Amador was probably lying about the betrothal. She would do anything to keep him by her side. And I didn't want to spend any of our time together talking about her.

Lucas rebuttoned his shirt while I smoothed my hair.

"Leave it," he said. "It looks good like that. You never wear it down."

"Okay," I said, and wrapped my ponytail holder around my wrist instead.

"Um, I have something else to tell you," Lucas said. "The page who was murdered, Marikit Baluyot."

"What about her?"

"I asked our kitchen staff to ask around the palace staff—you know, they know more about what's going on in the courts than anyone high up."

"For sure."

"She was the one who found your dad."

I looked up at him sharply. "What?" In my shock I had lost my manners.

"The king had called for her to pick up a note."

The letter my father was writing, he'd called for a page to deliver it. Of course, it never reached its recipient, whoever it was. *Temo was right. It's time to tell her the truth.*

Lucas continued. "And she found him dead."

"Do you think that . . . if the king was killed . . . whoever killed him killed her, too?"

He nodded. "I'm pretty sure they killed my father, too, you know," he admitted. "That's why I was looking into all this in the first place."

I did an actual double take. "Your father? I thought he was ill."

"That's what everyone thought. That his illness caused his death. But . . ."

"But?"

"It happened a year ago, while I was away at Sigbin. When I came back to Sirena, he was dead. I just barely made it to the funeral." He cleared his throat. "But I wanted to know how he died, and I discovered that he wasn't in his room at all. He was found dead in the palace, near the king's chambers."

Near the king's chambers. Lucas's father worked for the Court of Sirena, *and* he was murdered there? Lucas added: "I did a lot of digging through documents recording the *very* brief investigation, which ended with the conclusion that he'd suffered a sudden illness. But I discovered one intriguing detail."

I already knew what he was going to say before he said it: "There was a large black beetle in his mouth."

23

I DIDN'T KNOW what to say, but hearing that Lucas's father was cursed as mine surely was made me feel even closer to him. Someone was responsible for the losses we'd suffered. Someone had done this to us, to our families, to our futures. He was an orphan because of this killer, and I was practically one—my mother lay in a hospital in another world.

"I have to show you something," I told him. I ran to retrieve my father's note from the enchanted safe in my dressing rooms.

"Here," I said, showing him.

Temo was right. It's time to tell her the truth—

He read it and looked up. "My father was right about something?"

"Wait! Your father was Temo? I thought his name was Timoteo." Then I realized—Temo was his nickname. Filipinos never used their full names around family and friends. My father, Vivencio, was Jun. Lucas's father, Timoteo, was called Temo for short. I wondered if Lucas had a nickname, too. *Temo was right. It's time to tell her the truth—*

"Your father was head of security at the Court of Sirena," I said, thinking deeply. There was something here—something we weren't seeing but was just outside of our purview. "What if . . ." I said, my thoughts forming slowly, as if appearing out of the waves like a sirena. "What if he found the mambabarang? What if he knew the king was in danger?"

Lucas furrowed his brows. "Maybe?"

"Because your father was killed first. Months before mine. Your father must have known something."

"And who was this addressed to?"

"I can find out. I'll ask the pages—they always keep a record of where notes are supposed to go."

"Have you looked through your father's desk?" he asked. "Maybe there's more."

"I didn't have time. The last time I was there, I was, uh, interrupted," I said with a wry smile.

"Then we'll go back together," Lucas said.

He waited expectantly.

"Oh, you mean, right now?"

"No time like the present." He offered his arm. I liked this; I liked that we were a team.

We started for the other side of the palace. As we left my apartments, Ayo was watering the two large pots of flowers outside the doors—in other words, listening at the door for any funny business. He pursed his lips as if he still didn't quite approve. Royal permission granted or not.

"We're just going for a walk," I promised him.

"You don't intend to leave the grounds, I hope?" he replied.

I shook my head. "No worries. In fact, we're just staying inside."

He nodded approvingly. It was sweet that he was so protective over me. In some ways he felt like a surrogate father. I thought of my father and his long letters. I knew he had missed me; he'd said it in every letter. And I knew my mother missed him. I'd wished all my life we could have been a normal family, the three of us, together, but they both told me it was too dangerous. I tried to shake off my emotions and concentrate on the task at hand.

We were getting close to the royal wing. Few sconces were lit, because no one had reason to be walking around there. It was getting dimmer and dimmer as we got farther from the main passages. Shadows danced on the walls as we walked, like ghosts of ourselves. I looked over at Lucas, his handsome face determined, armed with a Biringan crystal dagger at his hip, directing me down a remote hallway in a massive, desolate wing of a huge palace. I was glad to have him by my side.

"Watch out!" Lucas threw his arm across me and pushed me back away at the same time I heard a scraping sound and saw something move in front of us. As he drew his dagger and prepared to take down whatever hid in the darkness, a figure appeared from out of nowhere.

I seized up and touched the anting-anting around my neck just as someone reached toward me and brushed against my shoulder.

"Ouch!" a familiar voice yelped. "That hurt!"

"Nix?" I called.

She stepped into the dim light, holding her finger to her mouth. "Ouch! That burned! How did you do that?"

I shrugged. It was the protection from the amulet, but I didn't want to tell her that. "Where did you come from?" I asked her. "What are you doing here?"

She ignored the question and instead waved for us to follow. "You gotta see this," she said.

Lucas was still on edge. He was breathing heavily, his eyes wide and alert, glancing in every direction, like he thought something else was waiting to leap out at us. His adrenaline must have been pumping, ready to fuel a fight.

I put my hand on his arm. "It's okay," I told him. "It was just Nix."

He put the dagger back in its sheath. "After you, Princess."

I walked in the direction Nix had gone but didn't see her anywhere. "Where are you?"

I heard "Here." Then I saw a tiny flame. She'd lit a match so we could see her. I followed it, with Lucas close behind me. "Check this out!" she said.

Nix was inside the wall. Part of it had been pushed open.

"It's a passageway," she said. "Can you believe this? Come on, before someone sees you."

I stepped into the space behind the wall. Lucas did, too. Then Nix pulled the wall back into place. It was pitch-black.

I thought of what Althea had said. *The darkness is all around us. It comes out of the walls.* "I don't like this," I said.

"Me neither," Lucas agreed. "You have two seconds to tell us what's going on, Nix—"

There was a click of flint, and then a blue flame came to life. Nix was holding a torch. "I didn't want to light it until we were safe in here."

"I assume you're using that word loosely," Lucas said. He still looked like he might kill the first thing that made him flinch.

"Calm down," Nix told him. "I'm telling you—no one will bother us here."

"But what are you doing here?" I repeated.

"I was trying to visit Althea without being seen. She's down in the dungeons, and I'm worried about her. All palaces have secret passageways, right? The maids use them all the time. That's how they pop in and out without being seen. I think this goes all around the palace, but I'm not sure."

"A secret passageway." I didn't like this at all. "Does it go to my room?"

"I don't know," she said. "Like I said, I haven't gone far. I just found it."

"Okay, then what *do* you know?" Lucas asked.

"I guess we'll find out," Nix said, raising her eyebrows. The torch began to bob away into the distance.

Lucas and I looked at each other. It was obvious we were thinking the same thing: This could be how the killer accessed the palace undetected. Who else knew about these hidden walkways?

"Come on, let's go see where it leads."

I hesitated. "Guys, guards patrol every hour, on the hour, and they keep tabs on my location. If I'm not back in the queen's chambers before then and they can't find me anywhere else, it's going to be a whole thing."

Nix and Lucas nodded. "Got it," she said. "We'll be fast."

We walked deeper into the tunnel. It was dark and grimy and smelled like damp stone and something mossy. I wanted to tiptoe, just in case we ran into something gross, but we were moving fast to beat the guards.

The hidden passageways followed the exterior walls of the castle, with the occasional trail branching off somewhere deeper within, but we decided to stick to the most straightforward path.

The last thing we wanted was to get lost or stuck—or who knew what else.

A couple of the turns from the main pathway even seemed unfinished or were deliberate dead ends that extended only a couple of feet before ending. I ran my hand across one of them. It felt smooth, like plaster, not like the rough stone everywhere else.

"Looks like those were covered over at some point," Lucas whispered when we passed one of the nooks.

"Or this was never completed in the first place," I suggested. "Maybe whoever designed the tunnels intended to but didn't get the chance."

Lucas nodded. "Could be."

Nix turned and held the light up to us. We both flinched away from the glare.

We continued around a corner, inching our way along the wall. The farther we got from where we'd started, the more cautious we became and the more every distant *drip* sound startled us. Nix began to have doubts, fear lacing her voice. "On second thought, maybe we should go back," she suggested. "We can try again tomorrow. I'm sure Althea's fine. Let's go to the library and see if they have any old maps of the building. Maybe we'll find something there. Don't you think?"

Neither Lucas nor I said anything; we just ignored her and kept walking. There was no going back now.

Lucas led on, searching the ground for any clue, no matter how insignificant. But so far, there was nothing other than dirt and cobwebs and tiny pools where condensation had dripped down the cool stone walls.

Nix was leaning into me so hard that I was having trouble

keeping my balance. I put my hand up to brace myself against the wall, and then we both lost our footing and began to trip over each other's feet. "Careful!" I shouted a second too late. We both tumbled to the ground. My knee hit the stone, sending a sharp pain through me. "Ow!"

"What happened? Are you all right?" Lucas rushed to kneel down and check on us. He shined the light on us.

"We're fine. MJ fell," Nix said.

"You were yanking on me!" I retorted.

"It doesn't matter. As long as you're both fine." He held his hand out to each of us to help us get up. I got to my feet and rubbed my sore knee. It'd be bruised tomorrow for sure.

Lucas swung the light all around us. "Nix is right. Maybe we should call it a day and try again tomorrow."

"Wait," I said. "Give me that." I reached for the light. "I think I saw something. Did you see that?"

"See what?" Lucas asked, handing me the torch.

I held the light up to the spot where I thought I saw—well, I wasn't sure what. A glimpse of something. A hollow or different pattern on the stone of the wall, maybe. I kept searching, and then, there it was. "Look!" I knelt, no longer caring about the pain in my leg. I inched the light closer to the wall. "Can you see it?"

Lucas bent down to see. Nix was still busy brushing herself off and fixing her skirts. My heart felt like it was pounding in my ears with excitement.

"Wonder where that goes?" Lucas asked.

There was a small door with a curved top in the wall. No handle or anything, just an indent where it could be pulled or pushed open. If we hadn't fallen, we would've missed it. "Should we find out?" I asked, locking eyes with Lucas.

"No," Nix said. She stood back behind us with her arms crossed. "I have a bad feeling about this. We need to go." She pointed her finger at the ground to emphasize. "Now."

Lucas took out his dagger. "You two stay here. I'll go." Before I could object, he was pulling the door open. There was nothing but blackness beyond it. "Hold the light over here," he said. I held the torch next to the doorway. He began to crawl inside. "There's no one here," he called back over his shoulder. And then: "Whoa! You have to see this. Give me the light."

"Come on," I told Nix. "Or would you rather stay out here alone in the dark?"

Reluctantly, she got down on the floor by the doorway. I told her to go first. After she went in, I scurried through, feeling like something was sneaking up right behind me, like when I'd go for a snack in the middle of the night and run back to my room as if being chased by a ghost.

On the other side of the door there was a little round chamber. I'd thought we'd end up in one of the rooms of the palace, but this was something else entirely.

"Don't walk there!" Lucas called out, shoving his arm in front of me so fast it almost knocked the wind out of me.

I looked down and saw that I had nearly stepped over a line on the floor. I held the light up. It was a chalk circle, sprinkled with what looked like salt. My heart pounded furiously, and I brought a hand to my mouth to suppress a scream when I saw what stood in the middle of the circle: a doll.

"What is this?" I asked out loud, though it was a rhetorical question; we all knew what this was. *Kulam*. Black magic.

"A mambabarang," Lucas muttered. "I knew it. They use the dolls to send the beetles to poison their victims. Stay back, both of you."

Nix wrapped her arms tightly around herself and backed up closer to the door like she wanted to flee. "I don't like this," she whimpered. She looked like she was about to cry.

"Neither do I," I said, because I just noticed that the doll was wearing Sirena school robes and wore her hair in a ponytail just like mine.

It was a doll of me.

24

NIX PICKED UP the doll because I couldn't.

"Let's get out of here," Lucas said.

I made my legs move. Someone—a mambabarang, an evil, dark witch—was definitely trying to kill me. I wanted to scream, but I didn't. I was too shaken and scared into silence. Numb.

We heard stomping overhead. It shook me out of my stasis. The guards were probably on the move. We'd been in there longer than I thought. "Hurry," I urged. The fear in me was starting to change, starting to morph into something else. Anger.

Nix was already starting for the door. "Hold on!" she said, stopping before crawling through. "What if the witch is out there?"

"Then we'll handle it," I said impatiently. "Come on, Nix. You're a resurrectionist. How can you be scared of death?"

She turned to me, shock on her face. "You knew?"

"Duh, it's in your name. *Phoenix?* And you can make wilted flowers bloom? And heal dying animals?" Plus, I was tired of cowering in the dark, and while Nix might have the power to resurrect things, I was the princess. And I was furious. Someone out there was definitely trying to get rid of me. Well, good luck with that. I wasn't going to be a sitting duck.

Once we were finally out of the room, Lucas pushed the door into place, and we all huddled together and made our way back through the dark passageway.

Somewhere inside the palace, the stomping continued as the guards made their rounds. They turned off down a hall leading away from where we were; we could hear their collective footsteps fade away.

"Come on," I said. "They're getting close to the queen's chamber."

We hardly spoke the rest of the way, other than the occasional "What was that?" when one of us heard a creak or a drip. I was positive the mambabarang would appear at any second, imagining their long, gnarly fingers reaching out of the darkness to wrap around my throat. But not if I strangled them first.

Finally, we slipped back out of the passage, one by one.

The guards were stomping toward us now. They'd come around the corner and run right into us unless we made it around the turn before them.

"Don't they follow your orders?" Nix asked me. "Why are you afraid of them?"

"I'm not afraid of them. I'm afraid of Elias deciding I need a shorter leash."

The three of us scurried through the hall. Thankfully, we made it back before they did, collapsing onto the oversized chairs in my sitting room with relief. "I guess I'm not going to visit Althea any-time soon," Nix sighed. Her hair was sticking up all over the place and dusted with gray. We all had dirty hands and streaks on our clothes.

"Yeah, that place was creepy." I shuddered.

"I have to admit I was getting a little nervous back there, too," Lucas told us.

"A little?" I teased him. With the threat of imminent danger (hopefully) behind us, we were slightly giddy.

"Mostly, I was nervous for you two. Clearly, I can defend myself, but you would be in trouble." He gave me a mischievous half smile to let us know he was joking.

I grabbed a toss pillow and threw it at him in mock outrage. "What kind of knight abandons a damsel in distress?"

He raised his hands in defeat. "You have me there, Princess." He put his hand over his heart. "In truth, I would never break a vow so solemnly sworn."

"Good." I nodded, satisfied. I felt like kissing him. Again.

"Now, who are you calling a damsel in distress?" Nix muttered, rolling her eyes.

"I was kidding! Anyway, can we talk about what the heck was going on in there—and how much danger we're in on a scale of 'a lot' to 'the most'?" I asked. "Do you still have the doll?"

Nix nodded. "I'll put it in the fire. That'll cleanse it of any dark magic that's imbued in it."

We watched as Nix tossed the doll that looked too much like me into the fireplace. It was made of wood and burned quickly until it was nothing but ashes. I exhaled.

"Okay," Lucas said. "Here's what we know: There's a mambabarang on the loose, and she—"

"Or he," I interjected.

"Or he," Lucas corrected, "is responsible for the death of the kitchen page and, judging by the presence of black beetles at each of their deaths, my father and King Vivencio, too."

"*Phew*, that's a lot! But why?" Nix asked. "What's the connection?"

I told her our theory, how Lucas's father had discovered something, and that my father was killed before he could act on it, while the page was killed because she had found my father's body and knew something about his murder.

"So who are our suspects?" I asked.

"First off, Jinky," Nix said.

I was offended. "Jinky?" Nix and Lucas looked at each other. They were in agreement, then.

"She has full access to the palace, and to you," Lucas pointed out. "Even the king's chambers. And knows the secret passageways."

"Exactly!" Nix exclaimed.

Once again, I didn't have anything concrete to refute their claims. All I could say was "Ridiculous." I thought about how much Jinky worried about me, what a rule follower she was.

"Think about it," Nix said, keeping her voice low. "How much do you really know about her?"

I didn't say anything, which was admission enough. Nothing. I knew nothing about her. And it was true: She had access to me, the palace, everything—and I wasn't tracking her movements. At that exact moment, I had no idea where she was. One more strange thing stuck out at me, too; all those times I snuck out and thought I'd escaped detection, sometimes by a hair. Maybe I didn't get away with it at all. Maybe she just allowed me to. Killed two birds with one stone: I wasn't watching her, and I was making myself vulnerable. I was gone when the page was murdered. And the killer made a fast escape, going unnoticed in the palace, or else sneaking through all the various passageways.

Again, though, my gut refused to believe it. "What would she gain?" I asked. She didn't want for anything, nor did she seem particularly interested in advancing herself.

"Maybe she's an insurgent," Lucas said gently.

My stomach sank. "No! I can't believe that. If Jinky's a suspect, then everyone in the palace is. Even Ayo. I can't believe they would all turn against my family. Ayo loved my father, and everyone here has worked for the royal family for generations."

"Okay, so if not Jinky or anyone in the palace staff, who, then?" Nix asked. "If it's not Althea, and we all know it's not. She's human and unable to wield dark magic."

Nobody spoke. We were all lost in thought and our own personal theories, none of which connected the dots, or else we would have offered them up.

"Speaking of insurgents, Elias recently traveled to Paulanan," I said pointedly.

Lucas frowned. Paulanan was in Sigbin territory. "What are you insinuating? The Court of Sigbin is loyal."

"Really?" My voice was cold. "They welcomed me to Biringan with the threat of usurpation. By Amador of all people."

Nix considered this. "Maybe when the insurgency didn't pan out—they weren't able to get to you—they went to plan B, scare you off the throne. And since that didn't work, they'll do to you what they did to Lucas's dad and your dad."

Lucas threw his arms up in annoyance, but Nix kept going. "You said it yourself, Lucas, that Marikit's death might be a warning to the future queen."

"But not from the Court of Sigbin!" Lucas roared. "You are talking of treason!"

"But how can you be so sure it's not Amador?"

His face screwed up with disgust. "Excuse me?" he exclaimed. "You think *Amador* is the mambabarang?"

Did I? "Not necessarily, I'm just saying, no stone left unturned . . ."

He crossed his arms and looked up to the ceiling, shaking his head slightly. "Like I said, the Court of Sigbin is a faithful subject to the Sirena throne. When the council ratified your ascension, there should have been no doubt as to where our loyalties lie. Perhaps House Oscura did mean to frighten you off your position at first, but when it was clear you would take on your father's mantle, they withdrew their opposition in order to keep the peace."

"There could be other reasons," said Nix, looking meaningfully at me, "for Amador to want MJ out."

"What reasons?"

Nix crossed her arms and stuck her face in his. "Boys! They're always the last to know!"

Lucas threw his hands up in defeat. "What do you mean?"

"She means . . ." I hesitated. "Amador hates me."

"Amador doesn't hate you," Lucas said.

Nix looked from one of us to the other and coughed. "Um, I . . . Excuse me," she said, and ran off to the powder room, leaving us alone to have it out.

Were we really fighting about Amador?

Here I was thinking we made such a great team, and yet I

had accused his kingdom of insurgency while he refused to believe his not-girlfriend could possibly be evil. Which was what she was. Evil.

"She doesn't," Lucas insisted. "Hate you, I mean."

I closed my eyes. Guys could be so clueless. Did he actually believe that, or was he just trying to convince me? I looked directly at him. "Yes, she does, because she thinks . . . I mean . . . Well, to be honest, she told me about your engagement."

"Our—*what*?" Lucas sputtered. I was even sure I heard Nix drop something in the powder room. Then he started laughing so hard he doubled over. I sat, stone-faced, and waited for him to recover. Finally, he straightened up and wiped his eyes. "Wait, wait. She told you what? That we're *engaged*?"

Now I was mad. I crossed my arms, too. Amador had made a fool of me. "She said you were betrothed as kids."

"Betrothed as . . ." He started shaking his head. "Did she really? You're not teasing me? Playing a joke on me?"

I shook my head.

"Why did she—" He clenched his fists, then smacked them back down on his thighs. "You know what, forget it. It doesn't matter."

"Well, are you?" I demanded.

"Am I what?"

"Engaged to her?"

"No! Of course not! I told you, she's not even my girlfriend! And if I was engaged already, why would Elias let me court you?"

"You're courting MJ?" Nix squealed from the other room. She ran back inside. "Well? Are you?"

I flushed, but Lucas only grinned. "Yeah, I am."

"I knew it!" Nix crowed. "I knew you liked him!"

"So, you like me," he teased. "Do you?"

"Not really," I teased back. "Not a lot, in any case."

Lucas laughed. Then his face turned serious. "Look—I know you don't like Amador, but her family is a loyal ally to the throne. She would never do something like that. The Court of Sigbin can be disorderly and chaotic like you said, but we aren't traitors."

25

THE NEXT DAY brought news that the high court was preparing for Althea's trial. Since they were moving faster than expected, I needed to move faster as well to prove her innocence. More than ever, I believed that someone was pulling invisible strings that led to some kind of trap. Whoever the mambabarang was, they were fully ensconced in court life. I had to cut through the spiderweb by freeing Althea.

I summoned Elias. Calling a councilors' meeting was my first official, independent act as the impending sovereign, so I chose a gown that commanded attention: a dark-green satin butterfly dress with a cape back that created long, drapey sleeves, accessorized with scrunched white satin elbow-length gloves and a delicate tiara with radiant pearls from our seas. Underneath, I wore my father's amulet as I usually did. I feared less for my safety knowing I had the anting-anting.

Jinky entered the room, and, remembering my conversation with Lucas and Nix, I instinctively reached for the amulet around my neck. Then I realized she'd come in contact with it many times already while helping me get ready, and nothing had ever happened. I was right; Jinky did not mean me harm.

I stepped in front of the mirror. The gown and tiara made me look (and feel) like I was in charge. Good, if I was going to be respected—especially by a bunch of older male encantos who would be fast to dismiss anything I said.

Elias arrived, looking drawn. "At your service, Princess. What can I help you with?"

"Thanks for coming so quickly. I'd like to call the council to discuss the upcoming trial of Althea Ramos, the healer currently imprisoned in our dungeon."

His left eyebrow raised. "Oh. Why?"

Instead of answering, I changed the subject. "Elias, when your patianaks fetched me, you asked if the insurgents had a mambabarang with them."

"Yes."

"Why did you suspect they had a dark witch among their ranks? As I understand it, the Kalahok was disbanded and exiled years ago."

He sighed. "Yes, but there is always the possibility . . ."

I waited for him to continue.

"That they survived and are hiding among us. Their Babaeng Pinuno was never captured."

"I see," I said. "That was during the war, yes? The one my father ended by winning the Battle of Biringan."

He nodded. "Your father won the battle decisively. The witches surrendered immediately. Everyone remarked on it."

"Why?"

"Because we were prepared for a protracted battle, everyone assumed the war would go on for years and years—but then the coven just surrendered."

"What happened to them?"

"The witches? Most of them were killed in the battle, but those who remained chose exile from the realm. They left Biringan. Why do you ask?"

"I was just brushing up on my history," I said. "I should know our past if I am to be queen, shouldn't I?"

I had promised Lucas and Nix that I wouldn't tell Elias what we had discovered about the beetles and how they tied to the three deaths. I didn't want Elias to worry, and I also didn't want him to tell me to stop investigating the source of the dark magic. He would probably lock me in my room till I was senile to keep me safe. Especially since he was already cognizant of the threat of the mambabarang.

"Anyway, I've called you here to arrange a special meeting of the queen's councilors. How do I do that?"

"You would send a formal invitation to each of them by page, with the date and time of your choosing."

"I was thinking right now."

Elias looked startled, and hesitated before he replied. "That's your prerogative. However, I must caution you, they may not be agreeable."

"They don't have a choice." I was getting tired of being told how I had to behave and how I had to bend to "the way things are done" when no one else seemed to do the same.

"They've become accustomed to doing things their own way, without interference. Let alone from someone so young, even if you are to be our queen." *And a hapcanto, no less,* I thought, but didn't say.

"I understand." I already suspected as much anyway. I pulled myself as tall and straight as possible and tilted my chin up. "But they'll have to become unaccustomed to the old ways of doing things."

THE MEETING TOOK place in the Aquamarine Room. It was a beautiful space, with iridescent blue gemstone walls and a massive rectangular white stone table right in the middle; a vaulted, beamed ceiling with skylights let in sunshine so it bounced off all the surfaces, making everything shimmer and sparkle, as if we were under the ocean.

I had been told my father always met with his council in the Oak Room, which looked exactly how it sounds: masculine, dark, with lots of wood and leather and the lingering notes of fire and cigars. It was a place where the councilors were definitely comfortable. Which was why I decided to call them to order elsewhere. I didn't want them to be comfortable. I didn't intend to try to fill my father's shoes and come up short either.

I stood in a small room off the side of the main one. I was shaking on the inside but determined to project nothing but calm leadership. I took stock of my reflection in a glass window. Nothing gave away how I actually felt. I might not have felt like a queen yet, but I was starting to realize I didn't need to; I only needed everyone else to believe I was ready to rule. *Fake it till you make it*, my mom would tell me when I worried that I wasn't good enough. I had to believe in myself, and then everyone else would, too.

Once Elias let me know the ten councilors—nine men and only one woman—had arrived and were seated at the table, I let ten minutes pass before I finally made my entrance.

When the doors opened and I strolled in, a hush fell over the room. Even if the spell didn't last a long time, for a few seconds, it still had the effect I wanted. I could tell the councilors were thrown off by the abrupt invitation, the new room, and my appearance.

"Her Royal Highness, the crown princess of Biringan," Elias announced as I strode in to take my place at the head seat. I'd even had a special chair brought in for me. It was bright white and had a tall, arched back.

The councilors stood and waited until I reached my place, greeted them, and sat down before they followed suit. So far, so good.

All their faces were focused on me. "I . . ." I cleared my throat. "I asked you here today because I want to discuss the unfortunate incident—"

"Are you referring to the murder?" one of them interjected. He was the oldest one there, or looked it anyway. I could barely see his actual face, though; it was covered by a long, bright silver beard, flecked with gray. Unlike the others, he wasn't wearing a barong Tagalog but a Western-style double-breasted suit.

"Yes, I am," I answered. I decided to let the interruption go.

Just as I opened my mouth to continue, he said, "The murderer is in custody. There is nothing else to say."

I gritted my teeth and forced a smile. "Well, I think that there is."

"Are you accusing us of imprisoning an innocent person?" the only woman there besides me chimed in, her tone defensive and borderline hostile. She definitely wasn't going to be an ally, then.

"No, I'm not," I said, trying to keep my patience. "However, I do have concerns about the rush to judgment and prosecution." The councilors all began exchanging knowing looks.

"With all due respect, Princess, we've been doing this a long time. Some of us, longer than you've been alive," one of the men said.

I didn't appreciate the condescending tone. I was thinking of a way to address it, but before I could, yet another councilor joined in the dissent. "The healer had access to the poison that killed the girl. There's nothing more to say on the matter," said the man.

"And she was captured at the scene!" the woman added, emphasizing her exasperation by throwing her hands in the air.

Lots of agreeable murmurs spread around the table. The old man—the head councilor—seemed to think he was the leader in the room, not me. He stood and said, "Once more, *Princess*"—he stressed my title to make it clear I was not a queen—"as Lord Beron said, if there are no further concerns at this time, we must get back to more pressing demands. I'm sure the issue of the healer is quite exciting, but there are many other things needed to keep the kingdom running."

"Sit. Down." The words popped out of my mouth unexpectedly, but I didn't regret them. In fact, I was proud of myself for taking back control of the room. To his credit, the old man didn't argue. He returned to his seat immediately, chastised. And everyone else got quiet, too. They all stared at me again, still with contempt—but also with thinly veiled fear.

But now my mind was spinning. After seeing how unfriendly they all were toward me, I was hesitant to share much of anything with them. Or to make them hate me more. *Fear is not the same as respect,* I reminded myself.

A wild thought crossed my mind then. What if the old man

himself was behind the killing? Maybe that had something to do with his animosity toward me. Elias told me none of the councilors were near the palace when the mambabarang struck, though, so it couldn't be him. But that didn't mean he wasn't working with the witch or the insurgents. They seemed determined to have an heir who would listen to them and do what they said. Someone *unlike* me. It was almost like they actually *wanted* a war—because then they could install whoever they wanted at the throne.

"I hear you," I continued. "And yet the healer proclaims her innocence. Is it possible she tells the truth?"

"She'll say anything to save her skin," a council member sneered.

I tapped my fingers against the table. "If you're going to imprison someone, I want to know what proof you have. And more than that, I want to know that, in your quest to punish someone for this crime, you haven't allowed the actual murderer to walk free with the opportunity to kill again." That did the trick. They looked ashamed of themselves. "Because if you're putting my household in danger, then you will be held accountable, to the fullest extent of the law, should anything happen."

"Yes, Princess," they all murmured.

"I want all the information concerning this case brought to me by this afternoon," I declared.

The old bearded man squinted at me. He did not like me. That was fine; he didn't have to. He just had to learn to respect me. Even that was going to be a stretch, though.

I dismissed the council while I was ahead. Then Elias escorted me back to my rooms to have merienda and await the papers I'd requested.

"You did great," he told me.

"Thanks. It was getting away from me for a bit."

"They're going to test their limits, like small children, though they think they are the elders, and therefore, in charge. They're also used to the relationship they built with the king. You're a wild card. They aren't sure if you'll be compliant, rebellious . . . though after today I think they have a much better idea." He smiled.

"Let's just hope they actually do what I said." I fiddled with the anting-anting. "Elias—about the insurgents—you still believe they are from Sigbin?"

He sighed. "It's hard to believe, but we found one of their safe houses, and it was filled with chaos magic. Their signature. As you know, most of our munduntug hunters are from the Sigbin Court."

I thought of those winged warriors who had come for me in that California school. It felt like a distant memory, but it had only happened a few weeks ago. Elias cleared his throat and looked uncomfortable.

"What is it?" I asked.

"Your young man, Sir Lucas," he said. "He wrote me asking for permission to court you."

"Yes?"

"I gave him my blessing for strategic reasons."

"Oh?"

"If the insurgents are from Sigbin, it's best to have their ear," Elias said. "And if his courtship is a ruse, we can keep close tabs on his movements."

Ah. Keep your friends close, and your enemies closer.

"You understand, Princess?"

Could Lucas betray me? Was he part of the insurgency? I couldn't believe it. I didn't want to believe it. But what if—what if he had taken advantage of the opportunity? I initiated our first kiss, after all. What if he was just playing around? Pretending to like me? If he wasn't with Amador, why was he around her all the time, then? What if I was just the butt of a cosmic joke? Pretend to fall in love with the princess, while we scheme to take her throne. I was the new girl, the newbie. I didn't know anything about Biringan, or about him.

"I understand," I whispered.

THE COUNCIL OF the Courts never did send me any of the documents pertaining to Althea's trial. They ignored my request, essentially thumbing their noses at me. The message was clear: I was not yet their queen. And until I proved my viability by taking the scepter and all the power imbued in it, my words meant nothing.

26

"OH, NO. THE weirdo is coming."

I looked to see who Nix was talking about. Fortunada was heading toward us. "Don't be mean," I admonished Nix. She'd surprised me by showing up at the palace early in the morning so we could talk about everything we'd discovered so far on our way to school. It was a week to coronation, and there was a mambabarang out there, and I still hadn't manifested any magical ability.

"Wait, you know her?" Nix asked. "That weirdo?"

"Yes, why? She helped me out on my first day here. She's really nice. I feel sorry for her. No one talks to her."

"Because she gives everyone the creeps."

"Why do you say that? Anyway, stop; she's coming."

"She just showed up one day and started, like, following people around," Nix managed to say just as Fortunada approached.

"Hello, Your Highness," she said while giving an awkward curtsy. Her shoes and thick knitted tights were strangely old-fashioned, I realized, and she wore yet another gorgeous jewel—this time a pearl-and-diamond brooch on her lapel. "I received my invitation to the Coronation Eve Ball."

"Oh, great! So you'll be there?" I asked.

"I wouldn't miss it for anything." She smiled, showing her crooked teeth.

Something else looked different about her. "By the way, I like your hair." That was what it was—she'd pulled it up with two jeweled clips.

She touched them. "Thanks, they were my grandma's. Like my brooch." She pulled it from her robes and waved it in the light so it sparkled.

Nix tapped me with her foot. "Do you know my friend Nix?" I asked, to cover the obvious nudge.

"Um, not really," Fortunada said shyly. "I don't really know a lot of people."

"I think I've seen you around," Nix said cheerfully. I appreciated that she was at least trying to be nice. I gave her a grateful smile. But her eyes looked dark. "What class do you have right now?" I knew that was code for "go away" but hoped Fortunada hadn't picked up on it. If she did, she didn't let on.

"Oh, yes. I have to run. I just wanted to say thank you. The invitation is beautiful." She gestured around. "It's all so beautiful." Referring, I guessed, to the decorations going up around the city.

"Thank you. I have to give credit to my lady-in-waiting, Jinky, and my assistant, Ayo. They coordinated everything."

"Well," Fortunada said, her voice abruptly serious, "I sure hope you appreciate what they do for you."

"Of course," I said. I looked at Nix. She gave me the slightest shrug, like, *Told you—weird.*

"We're gonna be late," Nix said.

"Oh! I'm so sorry to keep you," Fortunada said. "I'm sure we'll get to speak later?"

"Yes," I said. I had to admit, I was relieved when she finally walked away. "Okay, fine, you were right," I told Nix. "She's a little weird."

"Seriously, what was that? 'I hope you appreciate everything they do.' Okay? How about mind your business?" Nix was super irritated.

"No big deal. She's just awkward. You heard what she said— she doesn't know a lot of people."

Nix watched Fortunada slouch away, her back slumped like she wanted to crawl in on herself. "I guess."

THE NEXT DAY, Nix, Lucas, and I gathered at the round table in my apartments that was now our de facto planning area and laid out the next steps. Nix argued for searching the king's chamber right away. "We can't do anything else until we cross that off the list," she pointed out. "I think that's where we need to start."

Lucas agreed. "All roads do lead back there. We should do as Nix says, go back and comb through the rooms for any clues as to who the mambabarang might be. Maybe they dropped something or left a shoe print. Maybe the king wrote something down—a meeting with someone, a concern, who knows?"

"All right, let's do this," I said. "No time like the present."

I needed this off my mind so I could work on finding my magic. The other night, I had tried breathing underwater in the bathtub and almost drowned. I only had less than a week left, and so far, it wasn't looking good. At least this situation was something I could immediately control.

We made it from my rooms to the wing where the king's

chambers were located without any drama. But once we got there, I realized I'd forgotten something. I slapped my forehead. "Argh. I just remembered; we need to get the key."

"Actually, I've got it." Lucas pulled something from his pocket: a golden key.

"Where did you get that?"

"It was my father's." He slipped it into the lock and opened the door. "After you," he said, sweeping his arm into the room.

Nix went first. "Thank you, sir," she said in a faux-fancy voice.

Lucas waited for me to follow her. I looked down at the key and back up at him. "You've had that all this time?"

He straightened his shoulders. "Yes. Like I said, it was my father's."

"What other rooms does it—"

"None. If that's what you're worried about, don't. I wish you would trust me, Princess."

"MJ," I corrected him. "I told you, stop calling me Princess. Isn't that something we learned in P and P class? That once a couple is courting, they can drop the formalities?"

"Sorry, I didn't think it bothered you so much," he said.

It didn't. I was just being irritable, because I wanted to trust him, I really did. I liked him. A lot. And I think he genuinely liked me, too. But after what Elias had told me, about keeping our enemies close, I had to keep up my guard.

For now, however, we were already there, so I walked inside my father's old rooms once again.

Lucas closed and locked the door behind us. The sudden silence was overwhelming. It felt like we weren't even in the same palace anymore. More like an abandoned old mansion or something, between the thick layer of dust, the spooky sheets draped over the furniture, and the imposing oil paintings that seemed like they were either watching us or might come alive any moment. I could hear Nix's footsteps creaking in the next room over. "What's taking you guys so long?" she called out.

"I'll take this room," Lucas said. "Go with Nix." I thought I detected a slight edge in his tone, like he was annoyed with me or wanted to get me out of his hair, which made me kinda angry and sad at the same time. He didn't have a right to be upset with me as far as I was concerned; I wasn't the one with a secret key to his father's private rooms. It annoyed me, because somehow we kept falling back to being combative. I didn't know if I wanted to hit him or kiss him.

I left him to it and found Nix rummaging through the tiny drawers of a tall apothecary-type cabinet against the wall. I hadn't noticed it last time I was there. Most of the room looked different, actually. Probably because I was far more relaxed, less terrified. I saw a lot of things I'd missed before. "Anything interesting?" I asked her.

"Not yet," she said, shutting one drawer and opening another. "Most of them are already empty. Others have writing ink, quills, blank parchment, stuff like that." She kept opening and shutting. "There are, like, a hundred drawers, so this might take a while. I was curious about that, but I figured I should leave that for you." She nodded toward a mahogany rolltop desk against the opposite wall.

I went over and opened the top. I expected it to be locked, but it wasn't. That was good, except it also meant anything useful was probably already gone. And just as I'd thought, the desktop was completely pristine—not a piece of paper, nor an errant writing utensil, nothing. Just a black leather desk mat that appeared to have been wiped clean. To be thorough, I began opening all the little doors and drawers, but they were empty. "There's nothing here," I said.

Nix looked over at me. "I'm not having any luck either." She looked inside another cabinet. "This is getting boring."

I tried to pull out the last drawer, but it was jammed. I wiggled it and yanked, and then it came open, creaking so loud I was afraid I was about to break it. Much to my disappointment, it was also empty. But then I heard something metallic clinking around. I pulled the drawer a little more, and a silver coin about the size of a quarter rolled out from the back. I held it up to Nix. "Well, I found this, at least." It looked different from the ones I'd seen. Took a couple seconds, but I realized why—it was not a coin currently in circulation. The profile on the front was not of King Vivencio, my father; it was someone else—King Paolo IV. My grandfather.

She came over to get a closer look. "Well, at least one of us found something cool." She looked back at the cabinet. "I quit. Someone else already took everything. Let's try the other room."

First I peeked my head in at Lucas in the receiving room. He was patting down an upholstered chair, like a CSI investigator or something. He'd been inspecting every surface methodically. Sheets were pulled off the chairs, and one chair was lying on its back. "We're going to try the king's office," I told him. He nodded, deep in concentration.

I went back and joined Nix, already doing her own thing, checking the windowsill for footprints or anything suspicious. I decided to go through the desk where I'd hidden from Lucas last time. "Wait," I said, realization dawning on me. Nix looked my way. "Have you seen any bugs?" I asked her.

She tilted her head. "No, I don't think so? If I do, I'll let you know."

No bugs. I leaned and looked under the desk, checked the floor, inspected near the floorboards—definitely no bugs. They didn't get up and walk away; they were dead. That means someone had to come clean them up. I felt dread in my heart.

"We shouldn't stay here long," I said.

Nix agreed. "Let's just do one last sweep."

"Yeah," I said. I opened the desk drawers slowly, positive I'd find a beetle in one of them, dead or alive. Nothing. They were as empty as all the others. And then another thing occurred to me—all the handles were clean. Everything else was grimy. "Hey, did you happen to notice if there was any dust on the handles?" I asked Nix.

"Uh, I don't think so?" She looked at her hands. They weren't dirty. "Actually, no, they didn't. Wait." She ran out of the room and then returned seconds later. "I checked the drawers I hadn't checked yet—no dust." We stared at each other, both understanding what that meant. Someone had been here.

"The witch?" she asked. "Do you think the witch was here?"

I just shook my head. "I don't know. My first thought was the mambabarang, too. But we shouldn't jump to conclusions. Maybe just cleaning staff doing their job."

"Right, that makes sense," Nix said. I could tell neither of us was convinced, though we really wanted to believe it was just staff and not the witch returning to clean up evidence . . . or take something they hadn't before.

I put my hands on my hips and looked around the room. *If I was my father, where would I hide something?* If the witch was here, then they had reason to believe there was something to get their hands on.

Lucas walked in. "Nothing," he said, referring to the other room. He began running his hands down the curtains. Nix and I watched him curiously. "Something could be sewn into the fabric," he said, like it should be obvious.

That gave me an idea. I went back to the king's desk and pulled the drawers all the way out, checking the bottoms and looking into the empty spaces where they slid into the desk.

"What about the middle drawer?" Lucas said. He began tugging on the front of the desk.

"It's a false front. It doesn't open. It's just decorative."

But he kept yanking at the knob, and nothing. He stopped and stood back, staring at it.

"Told you," I said. "I already tried."

He got under the desk and began knocking underneath. "It's hollow," he said.

"Let me see." I got under the desk and lay on my back right next to him. Our shoulders touched; my hip rubbed up against him. He pressed a little closer, so I knew it was deliberate, and I felt butterflies in my stomach again.

"Try it now," he said.

"Right." I knocked on the desk. It did sound hollow. He smiled. I looked over at his mouth. Realized how close we were to each other. We hadn't been together like this since the day Ayo walked in on us. I thought he was going to give me a quick kiss, but instead he scooted out from under the desk, leaving me feeling abandoned.

"How do we get into it, though?" He was focused on the drawer.

"Yeah," I said. I tried to banish any thoughts of romance and get back to the immediate problem. I ran my hand all over, looking for a latch or handle or notch, something. "Wait!" I yelled. I felt a very small dip in the wood near the edge. It was too perfect to be an accidental chip.

"Did you find something?" Lucas knelt down near my feet.

"Feel right here," I told him. He reached under the desk blindly. I grabbed his hand and directed it to the spot. "Right here," I said.

His face lit up. "That's it," he said. He tried to pull from there, but nothing happened. "It's like it needs a key or something." He got up to search around for one.

I had an idea. "Actually, I think I might have it," I said. I took out the coin I'd just found in the other desk. *Found, or that was given to me,* I thought. It didn't seem like a coincidence. It was exactly the right size for the little notch. I lined it up and pushed.

There was a click.

"Ha! You did it!" Lucas yelled.

I crawled out from under the desk. Nix rushed over to join us. Lucas opened the hidden drawer. I was prepared to be disappointed again, as it looked empty at first, but then we saw it: a plain black book.

"Well? Open it," Lucas said.

It felt sacrilegious, but I told myself this was my father's. I had every right to open it, and I was just as anxious to see what it was. There was a folded piece of parchment stuck inside the front of the book. I unfolded it. "Just a sketch of some plants," I said. Ugly ones at that. Ragged and pointy, with spiky thorns jutting out like some kind of nightmare dandelion, only less pretty. "Looks like a weed." Biringan did a good job of keeping them out of gardens, because I'd never seen one.

Nix took the paper out of my hand and began examining it.

I turned pages. It seemed to be a journal. My father's journal. I began reading—it wasn't a personal diary; more like a record of something, sort of like a register. Lists. Sketches. I went back to the beginning.

I knew in my heart that, just like with the coin, finding this book had not been an accident; it was meant for me to have. Right as I was thinking that, Lucas pointed to a symbol drawn at the top of the page, a mermaid holding the sun. "The book is enchanted," he said.

"By the mambabarang?" I asked.

He shook his head. "Not at all. This is protective magic."

Meant to be hidden from anyone except the one it's meant for, I thought, as if somehow I already knew about this enchantment. "Wait, how do you know it's enchanted?"

"It's my talent," he said.

I stared at him. "Your talent is sensing spells?"

"No," he said, looking me in the eye. "Sensing danger and hidden threats. This book can be used for evil."

"Useful," I said, breaking away from his gaze and looking down at the book, "for a knight." I tried not to feel too jealous of his magic. Then something occurred to me. "Wait. Do you know what my father's other talents were? I know he could command the seas, but I heard he could do other stuff as well. But no one's ever mentioned it."

"He was clairvoyant. He could commune across the veil," Lucas told me.

"Like, talk to ancestors?"

"As far as I know. I don't really know the specifics."

I almost told him my secret right then and there by saying, *Maybe that will help me find mine*, but I stopped myself. I began reading out loud from the parchment instead. "'Heirs of Biringan, rulers of the Court of Sirena, descendants of Queen Felicidad.'" I looked at Lucas. "Does that mean I'm a descendant of hers, too?"

"Of course," he said. "I thought you knew that."

I was floored. Goose bumps rose on my arms. "I didn't," I whispered. I kept reading.

I, King Vivencio II, hereby vow to relinquish the firstborn of my blood to the Babaeng Pinuno of the Kalahok of Mambabarang, in order to guarantee victory in the Endless Wars between the four courts and thereby bring peace to the entire realm.

27

I FELT SICK. "Surrender his firstborn? Wait, what?"

Lucas studied the parchment closely. "Hmmm. It sounds like the king made a deal with the mambabarang coven to end the war. That's what they were called, the Kalahok of Mambabarang."

"Not just to the coven but specifically to the head witch—the Babaeng Pinuno," I said. "My *father*. My father made a deal to give me to the witches." I felt dizzy.

"When were you born?" he asked. He pointed to a date on the contract. It was in the Biringan calendar.

I did a quick conversion in my head. "Almost nine months after that, exactly."

"He didn't know," Lucas said. "He had no idea your mother was pregnant when he made this agreement. He probably had no intention of ever having any children."

My father had sacrificed having an heir to end the war. I closed my eyes. The truth flooded over me. "That's why me and my mom were hiding all along." I grabbed the edge of the desk. *I was an accident.* And then they had to give up so much of their lives, all for me. They couldn't even be together.

"Are you okay?" Lucas put his hands on my shoulders to steady me.

I nodded. "Just shocked." I felt tears welling up in my eyes. It was overwhelming. Realizing this. Realizing how much danger my mother and I were in all those years. Running and hiding to keep me from falling into the witch's hands.

"He thought he would outsmart the witch, but the mambabarang knew you had to come back to Biringan one day. The one true heir—you—would have to return when you came of age, or else the truce would be broken."

"And now he's dead, and I was brought back here, not even knowing I'd be closer to the danger my father was trying to protect me from." My mother couldn't have known the full extent of this bargain—she never would have let me come back here otherwise.

Temo was right. It's time to tell her the truth. Was this what he wanted my mother to know? Was he trying to warn us with his last note? That the mambabarang had come to collect what was promised?

I picked up the book again.

"You want to do this later, maybe?" Lucas asked me. He looked at Nix for help managing me.

She leaned against the desk with her arms crossed. "You good, MJ?"

"No," I said, in response to both their questions. "But I've waited long enough to know everything."

There wasn't much more in the book, except another contract with a smuggler—like one of the shady men in town—to hide me and my mother in the human world. So all this time, I thought we were running from these men, but they weren't after us at all. They were helping to *hide* us. Our very names were written on the bottom: "Queen Consort Michelle Robertson-Rodriguez and Mahalina Jazreel, Princess of the Court of Sirena, Heir to the Throne of Biringan."

I stared at the words on the page. Read them again. And again. And again. No one ever told me that was my real birth name. My encanto name. I always thought my name was Maria Josephina, but that was a lie, too.

Just another way they tried to hide me from the mambabarang.

"He wouldn't have signed the agreement if he knew your mom was pregnant," Lucas said.

I shook my head, still bewildered by my discovery. My entire life, I had been told that we were running because I was in danger from my father's enemies. But in truth he was the one who had put the target on my back. He was the one who had signed me away, promised me to the dark witch. I wiped my eyes. "Maybe he didn't, but he should never have made a promise like that—" I was interrupted by Nix.

"You guys! We have to go to the library," she yelled. She was already making her way to the door.

"What's happening?" I asked her.

"We need to know what this is," she added over her shoulder. "Right now." She waved the drawing of the strange plant that she had taken from me earlier.

"Guess we better go," Lucas said. "Besides, I have a feeling we've been here too long already."

*   *   *

ONCE WE ARRIVED in the palace library, I shut the doors behind us and set the latch in place, to avoid any potential interruptions.

"Won't that draw more attention?" Lucas pointed out. He was probably right. Should anyone come by, it would be hard to explain why they couldn't enter. It looked more suspicious, not less. As it was, we could simply say we were doing schoolwork. I unlocked the door. When I turned around again, Nix was already ankle-deep in a pile of books. She was yanking them off the shelves, flipping through the first few pages, scanning what I assumed to be the titles and tables of contents, then dumping them unceremoniously at her feet when she was through.

I walked over to join her, trying to avoid stepping on the pile, and began picking up the books and returning them to the shelf. "What are you looking for?" I asked her.

"I'll know when I see it" was all she said. Then she returned to flipping pages and tossing books on the ground.

"Hey," I said. "You're making a mess. And, worse, ruining the books."

She looked down at the growing pile and grimaced. "Right. Sorry." She turned a few pages in the dark-green leather-bound book she was holding and then placed it back where she found it when she was done.

"Thanks," I said. "Plus, someone's probably going to notice if they're all out of order. We don't want to leave a trail of evidence behind us. What if the mambabarang is onto us? They can see which books we've been through." Okay, that was highly unlikely, but I'd seen enough movies to know anything was possible.

And my heart told me the witch had been in the king's chambers right before we were. They could be someone working in the castle . . . *They could be watching us right now, in fact, maybe through the eyes of one of the portraits on the wall . . .*

Nix flashed me a finger gun. "Right. Cover our tracks. Gotcha."

Lucas had started on the opposite end of the shelves. He made his choices far more carefully, face scrunched in concentration, scanning the spines whenever they were labeled, gently pulling the ones from the shelf that were not and opening them to check the contents. If he decided they weren't relevant, he returned them and continued on. I watched his finger trace the spines, the way he was totally absorbed in the task, contemplative, deliberate. I found it all too attractive, how mature and serious he looked. I hated that I couldn't trust him, that Elias had put doubts in my head.

"Here," Nix said, her face inches away from the huge dusty tome she held open in both her hands, titled *The Mysterious Properties of Magical Herbs* and authored by someone called Lady Elowina. Nix walked over to a table with it and sat down. I shook off my trance over Lucas and joined her. He was paging through a brown leather book.

"Check this out," Nix said. She turned the book around to face me and pointed to a table of contents in the beginning of the book. I followed her finger to the chapter title: "Forbidden."

"Now we're getting somewhere," I said. I turned around in the chair and called out to Lucas, "Come see what Nix found."

He pushed a book back into place and came over to the table to stand right next to me. He crouched down to see better, and I could feel the heat coming off his body. I cleared my throat, a nervous reflex, but he didn't seem to notice. I scooched in the chair, and my leg accidentally brushed against his. "Oh, sorry," I said.

He put a hand on my leg and rubbed it. "No need to apologize."

Once again, when he stopped touching me, I felt it as a physical loss.

Lucas began turning pages in the book, looking for the ominously named "Forbidden" chapter. He stopped and turned back a few pages, then a few more, then began flipping forward again. "I don't understand," he muttered. He turned back and forth again, faster, frustrated. "It's not there."

"What do you mean?" I leaned over to look. He showed me one page, then the next.

"This is where the 'Forbidden' chapter should be." He picked up the book and opened it wider. "It was cut out." He showed me where the few pages that made up that section were cleanly removed.

"Holy . . ." Nix said under her breath.

Lucas put the book down. "Looks like someone was already here."

"Now what?" I asked them. "I mean, I guess the good news is we were on the right track. But we're a few steps behind."

"We need to find another copy of the book," Lucas said.

Nix clapped her hands together. "Guess we're going to town. The bookstore will have it."

28

ON THE WAY into town, we shared theories about the culprit.

"The witch cut out the information they used to commit the murders," Lucas said. "That's option number one. But we shouldn't jump to conclusions either."

"Maybe it was cut out to prevent anyone from using the information," I offered. "Maybe the witch didn't even need it. Could just be a case of good old censorship."

"Distinctly possible," Lucas said. "That's option number two." We sat in quiet contemplation for a minute. "Can either of you think of anything else?" he asked.

Nix shook her head. "I think it was the mambabarang. Who would go around cutting sections out of palace books?"

I had to agree. "True. At that point, why purchase the book at all, just to cut it up? Or cut it up instead of just getting rid of it?"

We came around the final bend in the road before arriving at the main street. The entrance into town still impressed me every time I saw it. Nix was gazing out the window now, too, taking in the magic of the bustling thoroughfare. It was a little different each time: new vendors, new people, new creatures. I saw a man in baggy trousers and a loose shirt, carrying a large glass jar with what looked like a small octopus inside, except I thought that I saw the upper body and face of a man. Before I could get a better look, he was lost in the crowd.

"Nix," I said, tugging on her sleeve. "Did you see . . ."

"Oh! The bookshop is right ahead," she said, oblivious to what I was trying to tell her. She banged on the roof of the carriage to alert the driver. We heard him say, "Whoa," and the carriage slowed down and pulled over to the side of the road. Once we had fully stopped, Lucas opened the door and stepped out, then offered his hand to assist the two of us.

"Thank you," I told the driver. "We should be back within the hour." He lifted his hat and nodded, and then the three of us were on our way to track down the missing chapter.

I looked up at the painted letters on the window: DAYEA'S FINE BOOKS AND MANUSCRIPTS. From outside, the shop appeared to be very narrow, but somehow when we walked in the door, it was huge. Shelves spread out in all directions, and there were tall piles of books creating walled paths twisting around them. It smelled faintly of wet paper and spilled ink and aged leather and incense. There were signs posted at various points on the paths, with arrows meant to point customers in the right direction. They said things like PAGHALAMAN, MAHIKANG BAHAY. (Gardening, House Magic.) Another pointed in the opposite direction and said: PAGHALAMAN, ASTROMANSYA, KASAYSAYAN. (Gardening, Astromancy, History.)

"How do we know which way to go?" I asked Lucas. "Both those signs say 'gardening,' but they're in opposite directions." I was whispering, even though this was a store and not a library. It had the same kind of vibe.

Nix seemed as lost as I was. I scanned the room, hoping to find someone who worked there, but I didn't see anyone besides us.

"Let's take a look around first," Lucas said. Nix and I followed him through one of the book-wall paths, which wound its way around to another room of the store. We walked under an arch also made of books, and I wondered how it managed to keep from falling. There was no rhyme or reason to its construction—it just looked like someone had piled books on top of one another and willed them to stay afloat.

"Excuse me," Lucas said. He was standing in front of one of the shelves. Except there was no one around.

"Are you . . . are you talking to one of us?" I asked him. He leaned forward and said something into the shelf.

"Thank you," he said. He turned to us and tilted his head to the left. "It's down this way."

On the way past the shelf, I saw a small fairy, about the size of a toy action figure, dressed in the long robes of a scholar and little wire-rimmed round glasses. He held a long sheet of paper in his hand, and he was walking across the front of the books, making check marks on the paper with a tiny quill. I tried not to stare, but I'd seen very few lambanas so far, aside from the flower fairies at school, and none who'd looked like a tiny monk.

We turned another corner and found ourselves in another maze of books, shelves, and various signs in metal stands on the ground, taped to the sides of the shelves, or attached to the fronts.

By now I felt really lost, but Lucas was determined. He forged ahead, trying to make sense of the signs. Finally, he happened on the right one: MAHIKANG HALAMANG GAMOT (Magical Herbs).

"Should be in this section," he said. We all scoured the titles, searching for the same one from the palace library. It wasn't a large section, compared to some of the others.

"It's not here," Nix said. "Now what?"

"Are you sure?" Lucas was looking over the same section for the third time.

"We're sure," Nix and I both answered. I was getting antsy. The book wasn't here, and even if it was, it was obvious we could spend days or weeks trying to find it.

Lucas straightened up and ran his fingers through his hair. "Fine. But before we go, let me ask."

We followed him again, begrudgingly, so he could return to the fairy bookseller and inquire about the book.

"Excuse me," Lucas said to him. "Sorry to disturb you again . . . Yes, I found it. No, see, the problem is, I'm looking for a particular . . . Yes, it's *The Mysterious Properties of Magical Herbs* by Lady Elowina." There was a slight pause, and then, "Yes, I see. I understand. Right. No problem. Have a good day." Lucas walked back to where we were waiting and brushed past us, in the direction of the entrance. As he passed, he muttered, "Let's go."

When we were back outside, I said, "What did he say when you asked for the book?"

Lucas was looking off into the distance, farther down the street, like he was searching for something. "He said they don't carry books by treasonous witches."

Nix and I exchanged a look. Her mouth was hanging open. "Lady Elowina was a treasonous witch?" she asked.

Lucas shook his head. "I guess? I don't remember learning about her in history class."

I crossed my arms, hugging myself. We'd spent a lot of time in there, for nothing. "All right. Is there another bookshop that might carry books authored by 'treasonous witches,' then?"

"I have a better idea." He started walking, but then stopped and said to us, "We'll go tomorrow. But you guys have to let me do the talking. Promise?"

"Cross my heart and hope to die," Nix said, making an *X* over her chest with her finger.

"A bit much, but I'll take it," he said. "Come on, let's get you back to the palace."

We walked to the other side of the main street, where Nix and I had seen the suspicious men not long ago. It was getting late, but there were still lots of people buying and selling and stopping to chat. I heard a couple of them mention the coronation.

The coronation—right. And still no sign of my magic.

29

LUCAS CAME TO pick me and Nix up the next day. "We have to go down to the docks," he told us, without explaining why.

I hesitated. The ceremony was mere days away, and I was caught up trying to solve a series of murders. But it was fine, I assured myself. I'd get to the bottom of this, and then I'd go out to the gardens again and try to summon my power. Or maybe there'd be something in the book, a spell, that could solve my problem. And maybe Lucas knew something I didn't.

We made our way back to the village, weaving through all the townspeople, following his lead. "Hold on!" I called when I noticed where we were going.

Nix turned and shrugged, but she kept following him, too. I ran to him. "Lucas, aren't the docks the other way?"

"Wrong docks," he replied.

We went past the edge of the main road and took a gravelly dirt street down a hill, into the southern edge of the Tikbalang Forest. "I don't like this," I whispered to Nix. We were getting farther and farther away from the center of town. Ancient trees reached over us, blocking out the light; their leaves crunched under our feet. We took a sharp left, into thicker brush, where there was no trail. I shivered—it was suddenly a lot colder. Large birds flew high overhead, their wings flapping in the leaves as they came to a stop on the branches above our heads. Somewhere, an owl hooted, and a large branch cracked. I got the feeling we were being watched. "How's that danger meter doing?" I asked Lucas.

"You're safe with me" was all he said.

Finally, in front of us, the trees opened up, revealing a glistening green river. Ships bearing flags from all four courts bobbed in the gentle waves. "What's this?" I asked Lucas.

"It's called Dwende Dock. But the kingdom doesn't use it anymore, ever since the Royal Dock was built, which became the official port. So this is the one the smugglers use."

"How do you know about it?"

"I told you. I do my homework."

"That or you've done business with them."

He ignored me.

The river flowed from the far west side of Lake Reyna, which was firmly in Tikbalang territory. That explained why it went undetected. Their court motto was "revelar nada"—reveal nothing.

Farther down, the water became choppier and more treacherous. "Is that a waterfall?" I asked.

Lucas nodded. "Talon Falls," he said.

"And the smugglers travel over the falls, or what?"

"Yes, sometimes. They go beyond Talon Falls, where there's a passage to the human realm that can only be opened with dark magic. You can't see it because you're not meant to."

"Where in the human realm does it go? They just appear somewhere, or what?"

"The oceans are vast," he explained. "They have ports of entry where no human ever goes. From there, they can travel freely."

I couldn't believe how much was going on right under our noses in the human world. "But what if they are seen? What then?" It had to happen sometimes. Yes, the oceans were huge, but they were also heavily trafficked.

He looked at me. "Then they disappear."

"Who does? The smugglers?" I asked.

"No, the witnesses," he replied, as if it were obvious.

"Like the Bermuda Triangle?" Nix blurted out. We looked at each other.

"If that's a place where sailors disappear, then probably yes," he said.

He left us slack-jawed and started down a steep wooden staircase that twisted down the edge of the bluff to the shoreline. There, human men were loading and unloading weather-beaten wooden crates. Some merchandise was being handed off to a few dwendes who wore the same ragged pants and leather sandals as the humans, along with knitted caps pulled down over their ears, which poked out the top.

I pulled up my hood and followed Lucas, Nix close behind. This was not a place I had any business visiting, let alone knowing about. If there was someone out there who wanted to get me, this was a good opportunity. Nix and I were unarmed and unguarded, except for Lucas and the dagger on his belt—little consolation against a longsword or multiple men. Or multiple men with longswords. A bad scene all the way around. But I did feel safe with Lucas. It was so confusing, to distrust him but also feel safe around him. I didn't know what to think.

We approached a group of men who looked like they'd been out at sea for decades. Their skin was thick and mottled with liver spots from many days exposed to the sun; their clothes were tattered and threadbare. One of them wore boots, but another was barefoot, and his feet looked a lot rougher than his face.

"Excuse me, *gentlemen*," Lucas said to them, sprinkling a touch of sarcasm on "gentlemen." They looked at him but didn't respond. "I was wondering if you could tell me where to find Romulo."

"Who wants to know?" one of them spit out.

I could tell by his accent that he wasn't from here; in fact, judging by his regular-looking ears, he was completely human. I wondered if they were prisoners like Althea or here by choice somehow.

"I do. I thought that was clear," Lucas said without a hint of irony. I closed my eyes and tried not to laugh during such an unfunny situation. But Lucas's lack of familiarity with certain human-world expressions was very amusing.

"Romulo isn't taking visitors right now," the man said to Lucas.

"I see. Could you please let him know that Sir Lucas Invierno came calling for him?"

The man chewed on that, looking Lucas up and down. "Hang on," he said gruffly. He walked across the dock and stepped aboard one of the ships.

We all waited. I kept glancing around us anxiously, afraid someone would jump out of nowhere and grab us.

After a few minutes, the man came back out again, and someone else was with him. The other man, who must've been Romulo, was bald and had a long, unkempt brown beard. He walked over to us and said, "I hear someone's looking for me?"

"I am," Lucas said.

"What can I do for you?" Romulo sounded polite enough, but there was something sinister lurking below the surface. I could tell he was irritated at the interruption and on the defensive.

"I'm looking for a book," Lucas said.

Romulo snorted. "I'm not a bookseller."

"I know. But you do deal in forbidden goods, yes?"

He narrowed his eyes at Lucas. "Sorry," he said. "I can't help you." He began walking back toward the ship.

"Wait," Lucas called after him. He added, "We have coin!"

"We do?" Nix quipped.

Romulo stopped walking. He looked down at the ground with his hands in his pockets, weighing his options. When he finally turned around and came back, his demeanor had changed. "Why didn't you say so from the beginning? Why don't you tell me what you're looking for, and I'll see what I can do." He put up a finger in warning. "No promises, mind you. And the price will be steep. Those coins better be gold."

"Of course," Lucas said, unfazed. "The book is called *The Mysterious Properties of Magical Herbs*, and the author is Lady Elowina."

"*The Mysterious Properties of Magical Herbs* by Lady Elowina?" Romulo repeated back, and Lucas nodded. "This some type of prank? It's just a book! Go and get it from the bookseller."

"We tried that. Apparently, the author was tried for treason."

"Ah," Romulo said. "That makes more sense, then. Should've just said that. I'll see what I can do."

30

ROMULO WAS AS good as his word. We weren't sure how he did it, but he had that book in our hands about an hour later—for a hefty price, which Lucas paid, because neither Nix nor I had more than a few coins on us, enough for food and a trip to the bookseller but not for Romulo's contraband.

Lucas handed over the money in exchange for the book, and we made a hasty exit from the docks. We still had to trudge back through the spooky forest, but I was relieved to get away from the place where all the outlaws congregated. As princess, I felt vulnerable and exposed, unsure whether my title endangered or protected me. I wondered if—or how many of—the men gathering near the ships were involved with the insurgents. Though we knew the mambabarang was behind the murder, that didn't mean none of them were working with the witch or up to schemes of their own.

"I'll pay you back," I told Lucas.

"Me too," Nix chimed in.

He made a face, like he was insulted. "No need. Frankly I'm offended that you'd suggest it."

I decided to change the subject. "Where do you think he got the book?"

"Smugglers will hang on to anything that might be worth something. And if it's associated with dark magic, that means it's banned, and that means it's worth quite a bit to the right person. There are enchanted safe houses, either in the Sombra Woods or the other realm, where they stash things. Treasure, weapons, whatever."

The three of us walked until we found a quiet spot near town, where some small children in linen play dresses ran circles in the grassy meadow. We headed for a copse of trees in the near distance and sat in a circle beneath them. Lucas placed the book on the ground in front of us.

I had seen this book at the palace library, and it was then that I realized I'd also seen it elsewhere. "Whoa! I just remembered something. I saw this book at school."

Lucas asked, "You did? Wait, how?"

"That girl. Fortunada. We ran into each other—that day in the cafeteria when Amador tried to make me eat black rice. A book exactly like this fell out of her bag." Another thought occurred to me. Maybe it wasn't Amador who gave me the black rice. "What do you think that means?"

"Probably means she's involved with the smugglers somehow," Nix said, scrunching her nose. "I told you she was weird. And not in a good way." She took the folded paper out of her skirt pocket while Lucas flipped right to the "Forbidden" chapter.

"Here it is," he said, turning the book to face Nix. "It's all there."

Nix held out the parchment and began scanning the pages. Every so often she'd hold the drawing up to one in the book, looking for a match. None of the plants were familiar to me; according to Lucas, they were all native to Biringan and could not grow anywhere else. "In fact, most of them are extinct," he told us. "Or destroyed."

"Didn't know you were a botany expert," I said. "Gotta say, I'm kind of impressed."

"I took the Hayop at Halaman class last year," he explained.

"Ah. Guess we haven't gotten to that unit yet." I shrugged.

"Wait," Nix exclaimed. "I think this is it!" She looked from the book to the drawing and back again a few times, then laid the paper down next to it. "What do you think?"

I studied the two pictures side by side. "Definitely," I said. "The drawing actually looks like it was copied directly from the book."

Lucas read the description out loud: "*Acalypha bitela*, a rare species of poisonous plant, distantly related to the similarly named Earth genus of flowering *Acalypha* . . . primary source of sustenance for the coleopteran species *Malificenti mortiferum*, likely extinct. . . . Its blooms may be dried, crushed, and utilized in various potions. . . . Indigenous to Biringan, once found exclusively in dense, shaded forestlands near the riverbed, it has since gone extinct in the wild. Use with extreme caution. In small amounts, causes severe illness. In large doses, death."

"This is it! This is what caused the king's illness," Nix said excitedly. "That's why the drawing was in his desk. He must have suspected something."

"Maybe he was sick for a while before he died. Like my father," Lucas said. "But why did the witch not just use a larger dose?"

"Either to draw out the agony or better escape detection," I suggested. "Or both."

"That makes sense," Nix said. She picked up the drawing. "Look!" She held it up to the light. "There's something written on the bottom." We all leaned forward and scanned the paper. After a few seconds, I saw it, too. Symbols, in what looked like white ink. "I can't read it, though," she said. "Can you?"

Lucas squinted at it. "That's an ancient diwata language. No one speaks it anymore."

"Can you read any of it?" I asked him.

"A little bit. I took a course, but it was rudimentary. This one is easy." He pointed to a square with a sun, moon, flower, and leaf in it. "That means 'the kingdom,' as in all of Biringan, or actually, it could also mean the throne itself. Let me try the rest." He studied the symbols for a while, holding the paper in different lights, muttering to himself. A few minutes later, he said, "Okay, I think I've got the gist of it anyway. It's a recipe. An incantation. Both, actually. How to make the poison and also how to administer it, I think." He pointed to a stick figure symbol. "That's the poppet. And then over here, there's the beetle symbol. The rest is harder, but in context, it's definitely a spell."

"*Malificenti mortiferum* is the beetle!" Nix exclaimed, taking the book from Lucas.

Lucas looked over her shoulder. "Yes!" he said excitedly. "The beetles are the vector. They carry the poison inside them. And since they can both administer and clear up any evidence of the poison, by biting their victims and then extracting the poison once it's done its work, the mambabarang enchants them and directs them to the target, represented by the doll. That way they keep their hands clean, evading detection. But basically, anywhere you see the beetles, the witch isn't far behind."

I remembered something from that last day I was in school.

"The day I came here, that morning when I was sitting in class, I saw a beetle. Not long after that, the assassins tried to kill me." It was all making sense now. The witch was working with the insurgents; I was sure of it. It was all connected. Lucas's dad's murder, my father's, the page's, the rise of the insurgents, and then the plot to kill me. Whoever this mambabarang was, they were after me and after the throne.

"What else is in here?" Nix began turning more pages. She stopped at the back of the book. "Look."

Lucas and I leaned in to look. It was an elaborate family tree. In the center, Lady Elowina. Some of her ancestral branches were dead ends, but one in particular went very far back, much farther than the rest. All the way back to one foremother.

Queen Felicidad.

"So technically, you're a distant cousin of Lady Elowina?" Nix pointed out.

There were handwritten additions, too—Elowina's direct descendants. It didn't take long to find a familiar name.

We all realized it at the same time. Lady Elowina was Fortunada's grandmother.

31

LUCAS STOOD UP. "Does anyone know where we can find Fortunada?"

"All I know is she lives in the Court of Lambana," I said, thinking of her school uniform.

"Her family was exiled from the palace, so somewhere in the village is my guess," Lucas said.

That was news. "They were exiled?"

"Supposedly. I don't know for sure, since it's not my court, but that's what I heard."

"Explains the ratty clothes and the fancy jewels," said Nix. "Lost grandeur and all that. Wonder what her family did to piss off the Lambana Court."

"Could be anything, could be nothing," said Lucas. "You know how it is. Politics."

"Have you ever seen her around?" I asked Nix. "After school or anything?"

She shifted uncomfortably. "Um, no, don't think so." She picked at the grass beside her.

I stood up, too, and brushed the dirt off my dress. "Well, why don't we go to your place and figure it out from there? Maybe we'll get lucky and find her." I was curious to see where Nix lived, anyway.

She didn't get up to join us.

"What's wrong?" I asked her.

"Nothing," she said slowly. "It's just . . . I don't feel like going home right now."

"This is about finding the witch, not a social call," Lucas said. I could tell he was getting irritated. Frankly, I was, too. We were on the verge of catching the mambabarang, and suddenly Nix was getting cagey?

"We don't even have to go to your place," I told her. "Let's just go to the Lambana Village."

Nix rubbed her face with her hands. "Argh! Fine. You want to know why I don't want to go there?"

Lucas and I looked at each other. "Yes, we do," he said.

Nix took a deep breath and exhaled slowly, raising her eyebrows. "Okay, but it's a lot." Neither of us took the out, so she said quickly, "All right. Here's the thing. I ran away, and I came here. So I don't really have a home. At least not one I want you to see. The end. Anyway—moving on!"

"Wait, what?" I shouted, genuinely shocked. So many questions. Lucas and I stared at her, waiting for answers. "Where have you been staying?"

She looked down. "An abandoned cottage on what used to be the emperor's estate, between the Lambana Village and the Sirena Palace. Near the Old Bumara Wall."

"With who?" I demanded, shocked, sad, and feeling awful that Nix had been basically living in a dirt hut while I lived in literally palatial apartments.

"Just me." Nix shrugged.

"Oh my god, Nix. All this time I assumed you were staying at the Lambana Palace." My heart went out to her. Here I was, constantly feeling sorry for myself, and Nix was a runaway, living alone on the edge of the village. "Wait, hold on. I heard about you! On the radio." I'd mentioned it around the time we first met, but didn't want to push. The headline from that fateful morning came back to me. *Phoenix Xing was last seen* . . . "You went missing!"

"Yeah. I'd had enough. I had nothing there. Here, I actually have something. Friends. An identity. A future, maybe."

"But how did you even know how to get here?" I stared at Nix, and remembered how nervous she was about running into encantos from Jade Mountain. "Nix, where are you from—*really?*"

She sighed. "You got me. I ran away from Jade Mountain. My father's the Jade Emperor. But I'm only one of, like, thirty, forty kids, who knows. My mother isn't a favorite concubine, even. I was sick of living there. I hated all their rules, so I ran away. First I went to the human world, where I was a foster kid. But then my father's guard found me, so I had to run away again. Avalon was too far, but I made it here. You won't tell, will you?"

"Why would I do that?"

"Well, you are going to be queen, and you'll need to keep good relations with all the other realms. But I swear, no one even cares I'm gone. I'm not like the heir or anything. Like I said, my mom wasn't even a favorite concubine."

Hmmm. I doubted no one cared, since they had sent encantos to find her in the human world. But I would deal with Nix's situation later.

"Well, I'm glad you're here," I said. "I'm not sure what I

would've done without you, actually. I never really had a real friend, you know."

"No need to get all sappy on me," Nix said, but bumped her fist against mine nonetheless.

This was the time to tell them about my problem. Since we were sharing. I opened my mouth to say it. *I have a secret, too. I don't have any magical gift.*

But before I could confess, Lucas was hurrying us along. "We still need to find the witch."

Maybe next time, I'll tell them, I promised myself.

BY THE TIME we arrived in the Lambana Village, it was nearly dusk. It was chilly, and though it wasn't actively raining, drops from the last storm still fell from wet leaves onto our heads or into puddles. Most of the villagers were already indoors for the evening. Smoke drifted out of their chimneys, and their windows shone with yellow light from within.

"Wish I was wearing boots." I pulled my skirt up to keep it from being dragged in the mud. Though the narrow streets were all stone, they were still damp and tracked with dirt from people's boots, horses, and carts.

"I should've warned you," Nix said. "Constant rain here. Biggest drawback."

"We didn't have time for a wardrobe change, anyway," Lucas said. He was looking around for someone to talk to.

"What's the advantage?" I asked Nix about living there.

"Also the rain," she answered. "It keeps people away."

"Unless they're looking for somewhere to hide," Lucas said.

We wandered aimlessly for a while as the sun lowered at the horizon. We were nearing the end of the village and hadn't found anyone to talk to.

I looked up at the darkening sky. "I need to get back."

"Soon, we'll head back soon. But first—Nix, see that house down there?" Lucas pointed beyond the village proper, where the official road became gravel and then dirt. Though not quite a forest, the area was full of trees. And within a group of them, there was a little nipa bungalow, just barely visible. "Who lives there?"

She shook her head. "Beats me."

"Let's go find out," Lucas said, marching right for the tiny house. We followed behind him.

"I don't like this," Nix said.

When we got there, Lucas pounded on the door. The little house was dark, and all the curtains were drawn. It looked like it was just one story—no upstairs and not even an attic window. There was a cracked clay pot next to the door, filled with weeds and some struggling flowers.

After a few minutes of knocking and waiting, we decided to look around the back.

It was even darker and more desolate behind the house. The trees made shadows against the siding, and the wind began to pick up, making spooky whistling noises. Nix peeked in a back window. "No one's home," she said. "But Fortunada *has* to live here, right? Take a look!"

I stood next to her and cupped my hands on the window to see inside. "You're right! That's a Court of Lambana uniform—and those are her jeweled hair clips!"

I wrapped my arms around myself and scanned the property. It did seem like no one had lived there for a long time. Except. I saw a small patch about twenty feet from the house that didn't look wild. "Check it out," I said.

We left the house and walked over to the garden.

There were tomatoes, carrots, various herbs. "Good crop," Lucas said.

Then I spotted it. *Acalypha bitela.*

Poison.

The same one my father had sketched.

32

JINKY FLUNG THE curtains wide open. "Rise and shine, Princess. It's a big day!"

I groaned and threw my pillow over my head.

"Come on, today's the rehearsal! Can't be late." She pulled the pillow off me.

All I wanted was sleep. My entire body ached from the day before. Plus Nix and I had stayed up half the night worrying about Fortunada's whereabouts. I heard Nix moan from the couch in the sitting room, where she'd slept. "Too tired!" she shouted. Yesterday I'd told Nix she didn't have to live alone on the outskirts of town; my rooms in the palace were big enough to accommodate both of us. I offered to ask the palace staff to set up a bedroom for her in the future. Nix insisted she wanted to stay where she was. She liked living on her own and didn't want to exchange her father's palace for mine, she explained. But since she was coming with me today to rehearsal, along with Lucas, she agreed to spend the night.

Jinky poured us some tea and then disappeared into the closet to prepare my rehearsal outfit. "Lucas will be here soon," she called out.

That got me out of bed.

Once Nix and I were ready to go, we met Lucas out front at the calesa. "Hi-*uh*," Lucas said, his greeting turning into a yawn. He was clearly just as exhausted as us. I was more than glad to see him; I was thrilled. I'd only asked him to join me for this the night before. I'd almost forgotten to ask, but he'd said yes right away.

He helped us climb in, and then we were on our way to the Council of the Courts, where the ceremony was scheduled to take place in three days.

Three days. Three short days until my coronation. My stomach turned. I was grateful to have two good friends supporting me, at least.

Lucas leaned forward. He was sitting across from me and Nix. "We need to tell Elias and alert the Royal Guard to the danger," he said. "They'll be able to capture Fortunada before we can. I've alerted my men to search for her, but they won't have as much lee-way as the palace does. Especially since I told them to keep it quiet."

I was touched he'd already mobilized the situation, but I didn't want to tell Elias what we'd discovered. "Not yet."

Both of them looked at me like I'd lost my mind. "If we tell Elias and the guard, then they won't let me go anywhere," I explained. "I'll be locked up in my rooms until I'm crowned."

"So what? It's only a couple days. Besides, they're not wrong. It's not safe for you to be out running around," Lucas said, worry in his voice. "Fortunada could be anywhere."

I was glad for his concern, but I didn't much like the idea of being a prisoner, even for my own safety.

"We don't really have a choice," Nix said gently. "It's for your own good."

"It's not just that."

"Then what is it?" Lucas said.

The truth was, I couldn't be locked up in the queen's chambers or kept under watch, because I needed *at least* one more night out in the garden. I needed some space so my magic would manifest.

"I have my reasons," I said. They couldn't possibly understand the pressure I was under. And I'd lost so much time as it was. Those last precious days could not be taken from me. If I was stuck inside with guards hovering, I'd never figure out my talent, and then it would all fall apart.

Lucas and Nix shared frustrated sighs. I ignored them. I was spooked, yes, but it was hard to feel scared of someone so timid as Fortunada. I didn't even really believe she could be the mambabarang. What if she was being framed, too? Just like Althea? How could we be so sure she was behind all this? And what possible motive could she have? Elias had always suspected the insurgency was a Sigbin plot, a power grab for the throne, and that was the most logical explanation for all this. But a mousy student from Lambana? Why would she want to take down the king? It didn't make sense.

"By the way, I did a little digging on Lady Elowina," Lucas said.

"What did you find?" I asked.

"That's the thing. There's nothing about her anywhere. There's no record even of what court she was from. It's like she never existed."

"Huh," I said. Curiouser and curiouser. I leaned back in my seat and tried to put it out of my mind for now. I still had a coronation to prepare for.

The roads entering the city were packed. There was a line outside the bakery and a steady stream of customers leaving with parcels—bibingkas and mango cakes for their coronation parties.

The boutiques were similarly crowded, as everyone rushed for last-minute outfits and accessories, and the taverns were stuffed with patrons. There were people on ladders, washing windows and putting finishing touches on decorations, and kids running up and down the walkways. They could feel the anticipation in the air.

All of this for me. And I was going to disappoint each and every one of them.

We didn't talk much the rest of the way. I stared out the window instead, out at those foreboding storm clouds over the mountains, bigger by the day; the feeling of impending doom—and guilt—gnawed in my belly.

Elias was waiting for us at the Council of the Courts. He led us inside, past the room where the council meeting had been held, then past other rooms where official business was conducted.

We finally arrived at a door with a sign on it.

—NOTICE—

PUBLIC TRIAL TO COMMENCE HENCEFORTH

The following day's date was written at the bottom.

"Is that Althea's trial?" I asked Elias.

He nodded.

I made eye contact with Nix and Lucas, and we all silently agreed we were going to be there.

We stopped at a sanctuary on the far north side of the building, where the service would be held. It was a huge space with a sky-high ceiling, all made of glass. At the far end was a dais, where three workers were busy polishing the ancient wood throne where I was supposed to be crowned.

"Can you believe it?" Nix said, squeezing my hand. She was a lot more excited than I was. "In a few days, you'll be queen!"

I managed an uneasy smile. *Maybe,* I thought. *Hopefully.*

A woman walked toward us. She was barefoot and wore a long, simple sheath, with her waist-length hair loose.

Elias introduced her. "Princess, this is the priestess Luzviminda. She'll be conducting the ceremony."

The priestess bowed. "Your Highness."

We followed her into the sanctuary. There were rows of benches for the congregants to sit on, but other than that, it was a simple space, clean and bright. A sharp contrast to the ornate palaces and festive villages and marketplace.

Luzviminda seemed to pick up on my thoughts. "Adornments distract from the sacred purpose of the ceremony," she explained. "There should be nothing coming between the being and the blessing."

I wondered if she could tell I had another problem, too. I decided I better not draw attention to my main concern. I nodded and asked, "What happens at the ceremony?"

"Are these your witnesses?" She gestured to Nix and Lucas.

I nodded. Since I had no kin of my own, I had asked Nix and Lucas to stand with me. I introduced them to Luzviminda, though she seemed familiar with Lucas already. I could tell she was surprised that he was there. I didn't have much time to ponder that, though, because right away, she began to walk us through the ceremony.

"The congregants will all be seated prior to your arrival, and then Don Elias will escort you down from the preparation room." She pointed to the upper floors in the center of the building. "You and your witnesses and attendants will gather here. They'll line up behind you, and inside, the musicians will play 'The Song of the Sun,' Biringan's ancient coronation music."

We lined up as she showed us, and she hummed the melody as we followed her lead. "And then you'll walk in."

We began to march down the aisle. Luzviminda's voice echoed: "Walk, walk, walk. Yes, just like that. You'll walk to the dais. Not too fast."

I began to feel sick. This made everything so much more real. It was happening. Very soon. In three days, those empty seats would be filled with people. Watching.

When we got to the dais, Luzviminda had more directions for us. Everyone moved around me, taking places, learning their roles. I knew she was still talking, but her words became muted background noise. All I could hear was the pounding in my ears.

The room was so hot. I wanted to wipe my forehead, but not with the sleeve of my dress.

I gazed out at the empty audience, picturing the seats occupied, all those eyes staring right back at me. Counting on me. Expecting a princess to become a queen.

Luzviminda stood in front of me. She put her arms out like she was holding something. "The box," she said. "At that point, the princess will remove the scepter . . ."

Right. Once I had shown my magic, I could touch the scepter. Thankfully, I didn't have to do that right now.

33

THE FOLLOWING MORNING, we arrived at the Council of the Courts for Althea's trial, as planned. I had the driver drop me and Nix off some distance from the entrance so we could approach without drawing a lot of attention. I shut the calesa door and flung a dark cloak around my shoulders, lifting the huge hood over my head. It didn't matter if anyone knew I was here—not like it was forbidden—I just didn't want to be bothered. Or start needless speculation.

I only had two days until I was supposed to stand in front of the entire kingdom and prove that I was worthy of being their queen. Two days and two major problems: no magic and no witch. I had to find both, or else I was going back to the human world, just in time to witness the apocalypse.

"This is nuts," Nix said. "I'll go find us some seats." There were various kinds of encantos everywhere, all waiting to go in and watch the trial. There were so few murders in Biringan that for most citizens this was probably a once-in-a-lifetime event. Then again, I thought as I watched them huddle in circles, speculating about the guilt or innocence of the accused, they didn't know about the king. Or Lucas's father.

As I looked around at all the unfamiliar faces, I wondered if Fortunada might be hiding somewhere among them. I still couldn't believe she could be the mambabarang. There had to be an explanation for it.

I waited around a bit, with a hood obscuring most of my face, looking for Lucas. People began going inside. I got antsy. I didn't want to miss anything.

Just as I was about to lose all hope, I spotted him walking down the path in front of the building.

"Hey," I said as I stepped up next to him.

He smiled. "Hey. I didn't recognize you."

"Good, then my disguise is working."

He held the door open for me, and we entered. There were tons of people still milling around, but most were heading into a set of doors at the far end of the building.

The courtroom was like a university lecture hall or a small theater. There were rows of seats for spectators. At the front was a stage with a long table and seven chairs facing the audience, while one chair was positioned with its back to the audience.

We spotted Nix and took the two seats she'd saved for us in the back of the room.

"Althea will sit there," Lucas explained once we were situated. "And the seven judges will sit in front of her."

"No jury of her peers in Biringan, I guess?" Nix said. "Oh, I forgot, humans aren't allowed to judge encantos."

The places were all filling up, and fast. It was a little unnerving how many people had arrived to bear witness. I reminded myself that it wasn't any different than at home, where we not only filled courtrooms for high-profile cases but also tuned in on our televisions, read about them, and listened to podcasts about them. Curiosity was natural, I supposed, but how was this trial more civilized than a public execution or a gladiator tournament?

We watched the crowd. There were encantos from all over, including creatures I hadn't seen yet, especially from the courts of Tikbalang and Lambana. One looked almost like a wolf, or a cross between a wolf and a gargoyle, maybe. It had a long, spiked tail and huge, spiky teeth. "Who is that?" I asked Lucas.

"A Sigbin. Guardian of the Court of Sigbin. Mostly harmless, until they're not."

There was a woman, sitting with representatives of the Court of Lambana, with thick, glossy hair down to the back of her legs, wearing a dress adorned with tiny mirrors; when she faced our way briefly, I saw that she had half a dozen eyes. Another encanto, from the Court of Tikbalang, had black feathered wings, which he expanded and tucked in close to his body at will.

Lucas noticed me staring. He leaned to the side and said, "The equinox courts attract those who live on the margins and prefer dawn or dusk above all."

Heads turned when two guards in blood-red uniforms marched in and stood one at each side of the door. They were followed by a guard holding a rope that trailed after him. A second later we saw that rope was connected to Althea's waist. Her hands were bound in front of her. Another guard followed closely behind. Once they were all out, the first two closed the door and then returned to their places.

They led Althea to the chair. She sat, and then they stood watch behind her, swords at the ready in case she attacked or tried to flee.

She looked thin and haggard, but her face was calm and serene, as if she had already accepted her fate, whatever it might be.

Another door opened, this time behind the long table. Again, two guards emerged, and one stood on each side of the door. Then the judges walked out one by one. They all wore black-and-gold robes. The crowd silenced as each of them took their seat, except for the judge in the middle, who stood next to his chair and waited for the others.

Once the room was quiet, he unrolled a parchment scroll in his hand and announced, "We have assembled to hear the evidence against Althea Ramos, accused of the wanton murder of Marikit Baluyot." He paused before continuing. "Will the prosecution please present your evidence?"

A woman in similar black robes, but with silver piping, stood from the front row behind Althea. "Marikit Baluyot was a page at the Court of Sirena palace. She was doing her job the night that Althea, a human healer, poisoned her using herbs that healers are known to possess as a matter of routine."

"Who will defend the accused?" the judge asked.

Another woman in black and silver stood on the other side of the front row.

"Sir," she began, "there is no doubt that Marikit met a grisly end, but it was not at Althea's hand. The deceased had already consumed the poison when Althea discovered her in the sitting room, writhing on the floor in agony. Althea was attempting to save her life. In fact, she is the one who called for help. That her benevolent actions have been met with this treatment is abhorrent. There is absolutely no proof that Althea poisoned Marikit. The prosecutor has no motive, no evidence that the poison was in

Althea's herbs kit, and in fact, they don't even have evidence for exactly what type of poison was used in this crime." She sat back down.

"Response?" the judge asked.

The prosecution stood again. "Sir, the poison does not need to be proven; the fact that it was poison and not, for instance, spoiled food or some other illness is not up for debate. Even the defense does not deny that poison was the cause of death. Only one person in the vicinity that evening had easy access to poison—a search was conducted, and no such substance was located in the palace kitchens or anywhere else on the grounds. The healer's kit, however, was present, in the same room as the deceased.

"As for motive, we contend that the palace page was not the intended target but merely a practice subject to test the poison's efficacy. Investigators concluded that the poison was consumed from a teapot the page was delivering to the sitting room. The healer invited her to share some tea with her, so the page poured a cup from the pot, took a sip, then promptly began to seize."

The defense stood once more. "We agree that the kitchen page was not the intended target. We believe the tea being delivered to the sitting room was intended for the crown princess of the Court of Sirena. Our initial theory was that the tea had been poisoned *before* Althea arrived."

My heart stopped. I grabbed Lucas's arm, and we looked at each other. Others were just as surprised. There were gasps and whispers around the room. I was glad none of them knew I was sitting there.

"What proof do you have?" the judge asked.

"Well, we knew a page would not have been called to deliver

tea to the healer. It was more likely that, upon delivering it to an empty room, Marikit had decided to sneak a sip of the poisoned tea, having no idea it was tainted. Althea, as she maintains, happened to be in the palace and heard her cries, and she rushed to Marikit's aid. Our theory made sense.

"But, sir, our initial assumptions were wrong. Because there was *no* trace of poison in the teapot. If Marikit Baluyot died of poison, it was delivered in a different way."

More gasps from the audience.

"And what way was that?" demanded the judge.

"Beetles. Althea did not poison Marikit Baluyot. She is merely a scapegoat to cover the truth that this kingdom is hiding." The defense drew a long breath. "Marikit Baluyot was poisoned by a mambabarang."

This time the room exploded.

"Order! Order!" the judge yelled.

When the crowd settled, the judge stared down the defense. "The Kalahok was disbanded and exiled after the Endless Wars. What proof do you have that a mambabarang caused her death?"

"I call Althea Ramos to serve as her own witness. Althea, please tell the court what you saw."

Althea stood up and bowed. In a soft, scared voice, she told her story. "I received a note saying to come to the palace and meet the page, who had something for me. When I got to the receiving room, she was confused as to why I was there. There was a pot of tea in the room, but neither of us took some. She said she didn't call for me. I was about to leave, when all of a sudden, the darkness came out of the walls."

"Darkness?" the judge said.

"Sudden, and complete. And then when it was over, the girl was lying dead."

"That is your testimony?"

"It's what happened. It's what I saw. I didn't harm the girl." Althea sat down.

"Do either of you have any further evidence to present to the court in this case?" the judge asked the prosecution and defense.

"No, sir," both of them responded.

"In that case, barring any further evidence, this case is concluded, and we will have a verdict in due time."

The judge sat down. I thought that meant we should leave, but Lucas stopped me when I started to stand. "Aren't we done?" I asked him.

"No." He explained, "They will have an answer any minute."

The team of justices conferred for a while, writing things down, passing papers back and forth. The entire process was baffling to me. They didn't even leave the room to do this. I added a mental note to do something, anything, about this inherently unfair system of justice.

Suddenly the judge seated in the middle of the row stood. "We have arrived at a conclusion," he announced. The courtroom quieted down. He waited until all whispering ceased. "Now we shall read the decision." There was some fumbling among the judges, and then they passed a sheet of parchment down to the middle of the table.

The judge put on his glasses, a pair of narrow, rectangular frames that perched precariously on the tip of his tiny nose. He read over the paper, then proceeded to take notes.

My leg was shaking, and my palms were clammy. Others in the

room were getting impatient, too. They started fidgeting and scooching around in their seats, whispering to one another again. The judge looked up over his glasses as if he was reprimanding some rowdy children.

Althea sat motionless in her chair, shoulders slumped. She stared at the floor in front of her. She was so still, it almost looked like she was sleeping, except every so often, she blinked.

"Ah, yes. Here we are," the judge said. "Per the rules, regulations, ordinances, and so forth and so on, et cetera, et cetera, concerning the application of laws and bylaws of the great kingdom of Biringan and all of its courts . . ."

"Oh my god, I wish they would speed it up," I whispered to Lucas and Nix.

"According to the ancient Book of Justice set forth by our esteemed ancestors and their rightfully anointed kings . . ."

"And queens," Nix whispered.

"We do hereby and henceforth declare the accused, Althea Ramos, a human healer residing in Biringan of her own free will and accord . . ."

"Wow," I muttered under my breath. "Free will?"

". . . is guilty of the crime of murder."

There was an eruption of voices and activity in the room, as people began shouting out their disagreements, while others were cheering the judge's decision. But Althea said nothing. She uttered not a word of protest even as the guards hauled her away.

She was resigned to her fate. Humans never got justice in Biringan, Nix had said. They were always found guilty of any crime in this realm. Althea knew she never had a chance.

"What now? How long does she go to prison?" I asked Lucas.

He pointed to the front of the room, where the judge was still standing. He was waiting for the chatter to stop again. Once it did, he made one final announcement: "Thereby, this board of justices has unanimously sentenced the convicted . . . to death." Then the judge banged his gavel.

34

I DIDN'T REALIZE I needed a date for the Coronation Eve Ball until Lucas mentioned it the day before. After we left Althea's trial and the calesa brought us back to the palace, he took his leave, saying he wanted to check in on his men and how they were doing with the search for Fortunada. "So, um, about tomorrow night," he said, with a strange look on his face.

"What about it?" I asked him.

"Do you need an escort, maybe?"

"Are you asking if you can take me?" It was the furthest from my mind after the shock of Althea's sentence. But the gears of the coronation kept turning—no matter what happened, I still had to participate in all the festivities that would ultimately see me crowned queen. (Or not.)

"Do you want me to?" He had his hand on the carriage door, and he looked so nervous I didn't feel like teasing him anymore.

"I would love it," I told him. "Thank you for asking."

In answer, he took my hand and pressed it to his lips once more. "It will be my honor."

"Okay! You guys can find a room!" Nix interjected. "Third wheel here!"

We laughed.

"It's okay, Nix. I can take you, too," he said with a wink.

"You sure will! I'm not going in alone!" she threatened.

THE NEXT EVENING when the door opened and Lucas walked in to escort me and Nix to the Coronation Eve Ball, I could not have been more nervous than I already was. Jinky had styled my hair into an elaborate French chignon, and this time I wore the gold circlet that marked me as the princess of the Sirena Court. I wore a gold-and-ivory dress embroidered with sampaguita flowers, with stiff butterfly sleeves and a deep V neckline, and carried a matching fan.

Lucas bowed when he entered. He was so dashing in a black barong Tagalog, his dark hair slicked back from his forehead.

"Wow," he said when he saw me.

I flushed with pleasure. "You look wow yourself."

"Ahem!" Nix said, clearing her throat.

"You look good, too, Nix." He laughed.

"Why, thank you, kind sir." She batted her eyelashes. In honor of the event and her heritage, Nix wore a red qipao, a tight-fitting silk dress with a mandarin collar, along with a beautiful pair of jade-and-diamond earrings. "My mom's," she explained. "And we wear red for celebrations."

"Shall we?" Lucas held out an arm for each of us. "It's a long walk to the other side of the palace." The ball was being held in—where else?—the ballroom.

It was off the back of the palace, an airy dome with floor-to-ceiling windows and French doors all around, leading out to the gardens.

"Dang," Nix said when the room opened up in front of us. The decorators had outdone themselves. It looked like the gardens were brought inside. Walls, ceiling, everything but the floor was covered in greenery and florals, all white and shades of purple and pink. There were gold chandeliers and candelabras and tall centerpieces on the tables, and staff dressed in white serving fizzy drinks in delicate flutes. The place settings were white with pale-pink stripes and thin gold trim, just like a play set I had as a kid. Ayo had coordinated the entire thing, going so far as to track down a special variety of pink roses that the Court of Lambana's master florist had bred to bloom with white polka dots. It definitely made up for all those formal dances I'd missed out on in the midst of constant moves. If only my mom could have been in the room, it would've been perfect.

One of the gloved footmen at the door announced our arrival. "The crown princess of Biringan and her guests, Sir Lucas Invierno and Phoenix Xing." To avoid the chances of anyone from Jade Mountain discovering Nix was in Biringan, Nix agreed to be announced but demanded she wear a "disguise"—which meant wraparound shades. I didn't think it would truly hide her, but there was very little chance anyone from Jade Mountain was in attendance.

It was all very impressive, and I was more than honored, not to mention extremely lucky to be standing in the ballroom at all. Except.

As soon as the string quartet had finished playing their first song, Lucas could tell I had something on my mind. To his credit, he didn't let on until we were alone. Nix said she wanted to go grab some sweets, and as soon as she'd walked away, he turned to me and said, "Out with it."

"What do you mean?"

"What's wrong? I can tell you're upset about something. But trying to hide it. And doing an awful job, by the way."

I didn't respond immediately. I looked over his shoulder to the landscape outside. "Lucky to have such beautiful weather for this special evening," I said.

Lucas huffed. "Nice try." Then he got serious: "Look, by the time you're crowned tomorrow, nothing will matter. You'll have the entire power of Biringan at your fingertips. Fortunada won't be able to touch you."

Tomorrow. It's tomorrow. At that point, it wouldn't even matter, because there would be much bigger problems in Biringan. "No," I said quickly. "I mean, it's not that. Not completely." Even if the witch wasn't an issue, I was still the problem.

"All right," he said. "Then what else . . ."

"Well, it's sort of that. Just not directly."

He waited for me to say more.

I closed my eyes and took a deep breath. I almost said it. The actual truth. But the words wouldn't come out. "It's Amador," I blurted out of nowhere, even surprising myself a bit. The thought went straight from my mind to my mouth before I had an opportunity to censor it.

"Ah," he said, nodding and glancing out the window. "I should have known." He looked down and then back at me. "I told you, she's nothing to me."

I had only said her name because I couldn't bear to confess my real secret. But now that I had mentioned her, I couldn't help but notice her presence. Amador was across the room; as a lady of the realm, she had to be invited. She was standing with the other courtiers from Sigbin. She looked spectacular, wearing a tight-fitting gown made of silver scales.

"She told me you guys were betrothed as children. Why would she do that?" I asked him.

He shrugged. "No idea. I told you I thought you were joking."

"What if she knows something you don't?" I asked.

He shook his head. "Impossible. Stop worrying about it. Like I said, if there was some kind of arrangement, why would Elias let me court you, anyway?"

Because he wanted me to keep you close, in case you were a traitor, I thought, but didn't say. Elias was wrong to doubt him, though. Lucas could only be himself, and I had seen his heart. He could never betray me.

Nix returned then, saving me from the awkwardness. "Want one?" She held out a chocolate truffle.

I shook my head.

"Did I interrupt something?" She looked at Lucas and then back at me. "Are we fighting?"

"No," we both said together. But Lucas was right. Something was bothering and had been bothering me for weeks. I needed to tell them; they were my friends. My witnesses. My allies. I needed them.

"You guys, I'm a fraud."

"Of course you're not!" Nix said. "You're just nervous."

I shook my head. "No, you don't understand."

They both stared at me. It didn't matter anymore. They would know within the next twenty-four hours regardless. "Let's go over there," I said, motioning to a quiet corner away from the guests gathered around the sparkling fountains.

We huddled there, and Lucas said again, "Out with it."

"Yeah, before someone starts eavesdropping. My dad used to say, 'If you want someone to hear you, then whisper,'" Nix said.

Okay, here we go. Time to confess. Okay, here goes nothing, literally. "I don't have magic," I said.

"What are you talking about?" Lucas frowned.

"Talent. Power. I don't have any."

"Be serious," Nix scoffed. "You're the princess! The heir to all of Biringan!"

"And I'm half-human. I think my human side beat out my encanto side."

Nix stared at me. "You're really serious?"

I hung my head. "Yeah. I've . . . I've been trying to figure out what it is, but I've got to come clean. I've got nothing."

Lucas shook his head. "No, that's not right. You just haven't found it yet."

"No, I don't think so," I said. I'd thought it would make me feel better, admitting it. But I only felt worse.

He took me by the arms and looked directly into my eyes. "You are your father's daughter. I believe that. You should, too."

I stared at him. He believed in me. I wished I did. But it was overwhelming. I knew I was going to disappoint everyone, him most of all. I shook him off me. I couldn't bear his care for me right then.

Nix grabbed my hands. "It doesn't matter! It's going to be fine. We'll think of something. Just act normal and enjoy the night in the meantime."

I nodded, my eyes watering.

Servers began gathering at the door. It was time for dinner.

"Come on," said Lucas. "Let's go. Like Nix said, we'll figure something out later."

We all went and sat at the head table: me, Nix, Lucas, Elias, and some of the councilors, whom, according to Elias, I should bestow some advance favors upon, in order to guarantee their loyalty.

"Professor Manatubay wasn't kidding. Check out all the forks," I said, trying to make light of everything and change the subject.

"You'll have to remind me which is which so we don't spark an *inter-court incident*," Nix responded. "Speaking of incidents, maybe after dinner we can sneak away and try to find a solution to your . . . you know."

"Yes, good idea," I agreed. We'd found so many secrets in books before; perhaps there was something in the library that could help this, too.

I spotted Amador all the way on the other side of the room, as far from my table as possible, with her back turned away from me. *We were betrothed as children. We are engaged to be married.* What if she wasn't lying? Lucas swore it wasn't true. But still I wondered. I tried to enjoy the night; after all, Lucas was next to me. He was courting me. He'd chosen *me*.

Eat your heart out, Amador. It was a far cry from when she tried to lure me into the incineration room or trick me into eating rice and making myself a prisoner in my own realm.

As servers began to bring out trays of food and drinks for every table, a steady stream of well-wishers filed past the royal table on their way to sit, to say hello, give congratulations, and offer their loyalty to the crown. "It's a little embarrassing," I said to Nix when there was a short break in the line.

"Nah, everyone's just excited to get a new queen," Nix said. "Enjoy it." She looked up at someone. "Here comes another," she said. Then she twisted around in her seat to speak to me more privately and whispered, "What is *her* problem?"

I thought she meant Amador, but when I looked, she wasn't even paying attention to us.

"Who?" I asked.

Nix motioned in the other direction with her eyes. I followed and saw one of the maids standing near the doorway, holding a tray, the white hood of her uniform pulled up. "I think she's just confused," I said. "She looks like she doesn't know what she's supposed to be doing."

Lucas stood. He picked up his fork and tapped it against his crystal goblet.

"And what's *he* doing?" I whispered to Nix. She shrugged.

The room got quiet. He tapped his glass again so everyone would look at him. "Thank you," he said. "In honor of this monumental day and before we are all wrapped up in the ceremony and celebrating our new queen, I wanted to take a moment to honor her myself and pledge, in front of you all, my fealty to Her Highness, as a knight of the Court of Sigbin, but also as a defender of all Biringan, no matter what the future may bring. We are, indeed, one people, encantos, no matter which court we call home, and I hope that moving forward we can continue to exist in peace and harmony for many more generations." Everyone clapped.

Except Amador and her table. She pursed her lips and glared at us.

As soon as the applause petered out, there was a loud crash. Glass shattered. All heads turned to the noise at the back of the room. The new maid was standing on a chair, staring at us from beneath her hood. Her arm was shaking slightly. The front of her dress was wet, and broken glass spread around her feet. She'd dropped her tray.

"Enough!" she yelled, and was met with shocked silence. I realized she hadn't dropped the glassware. She'd thrown it. "Enough of this kalokohan!" Enough of this nonsense.

A chair scraped against the ground, and a horned elder from the Court of Lambana, whose hair and beard were long and white, stood up. His legs were hooved, like a centaur's, but he only had two, not four. "Hoy!" he began, his voice deep and booming. "What is the meaning of this?"

"Guards!" Elias shouted from a few seats away. He stood up and pointed. "Arrest this woman."

"I'm not going anywhere!" she screamed, so high-pitched that those around her flinched and covered their ears. The hood fell back around her shoulders.

It was Fortunada.

I didn't want to believe it, but it was true. Fortunada was the mambabarang.

There was some clanking from the hall outside the ballroom, and then guards started marching in. But they weren't from the Sirena Palace, or even Biringan City.

They were wearing Sigbin uniforms, midnight blue with silver epaulets.

A couple of them even looked familiar . . . "What is this?" I asked Lucas, my heart pounding.

"I have no idea."

We both knew what was happening, though. We just didn't want to say it out loud. It was an insurrection.

A Sirena guard, a stout man, started toward Fortunada then,

but she lifted her hand in his direction, and he flew backward as if he'd been shoved. More gasps; some guests shouted out in surprise. The other Sirena guards, who had been moving from the perimeter of the room in that direction, stopped, unsure what to do. There were a few seconds of utter confusion as everyone tried to work out what was happening.

Lucas moved toward the front of the room, toward the guards from Sigbin. "What is the meaning of this? What are you doing here?"

There was a loud popping sound—familiar, almost—followed by a strange, wavy mirage. I remembered then—the popping sound at school before the assassins appeared, and the wavy mirage when the door materialized. And that was why I recognized a few of the Sigbin guards—they'd been among the munduntug warriors at school that day.

This was it—the insurgents—showing their hand at last.

The Court of Sigbin!

Except . . .

"Who are you?" Lucas demanded, when he reached them. "You're not my men!"

The popping sound continued, and when it stopped, Fortunada, or the person I thought was Fortunada, was no more. The woman standing in front of us was much older, with the same unkempt hair and a similarly dated dress, only her hands were longer and thinner, and her face was worn and wrinkled. She looked ancient, and that was when I knew. This person had never been Fortunada. Fortunada was only a mask she wore. A cover. A disguise.

This was Lady Elowina herself.

I heard someone shout, *"Aswang!"* Shape-shifter.

I wondered why she had rescued me that first day, when Amador had tried to get me to fall into the refuse room. Maybe it wasn't enough to just push me into the void—Elowina wanted *this*. She wanted everyone to see what she could do. Spectacle. A display of her power.

"Traitors!" Lucas brandished his sword, and the munduntug warriors attacked, converging on him. But he took them all on, cleaving them one by one, mowing them down in a whirl of speed and metal.

Multiple people screamed, and there was a flurry of chairs being pushed out and people standing to flee; meanwhile, Elowina put her hands up into the air, and some kind of energy reverberated around the room, like a magnetic pulse. It made me sick to my stomach, and presumably everyone else felt this, too; the guests sat back down, clutching their heads and bellies. The Sirena guards stood at attention but looked frozen. Amador still tried to make it to the door, but Elowina did to her what she'd done to the guard: She flung her hand in Amador's direction, and the duchess stumbled forward and hit the ground, twisting in pain.

"Now that I've finally got your attention!" Elowina shouted. There were moans, but no one spoke again.

Except Lucas. "Beware, witch!" he warned. He was the only one standing. He'd taken care of the insurgents all on his own. They lay in a tangled heap at his feet, blood seeping out from their armor, wings severed. He was breathing heavily, and there was an ugly cut on his cheek, but he was otherwise unharmed.

Now he started for Elowina.

But a knight, even as brave and true as Lucas, was no match for a dark witch.

I wanted to yell out, to warn him. But my words were caught in my throat, and it was no use anyway.

Elowina's hand flung out once again, and Lucas fell to the floor. I watched him struggle, writhing, his eyes nearly bulging out of his head. I wanted to run at him. To help. He started coughing. Retching.

To my horror, something even worse happened then.

Beetles.

A swarm of black beetles crawled out of his mouth.

This time, I did scream. I looked at Nix—she was on the floor now, too, squirming, clutching her stomach—then back to Elowina, the traitorous witch, the mambabarang. Her hand was lifted in our direction, pointed at us. She was concentrating hard. She looked very, very angry.

Then I realized why. It was because I wasn't reacting. I was calm; I wasn't panicked or fearful. I stood my ground.

Some others started to notice, too. Their eyes pinned on me.

"Do you know who I am, Princess?" she barked. She began strolling from table to table, idly picking things up and putting them down, curling her finger around a ringlet of one woman's hair. "Of course you don't, because you're not from here. You're a pretender. But everyone else here knows who I am, even though they tried to erase me from the history books. Isn't that right, Elias?"

Elias was paralyzed like the rest of us; he couldn't speak.

But she was wrong.

I knew who she was.

I knew I had seen those jewels before. In the portrait of King Paolo and his sister. *It was a gift from her brother,* she'd said, when I complimented her on the pearl-and-diamond bracelet.

The jeweled clips. The brooch. The ring.

They were royal jewels.

"Hello, Auntie," I said coolly. "Or should I say, Grand-Auntie?"

"Ah, so you do know who I am," Elowina said with a smile of satisfaction. "It was my book you and your little friends were reading, was it not?"

I tried to keep all emotion off my face. I didn't want to give her anything, not even the smallest flash of surprise or recognition. That was what she wanted—a reaction. Empty and blank would confuse her.

"Why did you do it?" was all I said. In truth, it was all I wanted to know. This woman had destroyed any chance of a normal family life I could have had; she had been the cause of my parents' painful separation and eighteen years of a life on the run. My own kin.

"Jun wasn't supposed to have children," she spit.

I felt my knees weaken. "You are the Babaeng Pinuno of the Kalahok ng Mambabarang. You made him sign that agreement. He didn't know it was his own aunt who demanded it."

She cackled. "It was the only way to stop the war."

"That you started."

"You're mistaken, Princess. War is what we do here in Biringan. The kingdoms have always been in opposition to one another. The truce barely holds. It barely holds now. All I did was seize an opportunity."

"But why?"

She sneered. "Your father was a fool to marry your mother. He sullied the bloodline by marrying that human whore. For that, I would never forgive him. I am the last full-blooded encanto with a claim to the throne. And I intend to take what's rightfully mine."

She kicked over a chair, laughing when the man nearest to it flinched and covered his head to avoid being hit.

She spun around again and narrowed her eyes at me, then started up another rant, directed to me but also everyone else in the room. "I am the last of the true line of Queen Felicidad. The princess will surrender the crown and pledge loyalty to me. Or else she will be responsible for the deaths of each and every one of you. And lastly, her own." She reached out then, and as if on cue, thousands of black beetles came out of the walls.

So many screamed. The rest cowered in terror.

I stood there, silent, with my shoulders pushed back, projecting confidence; all the while, my brain was swirling, still trying to come up with a plan. Lucas lay unconscious on the floor. Elias was paralyzed. Nix was knocked out cold.

I was going to have to do this alone. I reached up and put my hand over the anting-anting amulet hiding beneath my gown.

35

I SPOTTED ONE of the water goblets at the table. I recalled how I'd grasped the anting-anting and Nix had burned at my touch when I'd believed she was a threat. So a concentrated dose would do far more damage, or at least spread the damage out more. I hoped. It was the only weapon I had.

Slowly, I inched over to my right, until the goblet of water was just within reach. My fingertips could just touch it without leaning over.

"Once the hapcanto pretender is deposed and I am the ruler of Biringan, you all will see the heights we can reach, the power we can wield when we stop diluting our magic with the vile stain of human blood. We can be what we were, gods to the earth, wielding our magic as we see fit. Not hiding away, silenced, invisible!"

I put my hand to the amulet. There was no way to unclasp it without being noticed either. I tugged on it. The chain around my neck was pretty secure. I pulled again. Nothing.

She looked over at me. "The usurper! She taints the greatness of the encanto." She pointed a gnarled, decaying fingernail in my direction.

A chair screeched somewhere in the room, and her head snapped in that direction. "And you—" She pointed to the poor courtier who'd had the misfortune of moving his chair. "You refused to support my bid against King Vivencio when he married that wretch. Did you think I would forget such an insult?" She turned back again, pointing to the rest of the room. "Or any of the insults you have flung at me, and at all the mambabarang?"

I used my fingernail to pick at the jump ring holding the amulet to the chain. That worked. It bent just enough to slip the pendant from the necklace. I clutched it in my palm and put my hand down to my side.

Elowina was savoring the fear she'd created. She stopped in front of the horned man who'd stood earlier. "Remember when you had me exiled from Lambana? You promised me sanctuary, and you threw me out just like they did!"

I closed my eyes tightly, feeling the amulet in my hand, remembering my mother's words. *This is your father's amulet, an anting-anting. It's made of a very rare salt mined beneath the Paulanan Mountains of Biringan.* A vision of the protective salt transforming, becoming liquid, flashed through my mind. I opened my eyes and dropped the amulet in the water goblet. It hissed and fizzed. I put my hand over the top in an attempt to muffle the sound, just as Elowina turned back again.

She looked up at me, a sly smirk playing at the corners of her mouth. Just what I was afraid of. "And our princess, no, our *queen*," she said. "Whatever shall we do with Her Royal Highness? Her *Majesty*?"

It felt like everyone in the room was holding their breath. She continued sauntering up the center aisle, straight for me. One step.

Another. Deliberately toying with me. I had no doubt that once she reached me, she intended to kill me. I wasn't going to allow that to happen.

I took a sip of the water. Better aim that way.

"Our princess is thirsty? By all means, whatever she wants, she shall have." She bowed with a flourish, mocking me. That was fine. Let her have her fun. It wouldn't last much longer.

I locked eyes with her. Inside, I might have been quivering, my heart racing into my throat, but I wasn't going to let her see that. I'd had enough of being walked all over, here, in the past, and in both realms. I raised my chin.

"Haughty and entitled to the very end, are we?" she crooned. She stepped closer. Only a few feet from being able to reach out and grab me.

Out of the corner of my eye, I noticed Jinky struggling to get free from one of the Sigbin guards. She looked me in the eye, her brow furrowed. I could tell she was wondering what I was doing. I shook my head slightly. I didn't want her to risk herself for me. She'd only get herself killed.

That intensely salty water was starting to make my mouth burn; I had the urge to swallow or spit it out, but I controlled it.

Then the intense feeling completely disappeared. I felt a wave of something rush through me, like adrenaline, only far more powerful.

I had only one chance to do this. And if I didn't do it just right—or worse, if it didn't work at all—I was finished. But I didn't come this far to go out like that.

Elowina's hand rose, those spidery fingers reaching out like she was coming for my throat.

I waited, staring right at her scowling face.

The witch was inches from me now. *Come on,* I thought. *Just a little more.*

I could smell her hot, putrid breath. The edge of her sharp nail grazed my throat.

Now! I spit the anting-anting salt directly in her face, spraying it as forcefully as I could. She hissed like an angry cat and lunged to the side. I saw most of the water, which wasn't nearly as much as I thought it was going to be, splash against the long sleeve of her gown as she screeched.

My heart sank. *I missed!*

Her hand snapped out for me and, before I could react, wrapped around my gown's collar. She was yanking me toward her. Her lips curled into a snarl, and in the black pit of her mouth, I saw her jagged, pointy teeth, ready to bite.

I pulled back with all my strength, but she was stronger. I caught a glimpse of Lucas, as beetles crawled around his body.

Then I spotted the goblet with the rest of the anting-anting salt. It was my last hope.

I pulled against her grasp, managing to loosen her grip on me just enough. I reached out and grabbed the glass of magical salt water, nearly letting it tilt too far over. *Don't drop it. Don't drop it.*

Just as her face loomed up inches from mine once again, so close I could see the decay on her teeth, I splashed the contents of the goblet directly in her face.

Immediately, she jumped back, as if I'd hit her with a baseball bat, and let me go. She began fumbling around, clutching her face, screaming high-pitched wails like a siren. Her voice got louder and louder, until I had to cover my ears.

Others in the room did the same; I even saw guards drop their weapons as they brought their hands to their ears.

Everyone was in agony.

The witch dropped to her knees, hands scratching all over her face. Then she fell forward. Her face was bubbling so that it hardly even resembled a face anymore, just oozing red-and-purple sores, growing and bursting and spreading from where the salt water had made impact. The fizzing spreading down her neck onto her shoulders and arms and hands.

Normally this would've made me sick, but that witch tried to kill me.

Her head turned up to the sky like a wolf about to howl. There was one last window-shattering shriek before it ended, leaving only the reverberating echo hovering in the air.

The witch slumped to the ground.

Almost instantly, the room erupted into chaos. People ran toward me. Others ran for one another and hugged. Some gathered their skirts up in their arms and went right out the door.

The Sirena guards looked around, confused and disoriented. It appeared they'd been under her spell all along, unable to fight. Two of them rushed to the witch, or what remained of her. One of them kicked at the pile of fabric with his foot.

Something moved; the guard jumped back and held out his sword, prepared to fight. The mound of fabric wiggled more. Others noticed what was happening and froze on the spot, worried the mambabarang was about to rise again.

The movement intensified suddenly, almost like it was about to boil over, and then as quickly as it began, it stopped. The pile became very still once more, before a swarming mass of black beetles burst out from underneath, scattering in every direction while onlookers screamed and jumped on chairs to avoid them.

The bugs disappeared underneath the walls and fled through windows and doorways. The guard took his sword and lifted what was left of the witch's clothes. All that remained was a pile of ashes.

36

"HOW DID YOU know water would harm the mambabarang?" Nix asked me as the healers tended to her and Lucas's injuries.

We'd been ushered to my chambers while the guards took care of the mess downstairs. Jinky was pale, and Ayo kept fetching everyone snacks, but no one felt like eating. Elias hovered anxiously.

"It doesn't," Lucas chimed in. "So this seems like a good time to ask: What exactly happened back there?"

"It wasn't plain water. When the witch wasn't looking, I slipped my anting-anting in it so the salt would dissolve. Since it repels evil, I figured that would be a better weapon than the small stone alone." What would've happened if my mother hadn't given me the amulet?

Lucas and Nix looked at each other. "What do you mean?" Lucas asked me.

I was confused. There was no plainer way to say it. "Like I said, I put the salt stone in the water glass, and once it dissolved, I splashed it on the witch. So it would harm her even more."

"An anting-anting." It felt like a question, but Lucas said it as a statement.

"Yes. I got it from my mom. It was my father's. Why? What's the problem?"

"An anting-anting doesn't dissolve in water," Elias said. "It's made of salt crystal, yes, but it's hardened crystal, like a diamond. It doesn't dissolve in water."

"Maybe there was something else. Did you put anything else in the water? Recite a spell?" Lucas asked me.

I shook my head.

They stared at me.

Then Nix smiled. "I think you discovered your talent," she said.

I doubted that. "What do you mean? I just put the anting-anting in water." Not very exciting.

"No. The water didn't dissolve the anting-anting," Nix insisted. "*You* did."

Elias put his hands up, as if to say, *Stop.* "What do you mean, *discovered* your talent?" he demanded.

"Nix is right," Lucas said, nudging me with his elbow. "You made that happen, because you willed it."

"Excuse me. Princess, you never informed me that you didn't possess magic," Elias said. No one was paying attention to him.

My mind was spinning. I didn't believe what they were saying, but if it was true that anting-antings don't dissolve, then what else could have happened? I shifted uncomfortably. "You're saying I made the amulet dissolve with magic?"

"Yes. Some encantos are alchemists, able to transform natural elements into something else," Ayo piped up from where he was pouring tsokolate. "Are there any instances in your life when something like this happened?"

Nothing came to mind. I scanned my memories, searching for another time I'd done something like that. Maybe I wouldn't have known, though, just like in this case.

Nix clapped her hands together. "I know!" she shouted excitedly. "Remember that day at school, in the cafeteria, when Amador drank the water? After you thought she tried to give you black rice?"

Lucas looked surprised. "Wait, Amador did what, now?"

"Except obviously it was the witch all along, not Amador," Nix assured him. "Fortunada—I mean, Elowina must have sent us those tainted desserts."

He only looked more pained at that.

Nix continued, "But the water burned her throat, remember? You were angry, and you stared at her. You made that happen. *You* changed the water."

Everyone was staring at me now. "I guess I did?"

"If I had known . . ." Elias said. His eyes widened, and he exhaled a puff of air. "I suppose all's well that ends well."

Ayo smiled at me. "It appears you possess the same talent as your grandmother Queen Erlinda. She could also change matter. I never thought I'd see that ability again."

"What else have you kept from me?" Elias said. He rubbed his face with his hands like he had a headache. So we finally came clean and told him everything we discovered about the beetles, the doll we found, and my father's note.

Elias told us the note we had in our possession was a draft. A finished letter had been written, and Marikit had delivered it to Elias that very evening. In it, my father confessed to the agreement to surrender his firstborn to the mambabarang and exhorted Elias to find my mother and tell her the truth about the situation. My father had communed with the spirits and spoken to his father, who warned him that his sister was out there, meaning my father harm. Before his own death, Temo, Lucas's father, had spotted her in Biringan. He was the one who'd gotten the Court of Lambana to send her away. But the morning after my father sent the letter, before Elias could do anything, my father was found dead.

And so Elias kept everything to himself, because he didn't know whom to trust, and he didn't want to cause panic in the kingdoms. All he knew was that he had to fetch me and keep me safe until the coronation.

"Hey! You're going to be crowned tomorrow!" Nix said, hugging me.

Elias looked pained. I felt kinda bad. He'd had no idea how close we came to Biringan having no queen to crown. Perhaps I had the mambabarang to thank for revealing my magic, after all.

"There's one thing we need to do first," I said.

THE BIRINGAN GUARD accompanied us to the dungeons under the palace. Even without using the secret passageways, it was a dank, depressing place, with little light and no fresh air. "After this, no one is being held here any longer," I announced.

The guard commander took out a set of jangly keys to open the last gate before the cells. "Respectfully, Princess, it's a place for criminals, not a retreat."

"There are more humane ways to treat prisoners, Commander. And may I remind you that this dungeon currently has exactly one, and she is innocent."

"Yes, Your Highness," the commander said, bowing. She held the door open.

Althea was sitting on the floor in the last cell. She stood as we approached. When she saw me, she curtsied.

"Let her go," I ordered.

37

I WAS JUST about ready. From the private room above the sanctuary, I could see courtiers from all over the realm streaming into the Council of the Courts, decked out in their finest silks and linens, the men in warrior masks and draped in malong scarves. Those who didn't fit congregated outside the doors, spilling down the gently sloped hillside to the streets below. The sky was pale blue and nearly cloudless, the perfect backdrop for the rainbow of flower arrangements and plush green trees lining all the walkways and roads, where arches wrapped in orchids and waling-waling flowers had been set up for everyone to walk through. There were hanging pots on every street post, spilling over with white and yellow and shades of purple and pink.

I'd finally found my power—now I just hoped I'd be able to harness it again, and prove I was the rightful ruler of Biringan.

Children from all four courts played together on the steps below the building, their parents' rivalries forgotten, and peeked into the windows downstairs, waving purple flags and trying to get a glimpse of the activity happening inside. There was a sense of jubilation I hadn't experienced here yet—or, really, anywhere before.

I closed my eyes and took a deep breath. They were all there for me, to watch me be crowned, when I would vow to be a just and fair ruler, do my best to ensure the safety of the realm, the secrecy of the realm, and to maintain peace throughout all four courts. I intended to do everything in my power to uphold those promises.

Once I passed the test, of course.

"Are you ready for your gown, Your Highness?" Jinky stood in the open doorway with a heavy bundle draped over her outstretched arms. There were four more maids behind her, all carrying various pieces of the coronation ensemble.

I stepped into the skirt layers first. There were petticoats to keep the dress full, under a white silk skirt, and then a nearly black, dark-purple split skirt over that. The bodice was heavily beaded, with glittering crystals and a tall, wide, feathered collar, and there were voluminous slashed bell sleeves that matched the skirts, ending just below the elbow. There was a giant, fluffy train attached at the waist, in a shimmering iridescent purple, with silver trim.

Someone knocked on the door. "Come in," I called.

Elias peeked his head inside and said, "The priestess has arrived. It's time."

I took one last look out the window. I had the feeling that everything and nothing was changing all at once. I'd always be me, but at the same time, I'd never be the same, and I was acutely aware of it. Nothing in my life had turned out as I expected so far. If I'd been able to see into the future a year ago, I wouldn't have believed any of this would happen. Yet it all felt strangely right.

Jinky helped me walk down the spiral staircase. The other maids held the train of my gown. At the bottom, Nix and Lucas were waiting to escort me to the stage. I'd also asked Elias, Ayo, and Jinky to stand beside me as my chosen family. While I voiced some concern that Nix was being so visible, seeing as she was hiding from Jade Mountain, she dismissed my worries with a wave of her wraparound shades.

We all gathered in front of the door at the bottom of the steps, which led into the sanctuary. Inside, I heard musicians playing the ancient songs, and lots of excited chatter.

"Remember what we rehearsed. Once the procession music starts, you'll count to five, then walk out," Jinky said while she fussed over my dress. She seemed more nervous than I was.

"Don't worry, I remember," I assured her. I'd been so anxious for so long, and now that the moment was here, I felt a sense of peace wash over me.

So when a guard entered the room with a beautifully dressed woman, I wasn't surprised.

"Mom!" I cried, and rushed to hug her. "You're here."

She was thin and pale, but she looked every inch a queen. "Elias fetched me last night," she said. "I'm so glad I'm here to see this. Your father would have been so proud."

I didn't know I was crying until I felt her hand wipe the tears from my cheek.

"All right, it's on. I'll be standing by Elias," my mother said. "Good luck, just try to stay calm," she advised.

I released my mother, my heart full of love and hope. My father was dead, but I was his legacy. I would finish what he began.

The melancholy opening flute notes began. I counted to five as rehearsed, and then the doors opened up in front of me. I began to walk.

More instruments joined the first flute, until the only thing I was aware of was the intense music and each of my own steps as I neared the throne. None of the people around me registered; it was just me, the songs of my people, and the golden throne on the dais ahead of me.

The walk felt like both miles and feet; it was as if time had been suspended. All I could hear was my heart beating in my ears.

As soon as I reached the throne and turned to sit for the ceremony, I snapped back to reality again. I heard a baby crying softly somewhere in the crowd, the hushed murmurs of people commenting on the proceedings, the scrape of feet against the stone floor, and the echo of instruments as their notes faded and stopped.

Lucas, Nix, Ayo, Jinky, and the others lined up across the side of the stage. I looked over at Lucas. He looked back at me and smiled. My mother and Elias were on the other side, and I bowed my head to them as well.

Luzviminda stepped forward. She wore a simple, floor-length red dress, and her curly hair cascaded down her back. Her only adornment was a gold circlet engraved with symbols of the four courts: the mermaid's tail of Sirena, the wings of Sigbin, the dragonfly of Lambana, and the steed of Tikbalang.

She looked back and forth across the crowd before addressing them. "Welcome to all the beings of Biringan, from every court, and every station. We are all here today, as one realm, to anoint our new queen. We do so in the tradition of many thousands of years of our land and people." There was an outburst of applause, and then she said, "And thus, we begin."

A haunting, low song played, and the ritual started.

Two guards stepped forward from the hall, holding a large, square wooden box between them. They walked up the aisle to the dais as the music echoed across the sanctuary. My heart began thumping in my ears again. *This is where it can all go wrong.*

They made their way up the steps one at a time. *Step, step. Step, step.* They stopped in front of me and switched their hands around on the handle in order to face the audience. The box was sealed on all sides. There were no locks, no hinges, no way to open it. Nothing sticking out of it. I didn't even see how it was a box, instead of just a solid block of wood.

"This is the Puzzle of Truth," Luzviminda announced. She made a point to examine it on all sides, like a magician, and had the guards turn in a full circle so everyone could see for themselves, too. Only, unlike a magic show, this wasn't an illusion. I had to get the royal scepter out of that box, using only magic.

I swallowed, nervous. I'd discovered what my power was; the question was whether I could do it again.

Luzviminda spoke to the crowd once more. "The puzzle is an enchanted lock. There is no one way to solve the puzzle. But only the true heir to Biringan can do it."

She looked to me now. That was my cue to approach the box.

Time seemed to stand still. I rose slowly and stepped forward deliberately. I wasn't in a hurry—I was too busy concentrating. Praying, really. *Please work. Please work.*

I stood right next to the box. I wanted to reach for the amulet, but it was no longer there. I felt a pang at that.

I closed my eyes. The amulet might be gone, but my mother was in this room, and it wasn't only her; I saw my father, too.

Standing next to her. And beyond them, my grandparents Paolo and Erlinda, and more and more, all the encantos who had ruled Biringan. They were always with me, I knew then. My strength came from my blood, from the people who came before me. The powerful encantos with their magic, and my human ancestors, who were healers and made the world better with their kindness.

I reached my hands out toward the box, still with my eyes closed.

People in the room began to whisper.

I wasn't sure if anything was happening, but I kept my eyes closed, and I felt the strength of my bloodline rise to meet the challenge.

A surge pulled through me, and I heard more whispers around the room, and for a split second, I disconnected from my body, then abruptly returned. My eyes snapped open, and in front of me, the box was dissolving.

It didn't even open. It just . . . vanished. The crowd made some astonished noises. There, on a white silk cloth, was the Scepter of Aurora. Gold, with inlaid vines and florals, and on the end, an orb made of polished purple amethyst, veins and flecks of gold running through it.

I took it off the stand with both hands, feeling the weight of all those who had held it before me—all my ancestors. Most recently, my father. For the first time since I'd traveled over to this other world, I felt a true connection to him, not just my mom.

I looked up at the peaked ceiling and hoped he could hear my thanks.

"She has passed the Test of Viability," Luzviminda announced. The room erupted in cheers.

MOST OF THE rest of the ceremony was a blur to me. I was so focused on getting my parts right and not dropping the scepter or tripping over my voluminous skirts. The priestess sang in the ancient diwata language I had yet to learn, but I somehow felt like I could understand the meaning. I thought about all those who had sat there before me, those who would after me, and how I'd already ensured I'd be remembered for many generations to come—quite a lot for a girl who until so recently felt invisible and forgotten.

After a lot of reciting, Luzviminda turned to me and asked me to stand. I did, and one of her attendants stepped forward holding the Talon Crown, the royal crown of Biringan. She took it and carried it to me. It was large and looked quite heavy. There were four enormous jewels circling it, each representing one of the courts: Sigbin blue, Tikbalang maroon, Lambana green, and Sirena yellow. In the center: purple. The other color of the Court of Sirena and the color of royalty.

"Princess Mahalina Jazreel of the Court of Sirena, only daughter of King Vivencio Basilio Rodriguez II, once this crown is placed upon your head, you are hereby proclaimed the rightful sovereign of Biringan, with all the rights and responsibilities thereof. Do you accept?"

"I do," I said solemnly.

She lowered the crown onto my head. It was as heavy as I

expected, but it fit perfectly. The room—and even the crowd outside—was completely silent.

"Then I now officially decree you *Queen* Mahalina Jazreel, the first of the Court of Sirena, the one true ruler of Biringan, protector of the Magical Realm."

Raucous cheering and clapping exploded all around me.

AFTER THE CEREMONY, an endless line of aristocrats waited to congratulate me and genuflect to the new ruler. Including at least one of my former rivals.

Amador gave me her best half curtsy and polite, if somewhat reluctant, congratulations.

"Thank you, Amador," I said, responding with my widest smile.

Hers faded some. "I know this is your day, Your Majesty, but I wanted to be sure to be the one to tell you so you don't hear from anyone else first."

"What's that, Duchess?"

She acted like she was hesitant, or too shy to tell me. "Well, you'll see. I don't want to ruin it. Let's put it this way: Keep your eye on your mail." With that, she moved along, and the next well-wisher stepped up, and then another, and another, until I forgot about Amador and her pathetic attempt to ruin my day—with what? Her birthday party invite? She really was competitive about everything.

Once the line finally ended, I stepped outside to the roaring cheers of the crowd gathered in front of the Council of the Courts. I stopped to wave. They were all waving purple flags now, not just the children, many of whom were perched on their parents' shoulders. I couldn't believe they were there for me. An older woman at the front of the crowd reached out her hand. She held a huge white flower. "Your Majesty!" she called out.

I took a few steps toward her and accepted the flower. The woman looked surprised and happy; she bowed and then said, "You will be the best queen that Biringan has seen in centuries!"

"Thank you," I told her. At that moment, I felt a hand at my elbow.

Lucas.

"Afraid I have to steal the queen away from you," he told the woman.

She replied, "You treat her well, now!" as we climbed into the waiting carriage. He shut the door.

"Hey," he said.

"Hey, yourself," I said back.

It was the first time we'd been alone together in days. "You're too far away," he said. "Why is that?"

"Come over, then," I said, patting the seat next to me.

He came over and sat down.

"Thanks," I said.

"What for?"

I thought about how he'd slain all the insurgents on his own. How he'd been the one pushing to investigate the truth. How he'd helped me to believe in myself. But I just smiled. I was so happy.

He leaned closer and pulled me so that my legs were draped over his, and soon I was sitting on his lap, and there was no time to talk because we were too busy kissing.

WHEN WE ARRIVED back at the palace, Ayo and Jinky were already there, both dressed in brand-new white ensembles for the reception. "A lovely ceremony," Ayo told me.

Jinky nodded emphatically. "It was perfect. Best ever."

"Have you witnessed any other coronations?" Ayo teased. "You weren't born when King Vivencio was crowned."

"I don't have to to know this is the best one. The most eventful, for sure."

"They want you out on the balcony," Nix said, as the crowd roared outside. "Come on."

We went out to the balcony, all of us, including the Queen Mother. Nix was the most enthusiastic waver.

"I was pretty worried there for a minute," I admitted to them all.

"I'm sure you were," Elias said. "But we never doubted."

BEFORE THE CORONATION reception, as I passed through the sitting room that would now be where I read official documents and received councilors, I told Jinky there was something I needed to do first. It couldn't wait.

Now that I was officially queen, I wrote my first proclamation.

I, Mahalina Jazreel of the Court of Sirena, Queen of Biringan, hereby assert by royal decree: that henceforth, no human creature shall be retained in the realm, by means magical or otherwise, against their will, on fullest penalty of the law.

HRH Queen Mahalina Jazreel

I poured some wax from the candle and stamped my seal beneath my signature. While I waited for it to dry, I looked out the window, to the gardens, the rolling hills, the roads of my new home. *Home.* I was finally there. After eighteen years of running. This was where I would put down roots, continue one legacy, and begin a new one. I may have given up my human life, but I was ready to lead forever, as an encanto's daughter.

&PILOGUE

A MONTH AFTER the coronation, when the celebrations finally
wound down, I was having tea with Nix when Ayo walked in
holding the silver mail tray. Nix came over every day after school
to tell me the latest gossip. I hadn't been back to BANA, now that
I was queen. My education consisted of tutors and personalized
readings relevant to Biringan history and law. Nix was my
lifeline.

I hadn't seen Lucas in a while, and I missed him. He had been
called back to Sigbin, to rout any remaining insurgents there and
across the kingdom. Alas, Elowina had had a number of followers
around the realm, even in Sirena. The insurgents didn't come from
just one kingdom; they hailed from all over the realm. Elias had
advised me to be merciful, and I was trying to be, even though I
found it difficult. But I had to unite the kingdom somehow.

"Your Highness," Ayo said, bowing his head. He held the tray
out toward me. There was a square powder-blue envelope on it
addressed to "HRH Queen Mahalina Jazreel."

I pulled out the card inside. It was an invitation on thick paper
stock. My cheeks went pale as the blood drained from my face
while I read it.

Nix put her cup down on the saucer. It clattered, spilling over the side. "What is it? What happened?"

I read the words out loud.

We Humbly Request the Honor of Your Presence
to Celebrate the Union of

Grand Duchess Amador Oscura
and
Sir Lucas Invierno

at the Court of Sigbin Palace

—AUTHOR'S NOTE—

I AM SO proud of this book you hold in your hands. I have been in publishing for almost twenty-five years, and while I have written books that feature Filipino characters or characters that share my Asian ethnicity, I have never written a fantasy novel that draws from my heritage.

Growing up in Manila, my childhood was filled with superstition—my grandfather wore an anting-anting, and I shuddered at scary stories about aswangs (vampires) and mambabarangs (witches). Writing and imbuing this fairy tale with Filipino myth and sensibility, I felt an enormous amount of liberation—"This is allowed?!"—and no small sense of pride at the rich mythological soil I was able to layer into my story.

With that being said, as in my other books, I have tweaked and twisted parts of the legends in order to fit my story better. All deviations from the traditional norm are deliberate choices I made as an author. ☺

Maraming salamat!

XOXO,
Melissa de la Cruz

—ACKNOWLEDGMENTS—

A FILIPINO BUFFET of thanks to my amazing editor Polo Orozco, whose patient and thorough guidance was intrinsic to the book! Thank you to everyone at Penguin, especially my Jens—my mentors Jennifer Klonsky and Jen Loja. Thank you to Richard Abate and Hannah Carande at 3Arts and to Ellen Goldsmith-Vein, Jeremy Bell, DJ Goldberg, and Sarah Jones at Gotham Group. Thanks to everyone at YALLWEST and YALLFEST. Thank you to my friends and family. Thanks, Mike and Mattie, for putting up with endless wars (or deadlines). Thank you to my devoted readers.